Hotel

by Ray Sullivan

Chapter 1

And so, loyal readers, following my review of the Jungle Room, a long and savouring walk past row upon row of the King's gold and platinum records, I ended up outside in the relatively chilly Memphis October afternoon weather – mild by Blighty standards but clearly causing a few of the indigenous population to huddle into their long coats as we silently made the final part of our pilgrimage around the arcing path towards Aaron Elvis Presley's grand gravestone.

Regular readers will know that I've occasionally been harsh about the pedestal Presley has been placed upon by succeeding generations of fans, but even I was to be found wiping a solitary tear as I stood where presumably millions have stood since his untimely death in 1977. It may have been a blues pilgrimage to Beale Street that brought me to the doorstep of the King, but it was the tasteful way someone has presented Elvis' journey and home that made me weep.

Of course, I would commend a visit to BB's club, pop around to the Sun Records Studio, dance the night away on the Beale to anyone with a heart and a love for music, but if you're in the area, no matter what your musical tastes and loves are, pay the King a visit, you won't be disappointed.

*

Aiden sat back from the screen, ran a finger loosely along the word-processed words, corrected an infinitive split from arsehole to breakfast-time along the way and changed the tempo of the introductory paragraph before saving the document, packaging it into an email to the deputy editor of Music Monthly Review and pushing the send button. It was bang on three thousand words, not a syllable more than required and was, in Aiden's view, the biggest pile of pulp crap he'd written so far in a career that was spiralling downward at a steady rate.

He leaned back on the rear legs of his dining room chair, reaching for the bottle he'd left on the sideboard an hour earlier after accepting the invitation to write a review of 'Gracelands from a visitor's perspective' for MMR. It was ten in the morning and his hand shook as he uncorked the single malt. Putting the cork carefully to one side he slid the empty glass in front of him and listened as the smoky liquor poured into the generously sized glass, watched as the liquid bubbled under the force of being poured so aggressively. The second glass of the day would be poured more sedately, and drunk with more grace than this first shot, but would nonetheless be enjoyed as much. The third would probably be the last one he would remember with any real clarity as would the hour before lunch when he would drink it.

2

Sinking the first mouthful of the day Aiden reached out to his iPod and searched through the menu until he found what he wanted to listen to. As usual it would be Ricky Maggot, lead singer of Death Star and Aiden's all-time favourite singer and guitarist. As the power chords signalling one of Death Star's biggest hits reverberated around the room, amplified by a massive Bluetooth speaker setup, Aiden sank back in the dining chair, awaiting the inevitable request for some tidying up to be carried out on his submission.

He jumped as his cell phone rang. Brian Esk, the deputy editor of MMR who'd commissioned Aiden to write the piece on Graceland earlier that morning normally just emailed a scathing reply listing at most a few minor issues with the copy. Generally, the problems were trivial, but Brian liked to assert his position over Aiden, fallen Pulitzer Prize winning journalist that he was just because he could. Aiden's heart leapt as phoning meant only one thing - more work.

"Yes Brian," he said, pushing the glass away from him.

"Christ, you're quick off the mark," said Brian. Aiden felt his stomach flip - his love of single malts, hell his drink problem full stop - were common knowledge, but he doubted anyone had guessed he'd started hitting the sauce this early. He tried to evade the question.

"What's the problem, too many adjectives in the Gracelands piece?" he asked, glad he'd only taken the one sip. His voice wouldn't be slurring yet, would it? So how could Brian know, how could he tell?

"There are too many words, but that's not your fault. I've had to edge that article from the spot I'd reserved to accommodate the Ricky Maggot piece I'd like you to write,' Brian replied. In the background Aiden could hear the clatter of keyboards in the MMR office and his heart pulled as he recalled his journalistic apprenticeship in years gone by, in the days when he was a highly regarded staff writer, before the prize, when his ego was in check and he didn't work alone using the internet for research where only legwork would have done before. His brain pulled back on track; Brian wanted him to write a piece on Ricky. Perhaps he'd get to interview his hero at last, flown out to LA on expenses. Maybe he was in town, arranging the long-awaited tour?

"Sure, what's the angle?" he asked, reaching out towards the whisky glass with his free hand, turning the rim gently. He waited for Brian to pitch into his usual three-minute diatribe listing his ideas on a story before Aiden could demolish them one by one. The pause was longer than he'd expected.

"His obit, of course," said Brian at length. Aiden rocked back at this, the glass forgotten for a moment.

"Obit? For Ricky? Why?" he asked, flushing as soon as he spoke. There weren't too many reasons for commissioning an obit. One, usually.

"You don't know?" asked Brian, "I thought with you playing his songs in the background that you'd heard," he said, adding "he died this morning, in LA." Aiden felt his world start to crumble, the words just spoken bouncing around his head like bullets from a machine gun.

"I didn't know..." was all he could manage before pulling the glass up to his lips, sinking a slice of malt that would have had most livers running for cover. As the whisky sank down his gullet he felt his head straighten. "I always play Ricky after writing a piece," he said, wondering why he felt he needed to justify playing his favourite music in his own home.

"That's why I want you to write this piece, Aiden," said Brian, adding, "I'm clearing the front page for the news element - I've got a staffer working on that piece, trawling the news channels on the internet for inspiration. You: I'd like you to throw a ten-thousand-word obit for a commemorative centre-spread. I'll get the front-page draft emailed to you when it's got enough meat on it because I'd like you to top and tail your piece by referring to the news item," he said, unnecessarily as that was the industry standard way of dealing with these jobs. Nonetheless Aiden found himself scrabbling for some paper and a pen, trying to hold all these ideas in place until he found one.

"Could you email me all this?" he asked.

"Done already," replied Brian, hanging up. Aiden found himself staring at his phone, watching the Death Star logo fade in as a screensaver. He turned back to his laptop and opened his email. Sure enough, there was an email from Brian as well as a long list from fans, friends and Twitter correspondents regarding Ricky's death. "I guess the news just broke," muttered Aiden, pulling up his word processor program for the second time that morning. He looked at the half-full glass of whisky sat in front of him, concentric rings forming on the surface of the liquor as he slugged at the keys on his laptop mechanically.

After a couple of minutes of turgid pounding Aiden stopped. He knew his subject well; he was regarded in the industry as the leading authority on Ricky Maggot and Death Star. He knew pretty much every detail regarding Ricky's upbringing in a North Yorkshire mining community that had had its heart ripped out by the miners' strike and subsequent pit closure in the eighties, just as Ricky, then known as Jason Jones, was in the process of leaving school. Weeks that turned into months of standing on the dole queue and wiling away bored hours listening to punk rock singles on the radio while learning four of the five chords he ever learned on his unemployed father's Stratocaster guitar became his focus and his objective in life.

By the time Jason had turned seventeen he'd penned his first punk rock classic, 'Standing on the

6

edge, (stoning the bastards to death)', his view of watching scabs attempt to break the strike, describing the stones and rocks he and his friends threw at the miners who decided not to join in the strike and attempted to feed their families instead. Hooking up with three school chums, Jason changed his name to Ricky Maggot and formed Death Star. One month after forming his group he had a recording contract and a number one record on his hands, the first of fifteen that saw him dally with hard rock, soul, blues and a very unsuccessful attempt at Country and Western, which was dismissed by most aficionados as "taking the piss".

Aiden could write his ten thousand words on just this part of Ricky's life alone, never mind the glittering expletive splattered career he had, exporting his foul mouthed bon mots across the Atlantic. More hits in the Nineties followed, then a drop in popularity until Ricky allowed cameras to follow him everywhere, a fly on the wall reality show featuring the maddest, most unpredictable person to own a mansion in LA. Ever. Ricky released solo singles, turning his back on the guys he'd called friends since his mid-teens, casting them adrift without a lead singer and unable to use the Death Star name anyway as he owned that too. He'd always taken the lion's share of the royalties, now he systematically cut off their income stream. Even their drug dealers thought Ricky was being rotten.

All of this and more could and would cover Aiden's screen, but he realised he was jumping the gun. Ricky was dead, and he'd treated his body like it didn't have any value on many occasions, but this was a bolt out of the blue. People like Ricky didn't just die, someone else was always involved; a woman, a drug dealer, a mad doctor waiting to be struck off. Yes, Ricky was dead, and Aiden needed to find out why.

Chapter 2

"The passenger is being sick again," said the rating to the Chief Steward, more out of frustration than sympathy. Everyone, including the Captain, had felt the effect of the storm over the previous twenty-four hours. Most had managed to keep their mess inside of the buckets. The Chief Steward just shrugged; he understood the problem, the mess had to be cleaned up, the passenger treated with respect. Critically he didn't need to do that job, the rating did. The aft hold was his responsibility.

"One more day," he said. "And the storm has almost passed," he added. The rating pulled a face and returned to his duties below. He never expected any result other than the one received but it had given him a legitimate excuse to leave the aft hold, if only for a few minutes. Within twenty-four hours, possibly less, the cargo ship would be returning to its scheduled route, dragging its almost empty hold back to China having disgorged hundreds of containers of electronic devices at San Francisco docks for onward distribution throughout the United States. The passenger hadn't been scheduled, the diversion unexpected, the payment welcome. Empty cargo ships were hellishly expensive to run, any contribution to offset the cost accepted, even it did involve taking on a stranger just off the Western Seaboard and depositing them two thousand miles out at sea. No questions, obviously, asked.

Down below the man crouched over the steel bucket, holding it with both hands as he rocked back and forth on his knees.

"For Chrissake, make it stop," he mumbled to himself as another wave of nausea shook him. "Half a fucking million," he moaned. "And I don't even get an outside cabin, let alone a porthole." He knew the transport costs included more than the boat but also factored in the drop-off and pick-up, bribing Coastguards to look the other way, being snuck out of LA and of course there was the small problem of the body. He recalled the meeting that started it all nearly two years earlier, after a gig in Portland at the stadium.

*

"Great gig," shouted Derrick as he swanned into the dressing room, carrying a bottle of champagne. Ricky looked up and tried to stop shaking, causing Derrick, his manager for the last fifteen years, to stop in his tracks. "Problem, Ricky?" he asked, patting his pockets with his free hand, trying to work out if he had kept any cocaine back. "You need something stronger? A couple of hookers?" Ricky shook his head.

"No, well yes, of course I need all that, but that will only keep me going tonight. I need to get out of this," he said. Derrick looked confused; living for now was what defined Ricky, looking beyond tonight was almost unknown.

10

"How so?" he asked, putting the champagne glasses down and starting to peel the foil off. This had all the hallmarks of a bad day in the office. The least he could do is get some grog down his neck while the gravy train was still chugging. He knew Ricky had been knocked sideways by his divorce three years earlier and the constant court battles over the money dragged Ricky down every time he spoke with his lawyers, but he hadn't thought it was this bad. He popped the cork, letting it ricochet around the room. "Brenda?" The face was enough, but Ricky wanted to talk. He picked the glass of fizz that Derrick had poured, looked at the bubbles for longer than any drunk needed before answering.

"Yeah, she's part of it, a big part. She's bleeding me dry, bouncing me between courts over here and the UK, has taken half my houses, half my cash, some of the cars and kept the jewels yet she's going for more. She even took my Cessna, and she hates flying, for Christ's sake," he added. "My lawyers reckon she can keep touching me for cash as long as I'm alive and earning, will probably keep on touching me when I'm dead whether I'm earning or not.

"And the band are circling, got some hot shot legal team trying to winkle the rest outta me."

"They can try, but probably won't succeed," said Derrick. Ricky shook his head.

"Maybe, but I'll end up paying through the nose while they're at it," he said. "And I can't go anywhere, can't take a pee, buy a doughnut or screw

11

a hooker without the paparazzi stalking me. I don't need this shit anymore," he said waving his glass around the dressing room. "I've got enough income just from iTunes sales, I just need to hold onto most of it, drop from sight, disappear," he said. Derrick felt his face flush, he tipped the paparazzi off more often than not, got a backhander from his media pals for the information and kept Ricky's profile and income stream up. Whatever was good for Ricky was lucrative for Derrick. He took a deep breath.

"I'll fix you a meeting," he said.

*

Ricky had been impressed by the arrangements, the two car switches, the efficiency of the journey, the beachside tavern on what appeared to be a private beach north of San Francisco. Certainly there were no other customers, nobody on the beach and the serving staff were discrete, disappearing as soon as they had taken an order, delivered some food or put another beer on the table. Ricky sat opposite the black-haired American who provided a name that Ricky discounted immediately, it seemed that false. He noticed that although Derrick was on his second beer and Ricky, his fourth, the black-haired man hadn't touched his, just let the condensate stream down the side and form a puddle on the table. The black-haired man raised the subject.

"You want to disappear, I understand?" he asked, running his finger up the bottle slowly. Cold water streamed over the digit and trickled down the bottle. The black-haired man stared directly at Ricky, his eyes just visible through the Ray-Ban glasses. Ricky nodded, took a sip from his bottle as the black-haired man continued. "Did he," he asked, nodding towards Derrick, "tell you what I told him to tell you?" Ricky shrugged.

"You can arrange it, but I have to understand it's irreversible," repeated Ricky. "Yeah, he told me that."

"If you take my package you'll disappear from public view, into a world of luxury with anything you want – drugs, booze, broads, whatever, forever, but you can never return."

"Sounds great," said Ricky. The black-haired man held his bottle lightly, rocking it gently from side to side.

"I'm glad you think so, but I want you to think very carefully about this. If all you want is plastic surgery and a new identity, I can broker that deal. But if you want me to provide my package you have to be prepared to walk away from everyone you know, lose the chance to say goodbye, never speak to any of them again..." Ricky didn't know, couldn't know, that the black-haired man's predecessor but one had started this process off with some band members of one of the biggest rock bands in the world in the mid nineteen seventies and had screwed it up by not making it clear what it involved, yet told them too much before they signed the paperwork. The band members walked away and made a hit single out of the experience. The predecessor but one, however, found out how ruthless the company Human Resources team was. Contracts weren't the only thing they executed. Ricky was just letting the words about not speaking to anyone he knew again resonate around his head.

"Like my grabbing ex and former band members? Sounds like a plan to me," replied Ricky.

"Or, if you'd like to keep your current identity and just have those troublesome persons disappear, then I can broker that too," said the man, finally letting the bottle reach his lips. "I mention these options because they are cheaper than my services and much more flexible."

"Nah, they're a pain in the arse, all of them, but I'm no killer," said Ricky. He wondered if the 'package' on offer; vague, unexplained and held close to the chest of the black-haired man was going to be shared any time soon.

"Be very aware," said the black-haired man, "that if you sign up with us it's irreversible, with all your future royalties being directed to a holding fund that pays for this service. Those funds will be used to transport you in style, locate you in the finest accommodation you've ever stayed in, provide you with a life of excess and debauchery or just solitude, if that's what you prefer, for the rest of your natural," he said, sipping his beer again. Derrick seemed a little perturbed.

"I still get my cut?" he asked. The black-haired man didn't turn his head away from Ricky.

"Five percent minimum until the day you pop your clogs, and our investment team is very, very good," he said, adding, "as long as you keep to your end of the bargain. One wrong word to anyone outside of this deal and," he said, drawing his finger across his throat. "And of course, there's our facilitation fee," he said. Derrick seemed pleased – the royalty rate was less than he received at present, but it continued as long as he lived, and he intended living a long, long time. And the facilitation fee was intended to provide a worthwhile bridge between losing the monthly management fee and waiting for the scheme to be up and running.

Ricky wanted to know more details, but the black-haired man wouldn't been drawn. He asked Derrick for some financial information and before ending the first meeting urged Ricky to give the other options serious consideration before their next meeting.

*

"Transport me in style," grumbled Ricky, vomiting into the bucket again. "I'll never criticise Ryan-fucking-air ever again," he moaned.

Chapter 3

Aiden looked up at the clock; three p.m. in the UK, seven a.m. in California. Paper was strewn across his desk, folders with documents piling out were stacked three high and two more laptops had joined his Mac on the desk, one searching for news reports that would finalise his obit with sad-but-true details of Ricky's demise, the other constantly showing the live Twitter feeds about the rock star's death. Part of this was to help with his research, part was to help with his mourning. The first draft of the obit had been typed through freely running tears, now he was tightening it up with some little-known anecdotes about his hero that had been gleaned over the years and not so carefully filed away. Now he was regretting not being more organised, but deep down he'd never anticipated having to write all this stuff. He always figured he'd self-destruct before Ricky, not by much but by enough.

He rifled through the middle folder one more time, scattering clippings and handwritten notes everywhere before finding the scrap of paper he'd missed on the previous forays through the pile.

"Derrick's cell number," he muttered to himself, holding the slip of paper carefully aloft. Derrick had a public number that all music journalists had access to, one that he'd taken to turning off it seemed. But Aiden had obtained an alternative number from a friend of a friend of a drug dealer a couple of years earlier, a resource he'd avoided squandering. Now it was pay-back time. Checking the time again he tried to work out whether Derrick would be up and about. Ordinarily it would be a no-brainer; rock stars didn't wake up until after 2 p.m. local time, managers an hour earlier. But come a death and the rule book would be thrown out, plus it looked from police and ambulance reports in LA that Derrick had been at the hospital Ricky died in. He tried the number, got the voicemail message, decided against leaving a request for a call-back. Aiden reckoned Derrick had been the primary filter that had stopped him contacting his hero more often, so was withholding his number and betting on Derrick picking up on account of it being a very restricted number.

He turned to the news reports, now becoming fewer as America got used to the idea it was hosting one less rock renegade and more focussed on other news items. Ricky had died undergoing routine surgery in a top-notch medical facility, surgeons had worked tirelessly to save him but in the end his body gave out, probably thanks to the lifetime of recreational drugs and alcohol abuse he'd subjected it to. The coroner had called for an autopsy, but as there weren't any suspicious circumstances like firearms or complex dance routines involved, it wasn't expected to reveal anything exceptional and the body was likely to be released for cremation within the next few days.

Sad, but predictable facts about the end of a rock-star's life.

Aiden sat bolt upright as he re-read the coroner's office comments again. It was the reference to cremation that made his head swirl as he rummaged back into the middle folder for the notebook he'd flicked through looking for Derrick's cell number a few minutes earlier, but it was the "routine" operation that was really nagging him.

"Nothing fucking routine about that," he grimaced as he pulled the notebook containing one of his earliest interviews with Ricky out.

*

Derrick rubbed his eyes as he sat hunched in a waiting room of a Los Angeles Police Station. He'd wanted to be on the other side of the planet when the scheme unfolded, wanted the perfect alibi, the most plausible of plausible deniability. Ricky wanted him close to for the switch and the black-haired man had insisted, very persuasively, that Derrick had to be the "close friend" who identified the body.

The media storm had been brief; Ricky wanted to slip away as quietly as possible after being given the various potential scenarios. Derrick recalled that the black-haired man had smiled quietly when Ricky made the decision: he told Derrick that most came to the same conclusion but the bigger stars often wanted a media circus that rivalled their pre-disappearance publicity, had wanted a public show trial of a disgraced MD looking for a new life, one that inevitably involved a shed load of bribes to local officials and public defenders and a new life for the fall-guy MD. This was going to be a walk in the park compared to some he'd facilitated.

But the grilling from the LA cops hadn't been expected. He'd rushed Ricky into the Emergency Room, used a pre-arranged code, had Ricky taken into a private treatment room and from there on out of a back door into a waiting limo. The body that the Coroner now wanted slicing up again had been waiting in cold storage under a carefully managed clerical error in the mortuary, rolled up to a theatre where a well-compensated surgeon oversaw the practise of one of the medical industry's more common operations by a group of interns, who were glad to be allowed to make the cuts. Only the surgeon had any inkling of what was going on; the interns never linked the John Doe they sliced up and stitched with the British rock star who'd died from complications in another part of the vast hospital from a similar operation several hours later while they slept. The police should have been content, but clearly weren't.

"When did Mister Maggot first feel unwell?" they asked, as well as "why didn't you dial 9-1-1?" There were lifestyle questions, too, such as when did Ricky last take drugs? Where did he get them from? Who also took them? Given that Ricky took a line of cocaine on the drive into the hospital "to calm my fucking nerves", and that he'd got the drugs off Derrick, meant that Derrick had to lie continuously through the whole interview. He knew if he blew it the black-haired man wouldn't be around to save him,

19

there would be no protection. Plausible deniability was in place, but not for Derrick.

Then the call came from the Coroner's office, scheduling the autopsy and authorising letting Derrick go. "No need for bail, we've got your passport," the desk sergeant had advised. Derrick presumed the guy was trying to be helpful. It wasn't working.

He looked down at his cell phone again as he waited for the desk sergeant to arrange the taxi he'd promised. Several missed calls from a withheld number – he wondered if Ricky had managed to secrete a cell phone with him; wondered if he made the car switch okay, wondered what happened after that. What did make him smile was the first instalment of the facilitation fee had been credited to his account with an anonymous invoice "for services rendered".

The cell vibrated again, the number still withheld. Derrick cancelled the call. If it was Ricky he couldn't let him talk, couldn't speak to him again unless he took the same options as Ricky had. Above all he couldn't let anyone find out that Ricky didn't die on the operating table, the black-haired man had made that very clear. From this point on, it wasn't just money that was at risk, it was Derrick's life.

Chapter 4

By the time that Derrick had been released from questioning and Aiden had been finalising the first draft of Ricky's obit, Ricky was still on the mainland, rolled up under a pile of blankets in the trunk of a vast SUV driving at a sedate pace through California, carefully observing all traffic regulations and loaded up for a camping trip. The middle-aged couple with a map of the West Coast spread over the dashboard had chatted amiably to Ricky as they'd piled blankets on top of him, loading him up with drinks and some sandwiches, giving him a bottle "to pee in, try avoiding the need to shit", before loading more camping gear on top.

The vehicle had stopped a few times, Ricky had heard the surf clearly on one stop-over, overheard the woman ask a local about a good place to eat. Then the driving stopped for a long time and the light levels under the blankets, not generally good anyway, dimmed to let Ricky know it was getting dark outside. He was just easing his dick into the bottle to finish filling it with urine when the trunk door opened and the woman pulled back his blankets.

"So, it's true," she said approvingly as she offered an arm to help him get out. Thirty seconds later Ricky found himself half doubled up on a beach road that had virtually no light, his penis waving in the breeze and his trousers hanging around his ankles. As he put the bottle down and tried to drag his gear up his legs the woman pulled him at a brisk pace to a waiting boat, moored just offshore. Splashing through the shallow water Ricky found the man waiting in the boat, leaning over and reaching to pull him in. As night had fallen to an ink black the boat pulled out and headed for a rendezvous four miles offshore, a journey that would take a large part of the night and involve a very risky boat to boat transfer that would reinforce Ricky's doubt that the black-haired man shared the same view of what constituted stylish transport.

By this time his body double had been released for cremation, a fact confirmed by the middle-aged man tasked with transferring Ricky to the container ship or dumping Ricky's body overboard if the ruse had been discovered. Nobody enjoyed the services he'd signed up for if there was any doubt that his assets might be frozen. He didn't share the information with Ricky, in fact he'd hardly spoken all night except to suggest that Ricky "could pull his trousers up and put that dick away" when they'd first set off. Neither were aware that Derrick was a virtual nervous wreck, having fielded numerous interviews on local and national TV, contradicting himself enough to cause the detectives to consider pulling him back in for another conversation before the body was reduced to ashes. That event had taken place within minutes of the Coroner releasing the body, however the paperwork would conveniently state a date a few days hence, an administrative error that could be explained with blushes if necessary but would form part of the formal record otherwise.

However, the detectives were only concerned about "inconsistencies" with Derrick's statements on TV compared to his version of events in the interview room; inconsistencies that could be attributed to the sudden loss of a valuable income stream. What Ricky, the man on the boat and indeed Derrick were unaware of right now was the inconsistency that Aiden had turned up and was currently double checking in the UK.

*

The house Ricky had been brought up in was gone, replaced by a modern housing estate of starter homes, each of which could fit inside Ricky's dining room in LA had that been what he wanted. He'd requested more outlandish ideas to happen when he'd been a reality TV star. Aiden held the map carefully, blinking in the morning light, perching carefully on the bonnet of his trusty and relatively rusty Volvo estate. His hand shook as he orientated himself to the area, not having had a drink in nearly twenty-four hours. He'd sat on a bench in his garden watching the sun set while clutching his glass of whisky the night before, knowing that he did this regularly but appreciating that he'd actually remember it this time. The glass of whisky was sat on a sideboard with a coaster placed across the rim to keep the liquor free from passing bugs, waiting for him to return.

The drive north overnight had been uneventful; nowhere suitable to eat after ten p.m. and motorway services selling dried out inedible food

23

for extortionate amounts of money. At each stop he'd relieved himself and tried Derrick's cell phone, without luck. He'd fielded irate calls from Brian Esk, however, who'd become angry that Aiden hadn't completed the biog.

"What's the problem? You said you'd have it polished off in a few hours. I want to start subbing it ASAP," he'd complained. Aiden tried to explain that there were inconsistencies with the story coming from LA and he needed to check them out. There had been a long pause at this.

"Even if there are inconsistencies, and I'm guessing you're not going to share them with me right now, surely they don't affect the rest of his fucking life?" asked Brian, raising his voice.

"They concern events during his life," countered Aiden, wondering if Brian was right – push out the biog, let others report the death, then hit the world with his revelation. If it was a revelation. Something didn't chime right with his handwritten notes. Two things, actually. One was potentially a plausible change of plan, the other couldn't be attributed to anything other than gross medical negligence if his records were correct. He had to find supporting evidence, the old-fashioned way, by talking to people. "Okay, I'll send you the biog," he said, resignation in his voice "on one condition." There was a pause that made pregnancy appear brief on the other end.

"Go on," said Brian warily.

24

"If I find the evidence I'm hoping to find I want you to fund a trip to LA," said Aiden. Brian sucked in through his teeth.

"To do what?" he asked, wanting the biog on his screen ready for final formatting. The editor was giving him major grief over the lateness of the piece and he wanted it boxed off.

"I need to interview a few people over there," answered Aiden.

"Can't you email them questions?" whined the deputy editor.

"I need to look into their eyes, like in the old days," countered Aiden.

"Can't you just face-time them?" asked Brian, knowing in his heart Aiden had him over a barrel.

"Look Brian, authorise this and I'll deliver you a scoop that will get you promoted. Twice," said Aiden. Brian agreed, and Aiden found himself accessing his biog from the cloud and emailing it to London within minutes. Then he picked up the map and tried to find the local infirmary on it. As he oriented himself his mobile phone pinged. Looking at the phone he was surprised to see a message from one of Ricky's strongest acolytes, a fan who had tracked down Aiden and taken to messaging him on all matters Maggot, day and night. Generally Aiden didn't respond too quickly, he liked to keep this guy at arm's length, but he couldn't argue with the sentiment in front of him.

"How come Ricky's record label knew to release box set today?" read the message. Aiden racked his brain; as the foremost authority and generally most supportive music reviewer of Ricky Maggot's work he was always consulted about every release, new material and "best of" compilations, with a review copy sat in his study weeks before the official release, usually while the artwork was being finalised. He jumped onto Amazon and confirmed what the fan had spotted – a new box set containing all of Ricky Maggot's work including his Death Star period, was for sale released, it appeared, within a nanosecond of the news being released of his death. He replied to the fan immediately.

"No idea, not seen this before. Thanks," he texted, before opening iTunes up. Sure enough, the box set was available for download and was currently top of the iTunes chart. This was fast work, even for a record label. Shaking his head he returned to the map and located the infirmary, noting it was a ten minute walk away. Locking the Volvo Aiden strode out, purpose in his step.

Chapter 5

"So how does it work?" Ricky had asked the black-haired man as he signed sheet after sheet of paperwork, sat in the nondescript office in downtown LA. If he'd passed this office block the previous day he would have seen a "for let" sign up. If he returned tomorrow the sign would be up again. The man waited until Ricky had signed each and every page. He scooped the pile of paper up and checked each one carefully, looking back at the bank details Ricky had brought and compared them to the accountant's evaluation. Without saying a word he added the small amount of sheets that Derrick had signed too, checking them with the same amount of carefulness. At length he steepled his fingers and started talking.

"The papers you have just signed are legally binding. No matter what your family say, the tax authorities insist on or what your record company thinks is their right, my employer owns all your income from the moment you are declared dead," he said, his eyes not quite meeting Ricky's. "That doesn't mean we keep your money, we simply hold onto it to provide the services we're providing to you which will include – er," he said fishing out one specific sheet of paper, "that request about making sure your kids get a good education and your ex gets literally "fuck all"," he said, reading from the sheet.

"You're going to appear to die, disappear from public view, never to return. You'll live among

27

others who have made the same choices that you have made in accommodation that is second to none. You'll want for nothing; hookers, drugs, booze. Or just a good book to read beside the pool, whatever it is you want. There will be restrictions – no phones, no internet, no email. You won't be allowed to make contact with anyone in your current life again, ever," he said, leaning back. "You can still back out of this," he said, adding, "but there will be one mother-fuckin' hefty admin charge to cover releasing you from these," he said, waving his arm over the pile of agreements in front of him. "This is basically your last chance to do so," he cautioned.

"What about Derrick?" asked Ricky. He got it that this was some ultra-secret deal he was going to be read in on and that he would disappear from view for ever, but Derrick was sat right next to him, about to hear the same information and wasn't planning on going anywhere fast. The black-haired man nodded at the manager.

"I wouldn't be surprised if you're not the first artist Derrick has arranged this for. We accept that we need representatives in the real world and people like Derrick understand the balance sheet of rock and roll. You stay and he gets fed, you disappear and he gets a meal ticket for the rest of his life. As long as he keeps his counsel," he said. Ricky looked at Derrick and wondered whether he'd made this arrangement for any of his previous acts; he'd been Ricky's exclusive manager for so long he'd forgotten Derrick had managed a number of small groups before Death

28

Star needed a new manager fifteen years earlier. Derrick just examined his fingernails; what Ricky was about to hear was probably the worst kept secret in the music industry, with rumours and tales bandied around by managers whenever they got together.

"Where you're going was originally called Chattanooga Island," said the black-haired man. "Named by the original civilian owner," he added.

"Civilian?" asked Ricky. The black-haired man nodded before continuing.

"Until the US entered the Second World War the island was uninhabited, then in 1941 a forward operating base was built for disruptive operations against Japan. By 1943 it had outlived its usefulness and was abandoned, leaving behind a number of command structures that eventually formed the first accommodation blocks. Critically it had an excellent jetty hidden inside a mountainous cove, which had served to disguise its use from the Japanese and hide the base from prying eyes.

"Come 1944 and a famous band leader made Uncle Sam an offer, took over the ownership of the island in exchange for his disappearance and a purchase of US war bonds he promised would never be cashed in."

"Why would his disappearance be attractive to the US government?" asked Ricky, "surely, he was one of the most loved musicians of the day," he added.

29

"His music was and is in some circles, but the musicians hated him. He was regarded, in the words of your Prime Minister of the day, Winston Churchill, as an arrogant twat," he said, relishing using the word he'd picked up from his British colleague, "and increasingly the government was finding it difficult to find musicians that would play with him. Two of the best swing trombonists of the day had volunteered for literally suicide missions behind German lines rather than serve under him.

"He knew he wasn't liked. What's more, he was both tired and very wealthy thanks to his profile in the war, so he arranged to disappear, take over the island and set up a business that suited every government under the sun," mused the black-haired man. "Look son, it's not only musicians who need to disappear from time to time and the end of the war created a number of wealthy leaders who Uncle Sam didn't want to have to manage."

"Are we talking the likes of Hitler?" asked Ricky.

"Sure, who else, him and his inner circle," said the black-haired man, a mixture of surprise and admiration crossing his face as he judged the rock star. In his experience nobody else had made that leap, he thought. Then he realised that Ricky had been acting facetiously; he was as dumb as the rest of his ilk after all. No matter, he'd find out soon enough about the less musical residents.

"So, what's it called today?" asked Ricky.

"Officially it has a number of names, some catalogue style numbers used to list uninhabited islands in the general area that are not deemed to be especially useful or interesting, but in the industry, it's called...," the black-haired man said, looking across at Derrick.

"Hotel California," said Derrick, staring at his fingernails.

"Named after the Eagles' hit song?" asked Ricky, smirking. "What?" he asked, seeing the knowing looks exchanged between the black-haired man and Derrick.

"Let's just say the song came second, according to legend," said Derrick after a pause.

Chapter 6

Tony Morroney ran his fingers through his gelled, dyed black hair, negotiating clumsily over the headset as the Islander banked towards one of the rough airstrips that served the island. His second-in-command spoke over the radio on the secure channel, confirming that it was safe to approach.

"The locals haven't spotted your approach, as long as you're quick," he said, the nerves ringing in his voice. Tony tapped the pilot on the shoulder and nodded: he knew they were pretty much on the extremes of the aircraft's range and on more than one occasion in the last two years they'd had to abort at this stage of the flight.

"Land, turn around and if I feel it's safe I'll bail out," he shouted over the roar of the engines. He grasped his holdall with a firm grip and slipped the safety belt off his lap. He grasped the pilot's backrest tightly, his knuckles turning white as the aircraft lost height rapidly, the flaps fully lowered, killing airspeed. The pilot knew he needed to time this perfectly – wind shear was tight on limits, the runway, such as it was, too short, and the risk of deranged locals swarming out from hiding in the scrub too high a risk for what should be a routine flight. The wheels scraped the ground, the rumble rising dramatically as the propeller pitch was increased to stall the forward momentum as the brakes caused the tyres to drag across the rough ground. Dust billowed around the airframe as the nose ducked down, ploughing a furrow into the track, the tail waving side to side wildly. The Islander slewed to a stop momentarily, then the engines raced as the pilot spun the aircraft around to face the way he had landed, taxiing rapidly to where Tony's second-in-command was standing, waving madly as if the pilot didn't know where to stop.

"Ready?" he asked, looking over his shoulder, seeing Tony half stood, holding the door handle with one hand, his holdall in the other, his body waving from side to side as the aircraft rumbled to the waiting second-in-command. As the Islander stopped Tony threw the door open, launched the holdall onto the dirt track and jumped down, almost ripping his head off as the coiled cable spiralling out of the headset stretched taut. Ripping the headset off and throwing it into the cabin, Tony swung the cabin door shut and stood back rapidly as the engines roared up and the aircraft accelerated away, pulling up rapidly and taking to the sky, banking over the sea almost as soon as it was airborne.

The ground adjacent to the landing strip served as the resort's vehicle compound, specialist earth moving vehicles, fork lift trucks, mobile cranes for the periodic building upgrades and spare Land Rovers for whenever Moonie stole the keys and drove yet another vehicle into the swimming pool. Tony hated that man; the joke had well worn thin, but as it was usually Tony who erroneously left the keys unattended he really had to blame himself.

They stood watching the aircraft climb into the low clouds and disappear from view before Tony turned to Alec. Stooping to pick the holdall off the ground, dusting the majority of the dirt accretion off with his free hand, he held Alec's stare. "Problems?"

"It's getting worse, they're organising themselves. We need at least one more of us just to cover for the plane arrivals, getting away without alerting their suspicions is almost impossible." Alec often complained that the top-level management structure was too small, that they were too dependent on a team of pressed men and women who often had more affiliation with the bottom tier of workers than the corporate aims.

"I've been staked out in hiding for the last four hours, just to make sure," he blurted. Tony nodded and started walking; the Land Rover would be parked alongside the spare Land Rovers, keys in, ready.

"I need a drink," he said, slinging his jacket over his shoulder as the first drops of monsoon rain started to fall on him.

The half hour drive across rough ground and hidden tracks was difficult enough; in a torrent of rain it was as scary as landing on Beta wondering if a horde of locals were going to emerge and commandeer the Islander. Some of the locals were truly scary, not the kind of customer that had populated Hotel California in its heyday. Now many had track records of violence and skills that would

34

make most US Marines look like girl scouts on a bad day. Alec parked the Land Rover up outside of the main building, keeping the engine running as the rain pounded down on the vehicle. Both men knew the rain would stop suddenly and the sun would dry the ground up within ten minutes. Attempting to dash across to the door was foolish. Plus, it gave them the opportunity to talk business without locals eavesdropping.

"Good trip?" asked Alec, drumming on the steering wheel in time with the tattoo ringing out on the Land Rover's canvas tilt. Tony nodded, swigging from the bottle of bourbon Alec had given him.

"We've a new resident arriving, sometime later this week," he said, running his tongue over the liquor clinging to the front of his teeth, numbing the tip in the process. "A limey, like you," he added. Alec pulled a face that suggested approval; there were a few Brits amongst the locals, and Alec really enjoyed talking with accents that sounded normal to himself but was almost a foreign language to everyone else. Unfortunately, most of his countrymen caused him the most concern in his day-to-day dealings.

"Gangster or drug lord?" he asked, not really sure where one profession stopped and the other started. Either way, they tended to assert their authority rapidly, not really understanding that they had no power, no need for power, in Hotel California. As long as the money invested from their ill-gotten gains continued to flow into the accounts managed by the organisation, they could have whatever they damn well wanted without the aggravation.

"Neither, musician," said Tony, pulling another slug of bourbon. Alec raised an eyebrow.

"Wow, it seems ages since we had one of them,' he said, recalling the last great influx, in 2016, "Who?" he asked. Like Tony he preferred the musicians and other artistes, was fully prepared to manage the inflated egos, the ridiculous demands and weather the meaningless threats, mainly because many of the locals, as he and Tony called the residents, now came from less artistic backgrounds, were hiding from prosecution, sometimes for international war crimes, usually just for run of the mill violent murders, and most couldn't sing for toffee. Musicians made the place bearable, even the mard-arse Whitney who created mayhem every other night in the karaoke bar or the bloke who used to prefer being named by a meaningless squiggle and now accounted for a large percentage of recreational drug use on the resort.

"Some aging punk rocker called Ricky Maggot," said Tony, running his fingers through his hair, wondering if the humidity would deposit dye on them. Alec's eyes widened suddenly.

"Ricky Maggot? Deathstar's frontman?" he asked, incredulous. Alec loved music, that was one of the reasons he'd agreed to swap his life for an existence as the full time duty manager of Hotel California, as imprisoned as the locals, provided with a fabricated demise for his family in Barnsley, condemned to staying on the island for the rest of his natural life or until such time as Tony passed or retired - retirees were expected to spend their final days on the island – when he would take over the role of recruiting new locals. The upside of making it to general manager was the frequent visit to civilisation, mixing with celebrities considering buying a room and generally living the high life in the real world. The downside was knowing that it was a transitory position; that you could never relocate back to the real world and you'd never see your family again.

"Yeah. Know him?" asked Tony, not really interested. He was, in reality, just a money man. He never did care much for the background of the residents and was probably the main reason there had been a gradual drift towards gangsters evading incarceration in exchange for their ill-gotten wealth from the original concept of musicians escaping the pressure of 24/7 publicity. The investors who owned the complex didn't care who booked in as long as they provided an income stream. Until the turn of the Century musicians were still the biggest earners, who generated huge profits from sales of CDs after their faked death, but today record sales accounted for a small portion of the pie, touring was the cash cow and dead musicians couldn't tour. So, unless an existing megastar was willing to trade his or her fortune for a room in Hotel California it was down to rescuing bad guys from the reaches of the good guys that was proving to be the more lucrative business.

"I grew up listening to him, idolised him to be honest," answered Alec, his heart racing. Unlike Tony, Alec loved music, really enjoyed shooting the breeze with the old musicians in the communal rooms. Meeting the likes of Ricky was the high point of his working life. He stared out of the windshield, figured that the rain was stopping, felt the wave of warmth that inevitably followed the downpour. "Do we know when he's arriving?" he asked.

"Sometime this week, he's in mid Pacific right now, about to be transferred from a container ship to a pile of junk. That's taking him to a RV about one hundred miles away and he'll be picked up by our regular supply boat," said Tony. Alec wondered if now was a good time to remind Tony that he was supposed to train him up in the logistics of the organisation, ready for when he took up the reins, but he knew Tony wouldn't be persuaded; training Alec up would expose Tony to the threat of being deposed. He knew that was the way, he'd personally seen off his mentor with an entrenching shovel to the back of the head twenty years earlier. Both men sat in silence for a further minute before opening their doors. Tony grabbed Alec's arm before he stepped out of the Land Rover.

"The problem guy? Please tell me he's taken a turn for the worse?" he asked. Alec shook his head.

"I think he's got stronger than ever over the last two weeks," he said, adding, "and boy, is he stirring the shit with the new guys."

38

Chapter 7

Aiden had spent a few hours bugging the living daylights out of NHS staff working at the local hospital to track down the people he needed to speak to. His break came just as the hospital security were bearing down on him, his cover story of researching the ways the local health service had improved over the last thirty years worn as thin as cigarette paper causing staff members to phone for backup. Then one of the receptionists working nearby recognised his name and, more importantly, his connection with Ricky.

"I loved that piece you wrote a couple of months ago," she said, flicking through her Twitter account to prove she'd sent a similar message to Aiden at the time. Aiden showed more interest in the tweet than he'd shown when she'd first sent it, actually reading it this time.

"I remember that," he lied. Actually, he didn't even remember the piece, let alone any tweets, such is life as an award-winning alcoholic. The lie worked; she glowed with pride. Talking to Aiden was being with a virtual celebrity, talking with the man who wrote about her idol was a dream come true. She gave him the name and number of some of the older staff who had left a few years earlier, retired to less stressful lives. Most couldn't help, some didn't even remember the receptionist they'd entrusted with their personal details at some boozy leaving do a few years back. But one knew some of the even older guard, the ones least likely to have a mobile phone let alone internet access. Critically she had some names and addresses.

It was the third name on the list, last known to be residing in a care home on the outskirts of Selby, that provided the break he needed. Jack Fell was an octogenarian resident who'd been a doctor in Accident and Emergency in York hospital during the nineteen eighties. Unlike most of the residents sat dribbling around him, Jack had managed to avoid dementia and relished the opportunity to talk to someone who wasn't completely addled.

"If it wasn't for this arthritis I'd still be living at home," he explained as they sat in the visitors' lounge. Aiden asked about family, wondering why they would let their father live in a home with a bunch of burbling nut-jobs before momentarily wondering when he'd last called his own dad, currently suffering the same problem in Essex. "Daughter's got a career, also in medicine, gave up having a family to climb the ladder, wasn't going to let a parent too inconsiderate to not die stop her," he explained.

"Jason Jones," he interrupted when Aiden mentioned he was researching a story on the late Ricky Maggot.

"You knew him?" asked Aiden. Jack nodded and continued without being prompted.

"His family lived two streets away and I patched him up a few times, at work and sometimes at home. He got a bit carried away with the Miners' Strike up here and was always getting clobbered by badly thrown bricks, misplaced truncheons, the odd fisticuffs. I kept a weather eye on his progress as he became famous," he added. "Mind you, my daughter idolising him helped me keep up to date, I'm more of a Johnny Cash fan myself," he said, his eyes focussing into the middle distance as his memories flooded back. Aiden knew the look, checked the power light on his voice recorder, hoped he'd packed the USB charging cable as these sessions were often lengthy.

He sat back and let Jack start his tales about Ricky, starting sometime just after the First World War, waiting for Ricky's birth to occur in nineteen seventy. He didn't mind, he'd gone old school, spoken face to face with a witness and had a result. Life didn't get much better, the trip to LA was virtually assured

*

Ricky found himself shivering as he was lowered from the container ship onto the deck of the transit boat, a dilapidated ketch with both sails furled. The skipper and crew, that is, both occupants of the ketch, pulled on the rope guiding the rock star to the wooden boards, ostensibly attempting to help him land on the ones less likely to disintegrate in a puff of sawdust and woodworm. The skipper was going to get enough money to get drunk for a week for this transit and didn't know who the passenger was, didn't care. He cared to get him to the rendezvous point in one piece, to ensure he got paid, and then would wait for the next contact. These days the jobs were less frequent than in the old days, when he'd earned enough to pick up the ketch as a decent second-hand vessel and still get drunk, but work was work and booze was needed.

Ricky stumbled as his feet hit the deck and he struggled to stand still with the sway of the small boat amplifying his nausea. Grabbing the rail, he leaned over and heaved, felt his stomach ache worse than after a shed-load of dodgy drugs washed down with cheap champagne. "How long?" he asked the skipper, his eyes bloodshot and his face pale. The skipper didn't speak English but understood the question from the intonation. He gabbled an answer that Ricky didn't understand until the crewman leaned across.

"A few hours, maybe less," the young man said, smiling, looking closely at Ricky. Unlike his employer, who only watched TV in the bar and then to watch horse racing to support his need to gamble, he liked to watch the American channels, the comedy shows and the reality shows, even if they were a few years behind. Especially the reality shows, particularly the one with the crazy British musician who couldn't sing or play in tune. That one made him laugh, with the crazy antics in the massive house that would keep a village dry, with the trucks a village would kill for that ended up in the swimming pool that would water a village's crops for a year, with the

42

parties he would love to attend with crazy women who just liked taking their clothes off.

That man made him laugh when he saw the old reruns on the TV, and he was making him laugh now.

*

Alec braced himself as he approached the King's door, listening out for the Southern drawl burbling obscenities at the maids attending to him.

"Y'all need to get my karate suit, y'hear," he growled as Alec walked in.

"Sure thing, Elv," Alec replied, patting the eighty-something-year-old on the shoulder. "Just make sure you warm up. Why not book a session with one of the Thai masseurs first?" he asked, knowing the King's preferences beyond pain killing drugs. He noted that Elvis had trimmed down over the last two years, had started eating healthily and was taking regular exercise, which was a real worry. Tony had kept the old man of the island on a steady diet of burgers and prescription drugs for years because he feared that if anyone could trigger an uprising, it was Elvis. Hopefully Elvis had left it too late.

"We've got a new resident arriving," Alec said, conversationally. The old man liked to hear about new arrivals, believed his position in the pecking order entitled him to know about who was coming and when. Alec realised that Elvis probably

43

wouldn't believe that Alec often informed him literally minutes after he knew.

"Who? Another Russian gangster?" the old man spat out.

"No, a musician, like you," replied Alec, withering as soon as he realised what he'd said.

"I'm the king," bellowed the old man. "I doubt he's 'like' me boy," he added. Alec nodded, he'd been briefed long before to respect the old man's ego, advice he'd followed assiduously over the years.

"He was big after you left the scene," he explained, "but not as big as you were – or are," he added. "He was big on the UK Punk scene," he mentioned, wincing as he knew the old man wasn't a fan of the genre.

"Y'all know we've got enough punks around here," he said, pulling on his towelling robe. "Ah expect y'all want me to form the welcoming committee?" he asked, knowing the answer. Elvis was the de-facto leader of the residents, having taken over from Buddy in 1980. He missed Buddy, and Buddy had idolised Elvis until his own untimely death aged forty-four.

Since that day, after Elvis found himself the only resident who could be arsed to pay respects to the young Texan as the shallow grave was filled in, he made a point of visiting Buddy's grave every day. There were many more small mounds in the graveyard now, and as far as Elvis could tell he was the longest serving and probably the oldest resident left, but even when he hadn't been either he'd been the natural leader. And, as Jimi used to tell him almost daily, he was also leader of the escape committee, not that it ever made any meaningful progress.

*

Aiden repeated himself to Brian, even though the line wasn't bad. 'I said I don't think Ricky is dead, or if he is, he didn't die the way it is reported' he said one last time. Brian spluttered over the phone line as Aiden explained his theory. Eventually Brian broke into Aiden's tirade.

'Look Aiden, this is all supposition,' he said. It was Aiden's turn to splutter.

'Supposition? Look, I have absolute evidence that Ricky couldn't have died the way it was reported,' he said, fairly certain he'd been quite clear previously. Brian didn't break step as he attempted to demolish Aiden's theory.

'Right, first, doctors make mistakes. All - the – fucking - time,' he said. 'Worse, journalists these days don't check their facts like they did in the old days. You and your brethren just Google for facts and cherry pick whichever one suits,' he accused, unfairly in Aiden's opinion as it was people like Brian who insisted all research be started and ended with a search engine, with everything in the middle just made up.

'Finally,' he said, 'you just want a free trip Stateside. I know your type,' he accused, correctly this time. Aiden argued back; his source was a retired doctor with decades of experience and first-hand knowledge of Ricky. Plus, he hadn't relied on the journalistic output from the States but had contacted the hospital itself. Sure, it was a prepared statement he'd got, try getting better than that from a hospital in the most litigious country in the world. Eventually Brian caved in, partly because his coffee had been placed in front of him, partly because the travel had been signed off by his boss the day before. He'd just hoped to persuade Aiden to forgo the trip so he could show a saving to his boss or, better, bag the trip for himself.

'OK, I'll email you the authority. Bastard,' he said before hanging up.

*

Jack Fell finished the edit to his blog just before the evening meal was served. Unlike most of the residents of the home he'd kept up to speed on new technology, sporting Microsoft's latest Surface laptop, probably the only device hooking up to the home guest internet access point outside of visiting hours. He didn't bother during those periods as dozens of bored teenagers to fifty-somethings logged on while pretending to talk to their inheritance, sorry, grandparents. He'd been especially impressed with the journalist who'd eschewed accessing the internet during their discussion, preferring to take notes in shorthand. Shorthand, for fuck's sake. And to think doctors were criticised for illegible handwriting!

But he'd shown real interest in a neighbour and patient from Jack's past, so he wrote up the gist of the interview on his blog, for all five subscribed readers and anyone else who stumbled across it.

Pushing 'send' he felt a sense of achievement; which is reasonable when you consider he also signalled the end of his life.

Chapter 8

The ketch had proven worse than the container ship, pitching and swaying in the rough seas. Ricky recalled the man with the slick black hair drilling down to determine the date Ricky wanted to disappear.

"As soon as, tomorrow's as good a date as any," he'd answered. Tony had whistled to himself, flicked through a Filofax as though it was still considered cool. Who has a Filofax these days? asked Ricky to himself. He'd glanced at Derrick, saw he had the same look.

"Takes time to arrange. Earliest I can make it is late September, early October," the black-haired man said, sucking in again, furrowing his dyed brows.

"Ok, do it," Ricky had said, keen to get the ball rolling. The penny dropped with Derrick.

"Hurricane season. Might be a bit choppy," he said. Ricky gave it two, maybe three seconds thought.

"What the fuck, do it. What's a bit of wind?" he asked.

*

The ancient mariner shouted down the hatch some garbled language, but the meaning was clear. Hold tight, vomit in one place only, please. Or words to that general effect.

"Too fucking late mate," groaned Ricky as the ketch pitched constantly, the category four storm racking the boat relentlessly. He didn't know it, but the ketch had been selected for several operational reasons – the owner was considered reliable, confidential and disposable. So was Ricky, once the disclaimers had been signed. Sure, he was worth more if he arrived at Hotel California in one piece, but there was a one-off payment due if he didn't.

Plus, who the fuck would know he didn't arrive – it wasn't like he could send a text message or Skype home. Deep down Ricky started to realise that this might not be the paradise he'd sought, that he might have been sent to a version of hell dressed to sound like heaven. Then he remembered his last marriage, and it all seemed worth it.

*

Alec scanned the shoreline for the ketch, the envelope containing the relatively irrelevant amount of cash in the local currency that would satisfy the ketch pilot clutched firmly in his hand. The cove was as far away from the main camp as could be found, beyond the resources of those without access to the Land Rover. He kept a watching brief on his arse-end too, in case Elvis or one of the Russian Mafiosi had followed him by some means. They tried to keep the rendezvous locations as remote from the complex as possible, every guest was bed checked every night, although some found themselves in other persons beds such is the way with drugs, booze, hookers and conflicted orientation. Or sheer boredom. While the wind blasted his hair, ruffled his shirt and flicked sand along the shore he kept his eyes on the rocky outcrops that had shielded the island's occupations from the Japs so effectively. Eventually the wreck of the ketch appeared, listing heavily thanks to the wind and the woodworm, tacking towards the shoreline and the deteriorated jetty. Alec pointed the Very Pistol skywards and fired off the green flare that was the standard Hotel California method of saying keep coming. The red flare was in his pocket, protected from the occasional driving rain by a polythene bag – it meant turn around, find somewhere to hide for a day or so, and was way more important than the green flare.

He knew the boat owner wouldn't have a reciprocal flare to fire – if he had he'd have sold it years ago to fund his drinking habit. Strong on following orders, weak on cash flow, was Alec's take on the old man. The ketch pitched towards the shore, tacking here, drifting there, looking like it held more water than the bay itself at points. Eventually it drew up alongside the dilapidated jetty, a rope thrown haphazardly onto a skewed post and it dragged itself to the side. Alec wasn't surprised by the pale-faced passenger staggering to the edge – he'd witnessed this stage dozens of times, knew that Ricky would be desperate to throw himself onto the jetty, would have no truck with basic safety procedures, would be very pleased that they didn't bother with basic immigration processes. Plus, had Ricky managed to retain his passport it would just have found itself on a bonfire by the end of day.

"Ricky, welcome," said Alec, handing his arm out to the middle-aged rocker.

"You a Brit?" asked Ricky, taking the outstretched arm. Alec nodded, grinned like a Cheshire Cat and felt like spinning on the spot. One of his heroes – no, his all-time hero – was going to be his guest.

"Alec," he said in reply, "From Barnsley." Ricky looked at the young man, appreciated the accent like a fine wine or a line of the best cocaine.

"You live here?" he asked, not fully grasping the concept of the island. Alec got that, most residents assumed it was like the movies, or Lost, that civilisation was just around the bay.

"Sure do, under-manager, your day-to-day point of contact. How was your trip?" he asked, noting the expected wrinkle of the nose. "We have to do it this way to ensure you disappear off the face of the earth. I appreciate it wasn't pleasant, but everything improves from this point on," he said. Ricky didn't look convinced, but that wasn't unexpected. Wait until he's spent twenty-four hours with us, thought Alec.

During the half hour drive back to the main complex, which in reality could have been reached in fifteen minutes had Alec not been trying to confuse the living shit out of his new guest, they discussed the deal at the complex.

"Friday night is singers' night, where any of our guests can get up and belt it out like it's Vegas," he said.

"Sounds good, what day is it?" asked Ricky. Alec smiled.

"Every day is Friday here, every night is Friday night," he answered. "We have a very versatile house band," he added, omitting to mention that each and every member was a convicted murderer and that a deal had been struck with all of them that gave them immunity from prosecution in return for their musical skills.

"They can play anything from swing to punk, and I for one am waiting to hear you step up," he said, watching Ricky in the corner of his eye. Some guests, even the most musical, sometimes refused to perform, their issue with real life being that they just hated performing. If Ricky was one of them, he didn't reveal it then. They pulled up outside the complex, under the canopy. "We're here," he said, slipping out and running around the Jeep to let Ricky out.

"You going to show me the ropes?" asked Ricky. Alec was torn, he wanted to spend more time with his hero, but he knew the protocol, knew when he had to stand back. He could see the senior resident hovering in the background, waiting by the foyer doors.

"Our longest standing guest insists on doing that task, and I can see him waiting to do your induction," said Alec, manoeuvring Ricky towards

Elvis. Ricky had no idea who the old git was, noting the long, grey hair trailing down his body, but realised there was something familiar in the old man's appearance; he just couldn't put a finger on it.

"You going to show me round?" he asked the grey-haired man.

"Uh-hu," was the reply as Elvis curled his upper lip. Ricky realised straight away who his escort was.

Chapter 9

Aiden's heart skipped a beat when the call came through. He'd powered his phone back up to see if there were any voicemails from Derrick, having left his phone charger at home when he'd set off up north and consequently was nursing his phone charge until he could get a replacement charger. He was just amazed that it rang literally as it powered up, just felt his luck was in, even though it wasn't either of the numbers he knew Derrick held. Apart from cold calls from people trying to extract his credit card details he never got calls from unknown numbers these days. In fact, he hardly received calls from known numbers either, with Aiden taken to engaging the cold callers in mindless, banal conversations whenever they called, especially if he was drunk.

But this didn't feel like a cold call requesting his card details or its close cousin the "we've heard you were involved in an accident" call about the accident he'd never had. Maybe Derrick wanted to touch base using a new number?

"Aiden," he answered, brightly.

"Aiden McKie?" replied a cautious voice.

"The very same," replied Aiden, not placing the voice, but recognising the accent in general.

"I understand you visited a mister Jack Fell yesterday," said the voice.

"Yes, but..." replied Aiden, wondering who had complained. He'd blagged his way into the home, using all the usual subterfuge, but Jack had been happy to receive him, had had a great chat, inviting Aiden to call back any time he wanted. Aiden felt his hackles rise, this was likely to be some pointless do-gooder exercising their legal rights.

"I'm Detective Inspector John Morris, Yorkshire Constabulary, and I'm contacting you about your visit to mister Fell's residential home yesterday. Are you a member of his family?" asked the voice. Aiden felt his resolve crumble; he'd often broken the rules to gain access to people in the past and had got away with it most times. This was obviously one of those times he hadn't, but usually it was just a call from the institution warning him off. Calling the police was way too heavy.

"No, I'm a reporter," he answered. There was a pause before the voice continued.

"Not even a friend? A family friend?"

"No. Yesterday was the first time I met Doctor Fell," replied Aiden, wondering how much of a telling off he would get.

"Did he invite you? According to the staff on duty, you implied he'd contacted you." Aiden knew his face was glowing red but knew coming clean was the quickest way to get this guy off the line.

"No, I'm investigating a story about a previous neighbour of Jack's and I admit I blagged my way in.

But if you check with Jack you'll find he was quite happy to talk to me, and even invited me back," confessed Aiden, feeling better with every word of the confession. Another pause.

"I'm afraid that won't be possible. Could I ask where you are right now?" asked the policeman. Aiden told him the location of the hotel he was staying in, about five miles from the old person's home he'd visited the previous night.

"I'm just about to check out," he said. The by-now predictable pause was followed by a request for Aiden to call into the local police station, any time in the next half hour.

"We can send a car if you'd prefer," suggested DI Morris. Aiden declined, but mused whether he needed to extend his booking at the hotel.

"No need, we may only need to talk to you for a few minutes, and if we need to talk longer, well, we have accommodation at the station," replied the detective. That was when Aiden started to panic.

*

"That's Glenn's grave, number 23," said Elvis, pointing to a neatly tended mound in the yard behind the main building. "Someone told me that Hitler is grave number 1, didn't make it past the first day. Unfortunately, those Russian gangsters they take in last a whole lot longer," he added, wistfully. He'd already explained that he had been instrumental in ensuring the graves were kept neat and tidy, utilising some of the cheap labour used to clean rooms, cook meals, serve drinks and open their legs as required. "Weeding is a step up in their journey towards attaining some self-respect, if y'all ask me" he grumbled.

Ricky looked at the rows of graves, all unmarked, dozens in each row. "They number the graves?" he asked. Elvis raised his right eyebrow and tutted in an annoyed manner.

"When you're gone boy, your funding line is almost certainly at an end. Even if it isn't, they don't need to pretend to like ya, to even know y'existed. They bury ya, I guess grab as much funding from your estate, and forget ya. Glenn was long gone when I got here; back in the day one of the managers allocated the numbers, now it's me who does it," he said, pointing to grave number 206. "Jimi lies there, not a bad guitarist, lousy singer, but made fabulous meatloaf. I miss the meatloaf," he said. Ricky decided to ask the question he felt had been glossed over during the consultation with the black-haired man.

"What happens if your funds dry up?" he asked, seeing the look of panic in the King's eyes. "Don't worry, you're still selling great, doing duets and releasing new stuff all the time," he blurted, before adding, "I'm not sure how they do that, I know there's bugger all left of my back catalogue to plunder that hasn't been plundered already. Elvis turned his back on the graveyard and pointed to a building over in the distance.

"I don't know for certain, but have always assumed that if the cash dries up you're gonna end up in one of these," he said, throwing his thumb over his shoulder, "way sooner than God intended. But that building over there might help explain some of your concerns."

*

Aiden looked around the interview room, noted that the chair was bolted to the floor. A few hotels wished they'd done that when Ricky stayed, he thought. DI Morris placed a plastic beaker in front of Aiden and indicated to a glass pitcher of water.

"Help yourself," he said, leaning across to the side and slipping a CD into a double CD unit. "You want a copy too?" he asked, holding a second CD in the air. Aiden shook his head.

"Not unless it's on vinyl. I stream everything from the cloud these days," he said, finding his mouth became very dry as he clarified, "legally, of course." In reality he could download virtually every new release with access codes emailed to him by music industry execs pushing their acts. All music journos did. Most of it really was legit, too. The detective didn't seem too interested, he just started the recorder, stated his name, the date and the time, before asking Aiden to introduce himself.

"You're not under arrest and you're free to leave any time you like," he added after the preliminary introductions had been completed.

"Why would I be under arrest?" asked Aiden, the panic starting to well up again.

"You're not. I just want to know what your business with Doctor Fell was yesterday," said the policeman, scanning a foolscap pad with questions written on. "You said something about writing a story for a music magazine," he said, lifting the corner of his pad and reading some rough notes scribbled on there. Aiden nodded, wondered why it was important, suddenly realising that what he'd asked the good doctor to do was probably in breach of his code of ethics. Perhaps he'd dobbed himself in, along with Aiden?

"I'm writing an obit," he said, causing the policeman to look up suddenly. Aiden guessed that certain words had this effect on detectives, along with "I did it" and "you won't be needing that key for a while". Some phrases just didn't sound too good when expressed to a copper with a CD recording device or, Aiden guessed, followed by the words "your honour."

"Whose obit?" asked the detective, pen poised above the pad.

"Jason Jones," answered Aiden, swallowing hard. The look on the detective's face didn't show any comprehension, so Aiden added, "you probably know him as Ricky Maggot." DI Morris looked just as confused initially before scribbling something down on his pad.

"The rock and roll performer? He's local, isn't he?"

"He was, until the nineteen eighties," answered Aiden, realising that Ricky had probably left the area around the time the detective was born, or at most starting primary school. "Ask your parents," he suggested helpfully. DI Morris sat back briefly, clearly scanning his memory.

"He the guy who died a couple of days ago in the States?" he asked.

"Apparently," answered Aiden, regretting revealing his hand so easily. It didn't seem to make an impact on the detective, who decided that Jason Jones' death wasn't likely to be important as it happened across the Atlantic plus a few thousand miles on top away. His jurisdiction stopped at Huddersfield.

"Drug overdose, I expect," stated the policeman, scratching out the notes he'd made already, running his finger down his list of pre-prepared questions. Aiden squirmed: it was a reasonable guess, the first he'd made when hearing Ricky had shrugged his mortal coil, but the journalist in him liked facts to be right, unless writing them less than right provided a bigger fee or access to an award. Or a regular column in the Daily Mail.

"No. Natural causes, apparently. Died during a routine operation, it seems," he said. He realised that the detective had moved on from that conversation as he ringed a question on his pad. DI Morris looked up at the corner of the room to search for a delicate way to ask the next question. When he looked down he noticed Aiden's hand was shaking as he tried to pour a beaker of water. He leant over and took the jug and finished the job, mainly because he was responsible for cleaning up any mess made during the interview.

"Your hand's shaking. Nervous?" he asked. Aiden shook his head, but wasn't convinced, wasn't expecting the detective, if he was true to his job title, to be convinced either.

"I haven't had a drink for nearly thirty hours," he confessed, "apart from coffee, which doesn't count." The detective looked at Aiden closely; no sign of dehydration, skin pallor looking normal. Then the penny dropped.

"Ah, you've a drink problem. Drugs too?" he asked. Or at least it sounded like a question, but Aiden felt it was more like a statement. He shook his head.

"No, drink. Whisky, mainly. Occupational hazard along with splinters from pencils and headaches from staring at blank screens," he said, hoping his candid approach would help. There was a long pause, way beyond pregnant unless the gestation period of a sperm whale was being considered. Aiden took a swig of the water, spilling half down his front. "OK, I work in the music industry, drugs are always around, I've used some recreationally but nothing recently," he admitted. The detective scribbled down a few notes, before asking the next question.

"Would you object to a full body search?" he asked. Aiden knew his eyes would have dilated immediately – he'd heard of these searches from rock artists, with graphic descriptions of what to expect as you tried to touch your toes.

"No, well, actually, yes," he blustered. "Am I under suspicion of drug related offences?" he asked, considering the option to leave seriously. The policeman sat back, having circled another question.

"How well did you know doctor Fell?" he asked, pointedly not answering Aiden. Aiden shrugged.

"Until yesterday I'd never heard of him, let alone met him. I spoke with him last night for, what, thirty minutes," he said. More note taking, more silence. "Look, I can share my notes if you like," said Aiden, if only to break the silence. "Or you can just ask doctor Fell, he'll back up everything I've said," he added, noting the raised eyebrow facing him.

"That would be difficult, seeing as doctor Fell was found dead unexpectedly this morning, and you're the last person known to have seen him alive," stated the detective.

Ricky stood in the middle of the recording studio, recognising that it was probably ten years out of date but essentially as good as the one he'd left behind in California in one of his houses. The mixing desk was new, better than the ones he'd used in pro studios. From the outside the building had looked like most of the non-accommodation buildings in the complex; single floored with a wide frontage like a nineteen-fifties cinema. Inside the front doors, in a foyer like space, were posters of recording artists from the past seventy years, some seemingly still undecided about joining Hotel California, and a pair of double doors with the legend "Recording Studio" emblazoned above. To the side and at right angles to the doors was a huge stack of Marshall amplifiers that Elvis said were used "now and then" to sound check new recordings. He walked through the door to the control room and ran his fingers along the mixing desk.

"So, if you're losing revenue they get you to record new material and arrange for it to be found", he said, crooking his fingers around the word "found". Elvis nodded and walked Ricky across to a steel cabinet, one Ricky recognised as a storage for raw music media. In Elvis' day it would have contained two-inch tapes, in Ricky's studio it stored solid state media disks. These looked like the DVD storage his old studio used to hold. Elvis pulled one out and slipped it into a disc drive, walking around to the mixing desk.

"This'll sound a little rough boy, 'less I get the mixing levels right. Some dude in London usually does the final mix, makes sure it sounds a little rough. I guess some critter creates a back story to explain why it's remained lost for so long, then passes it to an innocent but talented producer who remixes it properly and wham! A hit. That's my guess, they don't provide us with any information from outside the island. No radio, TV and certainly none of that internet thing you new guys keep banging on about. They sometimes bring a newspaper in and make us pose with it for a photograph," he said as a reggae beat kicked off.

"That Marley's new hit?" asked Ricky, impressed, wondering about the newspaper story. Elvis nodded, messing with the mix to increase the bass, too engrossed to complete the story.

"I'm none too good at this. Usually get one of you Brits to do the honours," he said. "Paul McCartney wasn't too shabby, as he called it, behind a mixing desk before he passed – number two hundred and eighty-four," he said, still adjusting. Ricky had to agree – Elvis wasn't too good, but for an octogenarian he wasn't too "shabby" as he called it, either. He couldn't agree about Macca though – they'd shared a beer a week before Ricky made his trip, at an awful benefit concert in New York. Elvis saw the look.

"The original one, who came to see me in Bel Air with Lennon. They used to make a great double act here before they passed," he said, looking

64

crestfallen. "John was number three hundred and forty-five," he added. Elvis turned and looked straight into Ricky's eyes. "Look kid, when I arrived here I must have been about your age. Fed up with the rock and roll life, the pressures, the constant intrusion. I bet you've got some of that too. Back then this was still a great place, some real characters, it was a laugh every day and all night long.

"But back then the staff, including the hookers, were on short term contracts, lifted from nearby islands, a two-year job at most. To be fair, two years is enough – we always gave them a hard time, now the Russians are ruling the roost it must be harder again on the girls, know what I mean boy?

"Back in the day they could be returned to their village, technically wealthy in their terms and no risk to the island. We were just white or black dudes who got smashed every night and occasionally drove cars into the swimming pool. Moonie still does if he gets his hands on the management Land Rover keys.

"Now, if they wear out, if the girls fail to please, if anyone complains then they're finished. But they can't go back to their islands anymore, that internet thing I mentioned, it's everywhere apparently. Seems nowhere is really isolated in the world any more, except here." Elvis was staring at the console, his hands resting on the sliders, pulling the reggae beat down to silent. Ricky stared at the King's hands and wondered when the induction would get to the bar. He felt he had to ask.

"So, where do they go now?" Elvis looked up, tears welling in his eyes.

"Where I took you first. There's over a thousand graves in that plot, only about fifty belong to musicians. Perhaps management account for low teens, and that's only because offing each other is the only route to promotion in this game, it seems. The rest are members of staff that have failed, disappointed or upset somebody just for being human. Some thanks to the medical care," he said. Ricky held up his hand.

"I was told the medical care was second to none." Elvis smiled.

"Boy, when there's no competition, anyone with a first aid certificate looks good. To be fair, the medical facility is well stocked, most of the staff quite competent. But they're here just like you and me, they can't leave, drawn to this life because of the excesses, the climate and I'm guessin' that each and every one of them have been struck off for one failing or the other back in the day.

"Try not to get ill after a major party as they're usually all smashed on cocaine," he said. "I guess y' wanna find the bar"

*

DI Morris had explained that generally an eighty-year-old man waking up dead in a care home wasn't considered unusual, it's what eighty-year-old men did in care homes up and down the country

66

every day. "But his GP wasn't happy when he was informed. It seems he carried out a routine health check on Mister Fell yesterday morning and found him in fine health, with no worries. He wasn't happy for the death certificate to be signed off, consequently the Coroner authorised an autopsy this morning," he said. "We're expecting preliminary tox screen results any time now," he added. "Might be a good time to clear up any omissions in your story, better than making us take every step unaided." Aiden's head spun; "this guy thinks I've killed the old man," he thought.

"He was fine when I left him, I didn't give him anything. He had a cup of coffee when I entered, he drunk it during the interview, I don't know if he ate or drank anything after I left," he insisted. DI Morris doodled on his pad, spoke without looking up.

"Staff say he ate before you arrived, never saw him after you left until this morning when he was found dead, stone cold. Time of death given to be around the time you visited," he said, failing to mention that time-of-death estimates varied hugely over a three or four-hour time limit. He looked up as the door opened and a constable brought a folded sheet of paper into the room. Unfolding the paper, Morris scanned it briefly, then re-folded it. "It appears that Doc Fells died from a mixture of barbiturates and heroin, delivered in a cocktail injected into his neck," he said, staring directly into Aiden's eyes.

"Preliminary results suggest that both drugs are standard street quality but delivered in a lethal concentration. The kind of drugs often found in the music industry," he said.

Chapter 10

Tony Morroney parked up on the promontory as the sun was making its way to the horizon. Within minutes the whole area would be pitch black, with no light pollution this far from the complex. Double checking the hand brake on the Land Rover, he got out and climbed on the hood, standing as high as he could, looking around for any sign of movement, any colours that shouldn't be there. Satisfied he was alone he jumped off the vehicle and paced ten steps to the left, feeling for the one-foot diameter rock with his foot as the light was falling fast. Bending he pulled the rock up and extracted the key under it, then backtracked to the Land Rover, finding the metal strongbox welded under the driver's seat and unlocked it using the key, a duplicate of the one held in the office safe.

These days the sat phone never travelled anywhere outside of the box, and the key to the box never travelled with the sat phone. Apart from being the only reliable method of contacting the outside world, the sat phone provided the only internet access on the island when hooked up to his laptop, and that combination would be a real game changer if the locals got hold of them.

Extracting the sat phone he scanned around one last time before hitting the speed dial. His boss answered straight away.

"How's the new arrival?" he was asked. Tony sighed deeply.

"Arrived, on time, fit and well," he reported. "Courier paid and gone." There was silence, presumably as the message was conveyed, probably by means of written notes or just hand signals. "Have you dealt with the leak?" he asked. He'd heard about the problem yesterday, during the comms briefing from this promontory, understood that if Ricky hadn't been so far advanced to the island they would have terminated his contract.

"We've quashed the messenger, have the laptop. Our specialist is confident he can crack the passwords soon and take the blog page down. Distribution is minimal, once we have access to the blog we can see who has opened that page and eliminate those eyes too, if needed. We're evaluating the options. We have a task for your team," said the voice, making Tony's blood run cold. A task for the team wasn't a euphemism for a good time, and his team was essentially himself and Alec.

"I'm listening," he said, looking into the pitch-black night.

*

Aiden sat in the cell, looking at the coffee cup, watching the brown sludge form concentric rings every time someone walked outside. He hadn't been charged, had been offered the chance to contact a lawyer, was reviewing his options.

70

Suddenly the door swung open, a police sergeant beckoning. "This way, sir," he said. Aiden stood, threw the cup of cold coffee into the waste bin in the corner and followed. He'd never had a lawyer, wondered if this was time to break that habit. He was ushered back into the interview room and was joined shortly by DI Morris.

"It seems doctor Fell updated his blog half an hour after you left the building. We've checked all relevant CCTV at the home and at your hotel and can confirm that it looks like he was alive at least thirty minutes after you left. The pathologist is adamant that death would have occurred within twenty seconds of the injection being applied, so it looks like you're probably off the hook," he said, holding out a sheet of paper.

"Probably?" asked Aiden. DI Morris nodded.

"We've checked his blog entry and compared it to his previous entries. Let's just say doctor Fell has a certain voice on his blog and the latest entry sounds one hell of a lot like his. Couple that with the time stamp of the entry, including two minor modifications for typos, we conclude he blogged way after you found your way to your hotel. Only problem is we can't seem to find his computer, and staff have confirmed he had one." Aiden nodded.

"A Surface Pro, one of the latest models I think. He showed it me briefly, was proud that he was up to date with technology, laughed at me for using shorthand," he said. "Could it be a robbery gone wrong?"

"Maybe, maybe not. He mentioned you in the blog, though," said Morris, waving at the paper in Aiden's hand. Aiden looked at the screen dump, waded around the pop-up adverts and found the text. The blog was, seemingly, named "Voice From the Home".

"Readers, a visitor tonight, unannounced and unknown (to me). Not family, of course, that would never happen without a three week notice and the right to cancel at any time. Grumble over.

"Visitor is a journalist, actually makes a living writing for magazines, has won awards, too. Gosh, that's me honoured. His name's Aiden McKie, and he's writing a piece on an old neighbour of mine. I knew the neighbour as Jason Jones, but you might know him by his stage name Ricky Maggot. You might have heard he died recently, tragically, at the hands of my brethren over in America. Aiden smells a rat and, having looked closer at the reports on the web, so do I. I'm not going to spoil Aiden's fun for him, but when he publishes his shock expose then I'll provide a link to it, you can be sure. He'd better name check me while he's at it!

"I'm going to do a little more research before I turn in at the sleepy hollow home for the aged and demented, because I'm sure Mr McKie has a webpage or blog I can link you guys to. Good night and God bless. Jack."

Aiden held the printout limply, re-reading words typed up minutes after he'd left. He'd guessed that Jack didn't get many visitors, missed his family and seemed to enjoy shooting the breeze with a "real life journalist". He looked at DI Morris, who cocked his head before asking his question.

"The rat you both smelled? Is it relevant to my investigation?" Aiden looked at the blog printout again and shook his head.

"I can't see how, what I'm looking at is possibly a reporting error, but more likely a cover up for some degree of medical negligence in the US." He looked at the timestamp on the printout, showing when the last update had been saved. "Christ, this was finished an hour or so after I left, if what you say is correct he was killed shortly after. That's quick work by any measure, even if it was worth killing for. My guess is the missing laptop is the bigger clue, those devices don't come cheap and you know better than I do that violent crime and drugs are often bedfellows." Aiden felt sick to the core that some drug addled kid could have taken this man's life for something like his laptop; he'd only known doctor Fell for half an hour but really felt a connection. That Jack Fell had made the same link after Aiden's questioning showed that he was still sharp, sharper than practically anyone else involved in Ricky's death.

*

Tony pulled Alec aside, insisted they relocate to somewhere private, which generally meant a drive.

Alec pulled away from the residents' bar doorway, reluctantly leaving Elvis and the new resident in deep conversation. "He's poisoning him already, on day one," he grumbled. He saw the look in Tony's eyes and stepped up a gear, checking that staff were in position to carry out all the necessary duties before exiting the main building and stepping into the Land Rover outside. Tony gunned the gas and drove off into the dark, moonless night, pulling over after twenty minutes of silence way into the depths of the island.

"You're going home, well, Stateside," said Tony, keeping his hands on the steering wheel. Alec tried to comprehend; the Deputy Manager leaving the island alive without promotion was unheard of; he'd resigned himself to staying on the island until either he or Tony died. He didn't say anything, just waited. Tony broke first.

"That new guy, Ricky whatever, has started a wave of problems," he said, grimacing. "Well, he hasn't himself, but there's been some loose threads that are unravelling. Some journalist has been knocking on doors back in your country, asking questions that have attracted the wrong kind of attention. We've had Cliff working the ground over there," he said. Alec nodded; Cliff was legendary, a fixer, ruthless and resourceful. He'd never met him, he suspected Tony hadn't either. Rumour had it that whenever there were problems that money couldn't fix, and money fixed most things, then Cliff was sent in.

"Seems that the journalist has been asking questions, has bugged his boss for a commission to investigate some loose ends. His boss has been emailing left, right and centre and we've picked up on it. Cliff's got his work cut out in blighty doing some damage limitation, but we need to sort out Ricky's manager," Tony said.

"We?" asked Alec.

"You. I brokered the deal and he knows what I look like, so you need to pop over to the States and off him," said Tony, looking at his cuticles in the dark. Alec felt his bowels loosen; offing someone had always been a possibility, but he'd assumed it would be Elvis or Tony, possibly both. Killing a stranger in the US where they actually had laws was a different proposition, which is where Cliff generally came in.

"Can't we just take a contract out on him?" asked Alec, suddenly not as keen to leave captivity as he normally was. Tony said no, there were too many loose threads already. The manager, named Derrick, had fluffed loads of interviews, had raised eyebrows and almost certainly created the environment where backwater journalists were not fully believing the back-story Tony had carefully crafted.

"It was watertight, I spent hours coaching him on how to answer the questions. Man's a moron, you should have no problems offing him. It's not like he has any friends. You're to leave with the next delivery ship, arriving and departing tomorrow. You should be in the States sometime next week," he said, gunning the engine again.

*

The bar was almost empty, the entertainment for the evening slumped over the amps, scattering cocaine everywhere. Ricky was starting to enjoy the buzz of the liquor, having drunk enough to not feel his legs, always a good sign. Elvis had stuck to soft drinks, explaining he'd been clean for nearly twenty years, followed a sensible diet and had returned to daily exercise and was teaching Shotokan twice a week to a handful of students.

"I nearly got away, in 1998," he said in his Southern drawl. "Got my hands on their bat phone when the manager wasn't looking," he said. Ricky screwed his eyes at the sentence, trying to work out what the old git had said.

"Do you mean sat phone?" he asked. Elvis shrugged, it sounded like bat phone to him, but wasn't going to get into a fight with the new kid on the block.

"I'd arranged a signal with one of my management team, said that if I didn't like it I'd get in touch, let him work out what to do. Must've been 1987 or 1988 that I decided I'd had enough, took the best part of ten years to get hold of the bat phone. It had connected and was ringing before they realised it was missing, my man had answered before they snatched the damn thing off me. I was that close," said Elvis, clasping his fingers together. "Manager didn't last long after that, turned up in plot three hundred and thirty-two, just two weeks before Lennon bought it.

"I dug a tunnel, to get outside of the wire, but never got the chance to use it. Took me years of digging, entrance my best kept secret," he admitted, unburdening himself on the new guy. He quite liked the Brit, felt he needed to persuade him to consider leaving if he got the chance.

"I'm never going to leave here, no matter what happens. I may be fitter than most, certainly fitter than when I arrived, but I'm old, boy. It's you I'm worried about. Once myself and the remainder of the old guard go it's going to be just you, a handful of other musos and the damned Russians left. Those Russian guys came here about the turn of the Century, clearly running from lives of crime, but now they're looking at leaving, going home. My worry, boy, is that they will take out anyone and everyone who isn't one of them." He raised his glass of fruit juice and tapped the side of Ricky's tequila glass. "Think on it, make your own mind up, but consider getting out before it becomes impossible.

"I could never walk back into the real world now, whatever the backstory. You could, just. Talk about a mistaken identity, say you went for a long vacation, claim brain damage – you can get away with that if you try," he said. Ricky swilled the liquor, then drained it.

"Where do I sleep?" Ricky asked.

77

The geek turned around to the white-haired man who called himself Cliff. "Cracked it, password guessable, used the same one for the blog entry too," he said. He'd done work for Cliff before, knew he was reliable, paid up straight away. Cliff picked up the laptop and slipped the piece of paper containing the password in his jacket pocket.

"How many read the blog entry?" he asked. The geek turned to a pad to his side, run his fingers down it.

"Three of the usual four plus it looks like West Yorkshire Police also viewed it. I've taken it down now and changed the password to your normal one, just in case." Cliff wondered whether he needed to focus on the police aspect, or whether to disregard it. He wasn't convinced the three other blog readers presented any risks, such was the vagueness of the blog entry. He decided he'd look at that once he'd sorted this Aiden guy out, once and for all.

Aiden phoned Brian Esk's assistant, Sarah, explained that he'd never make the flight she'd booked for him thanks to following up a critical lead. He felt explaining the discussion with the West Yorkshire Police would send a shiver up the corporate spine and might just put the kibosh on the trip. Sarah just sighed and muttered something about Aiden being pissed again and asked if he needed to talk to Brian.

"Only if he's needed to approve the change," he said. He knew the magazine had an arrangement that allowed for missing flights, and that the airline would have reallocated the seat to a last-minute customer who would be flying over the Atlantic as they spoke. He listened as Sarah's fingers floated over the keys, marvelling that a secretary working for a publishing company could survive with two fingered typing.

"OK, you're booked on the eleven-a.m. flight tomorrow morning. Are you close to Manchester Airport?" she asked, only marginally interested. Aiden confirmed he was about twenty to thirty minutes away, hanging up as soon as he'd written the new flight reference down. He powered his phone down before he didn't have a choice. First priority was to blag a room at the hotel next to the airport; second, a seat at the bar; third, find out if he could pick up a charger from the Duty-Free shops in the terminal.

*

Somewhere over the Atlantic, on the dog leg leading to overfly Goose Bay in Canada before turning south to head across the Great Lakes bound West for Los Angeles, Paul Riggs pinched himself again. He'd had a chance to pitch his script to a Hollywood producer "as long as he could get here before the end of the week", with the production company picking up the tab. All he had to do was find a flight at short notice. All the direct flights had been booked months in advance and it looked like he was going to have to try and take an indirect flight, adding a day or more to the journey when a seat came available. The girl in Manchester check-in said it was the second time the seat had come up for a short notice passenger in three days. It was fate, the script was in the bag. Paul ratcheted the seat back the fraction that cattle class permitted and eased his feet out of his shoes to cool down. He just knew this pitch was going to work out.

*

Cliff sat in his hotel room working out his next move. The guy Aiden wasn't appearing on any radar he had access to, it was like he was a dinosaur. Considering he was a journalist he didn't seem active on social media. He hadn't accessed his Twitter account for several days, since he'd had a lot of banter with followers over the death of Ricky Maggot. After that his phone had been switched on for a minimum amount of time, powering up, making a call and powering down. Last pinged somewhere near Manchester, England it was dark again. There was a call logged to his magazine desk and Cliff had established Aiden worked for a guy called Brian Esk.

Esk had been the opposite of dark, broadcasting on every topic under the sun that was musical. He'd alluded, like that doctor Cliff had visited last night, that he knew there was something fishy about the Ricky death but hadn't published anything on social media so far. He pinged Esk's phone and got a location just outside of London. Interrogating the call log he worked out that Esk had called a restaurant about ten minutes earlier. Chancing his arm, he called the restaurant, said he was meeting a colleague there but couldn't remember who was supposed to make the booking. When he mentioned Esk the girl on the other end remembered the name and confirmed that the table had been booked for eight. That, decided Cliff, was just perfect.

*

Ricky found the residents' restaurant and figured it was a mixture of self and waiter service, resident decides. He filled a bowl of muesli and sat next to Elvis, who was eating something that looked way too healthy to be rock and roll. "At least I've poured Jack Daniels over mine," he thought. Elvis looked up and nodded while he chewed on his breakfast.

"Y'all sleep well?" he asked, eventually. Ricky nodded, took a mouthful, decided that single malt might make a better mixer for the cereal in future. "Did ya consider what I said last night?" Elvis asked. Ricky swallowed; he'd thought about little else since waking that morning.

"I woke up with a splitting hangover, next to a girl I hardly knew, with a name I couldn't pronounce even if I could remember it," he said. Elvis nodded, swallowed another mouthful.

"I know it appears great fun for a while, boy. It could take weeks, months, maybe years but the novelty will wear off, believe me," he said, pouring himself a cup of coffee, offering one to Ricky, who accepted with a nod.

"That's just it, though. Last week, the day I pretended to go into hospital, I woke up with the same headache, next an indistinguishable girl with a similarly difficult to pronounce or remember name," he said. "I've swapped Los Angeles for Los Angeles, paying my entire fortune for the privilege," he said. "The only thing I don't have to do here is tour," he added. Elvis nodded, waved a fork at Ricky.

"For me it wasn't even a difference in performing; coming here was just the same as a Las Vegas residency. Just without the crowds, the constant pressure." He leant forward conspiratorially. "To be honest, this was my last choice. All I wanted was to be able to walk down a street again. My ideal job would have been working at the checkout in a supermarket," he said. Ricky agreed that had a ring to it.

"Ever think about a career in fish and chip retailing?" he asked, noting the bemused look on Elvis' face. He couldn't believe nobody had mentioned it before. "I'm going to see if I can back out, but I'd like to take you back with me. You deserve to spend the rest of your natural in some sort of normalcy. I'd get my mum to put us up, we could get part time jobs in the local pub, maybe start a duet, gigging. It's not like anyone would believe it was you after all these years," he said. Elvis was shaking his head.

"They'd never let me go, probably won't let you go either. But definitely not me. Even if they did, I'm too old, too institutionalised. And all that talk about the internet gives me the willies," he said. Ricky marvelled at how Elvis had picked up on the varied and disparate terms through living on the island, and realised from his sparse understanding of the King's last years before the island that he had probably been very isolated and lonely. If he got Elvis out of this hell hole he'd make sure he was never lonely ever again. The king leaned forward.

"There's a saying around here – y'all can check out anytime you like."

"But you can never leave," said Ricky. "What's that all about?" he asked, understanding dawning as Elvis flicked his eyes in the direction of the graveyard.

"I'm going to give it a go anyhow," Ricky declared, spooning the last mouthful of Jack Daniels' infused muesli into his mouth.

*

Alec wasn't coping too well; violence was always an option on the table, that had been made abundantly clear at his interview with Tony four years earlier. He'd had a pretty rough upbringing, been beat up more times than he'd care to remember, had reciprocated to maintain a sense of balance more times again. But music was his main thing, hotel management was his fallback career that had, in a bizarre way, led to him managing the most musical hotel ever.

He hadn't left the hotel since arriving, had developed systems and processes that ensured that, in the main, it ran like clockwork. But clockwork mechanisms need winding up every day, checking regularly and benefited from regular maintenance. That was what Alec did best, so an unannounced trip to the States, although on the face of it exciting if you forgot about the purpose, was a major disruption. He was always on-site, never sick, didn't bother with R and R so he never had to depend on anyone else for help. And it wasn't as though he could depend on Tony for any help anyway.

So, Alec was preparing for an indeterminate trip away. The next supply vessel was due to arrive at port B in a few hours. As usual he would take a selection of staff members on a blindfolded trip around the island, disorienting them wherever possible, and then set them to unload the boat into the storage containers on the dockside. He and Tony would unload the containers incrementally based on demand and potential for spoilage. Now it would be Tony on his own, who was supremely inefficient at managing the stocks and rarely re-ordered as he went.

The boat would sail a few hours after arrival, dependent on the tide, and would offload Alec on the nearest island with an airstrip before the day was out. After that it was down to the logistics skills of the senior management team as to when he arrived in the US. He sure hoped they remembered that the under-manager always had his passport taken off him on arrival.

All of this would be difficult enough, but in the way of the organisation it was imperative the residents didn't get wind of a change, or indeed of an impending supply run. Because they didn't know Alec was way busier than ever in his time as under-manager, they kept coming up with their usual litany of daily demands, generally unreasonable, but that's what you get for taking prima donnas as guests. He'd just sorted out a critical champagne temperature issue by putting the offending bottle in the fridge for precisely three minutes and was hoping to get back to his packing when Ricky Maggot approached. Alec put his best hotel manager smile in place.

"Hi, how are you settling in?" he asked, "hoping the answer would be "fine" and be all they would say to each other. But Ricky had a look about him that suggested otherwise.

"We need to talk," said Ricky, indicating the manager's office. Alec tried to deflect.

"I'm terribly busy, perhaps we could talk later?" he suggested, but Ricky wasn't being fobbed off.

"We need to talk now," he growled, in a way that let Alec know his fellow Brit meant business. They walked into Alec's office and Ricky closed the door.

"I know you're not going to like this, but I've made a terrible mistake," he said. Alec felt a wave of relief flow over him; most new residents took a few days to settle in and wanted to leave by the next boat initially, but this sounded normal rock and roll.

"No problem, housekeeping will dispose of the body. We can provide a new one tonight," he said, noting the look of horror on Ricky's face. "Or earlier, if that's what you need." Ricky shook his head, this was going to be harder than he thought. He was just about to launch into a speech about how he was leaving, didn't give a stuff about the money, wouldn't breathe a word and, by the way, Elvis was coming too when they both become aware of a huge commotion happening in the restaurant.

"Bloody Elvis again," muttered Alec, storming out of the office. In the restaurant Elvis had squared up to one of the Russians, accusing him of taking all the vodka and was throwing Shotokan kicks that were just missing. "If any of those kicks connect, Elvis is dead," thought Alec, desperately trying to suppress his management training, but failing. Wading in, he placed himself between the two men, holding them apart with palms on both chests and slowly diffused the situation. The Russian looked like he wanted to resume the fight now that he'd had the chance to get back on the front foot, but Elvis suddenly shrugged and walked away.

Alec returned to his office and was relieved that Ricky had decided to leave, making a note to ensure that housekeeping had disposed of any bodies in Ricky's apartment – by rights they should have, but he had a few staff issues to work through. Picking his keys off the desk he walked out of the office and carefully locked the door behind him, a routine he never failed in. Sighing heavily, he started the long and disruptive route back to his room to resume packing.

*

Cliff had stood outside the small Greek restaurant as it was closing after the lunchtime session, waiting for the last customers to stand at the till, running their credit cards through the reader and fumbling in their pockets for suitable change for the tip. He entered the restaurant and smiled as the waitress approached to tell him the restaurant was closing for a few hours.

"That's OK," he said, "I'm meeting a lady friend tonight, and would like to take her somewhere special," he said, looking around at the small, dark room. He hoped there were spaces, because this was perfect. The waitress, keen to finish her shift, sighed and walked around to the booking chart for the day. Cliff practically followed her around and scanned the chart, spotting Esk's name straight away, noting the table he preferred to sit at. The girl picked the first table she come to that was free, one of four not booked, and asked Cliff what time he wanted. He just looked down the length of the room, orientating himself to see where Esk would be seated, and pointed to the table he wanted which, unfortunately, was already booked.

"Could I have that table, the one opposite the booth?" he asked. The girl was just about to deny him the table, but Cliff turned on the charm. "It's such a lovely restaurant and that table looks just perfect," he said, smiling. The girl looked at the name against the table, realised it wasn't a regular, so scored through it and allocated a different table. She took the false name Cliff offered and followed him to the door, where he smiled a lot and thanked her profusely for her help.

Ten to eight saw Cliff back at the door, claiming his table having watched the restaurant for the previous thirty minutes, watching to see if Esk turned up early. Being shown the table he'd booked he declined the seat offered and positioned himself so that he could see the door. "My girlfriend says she is running late," he mentioned, and asked for tap water to drink while he perused the menu in anticipation of her arrival. At ten past Esk and a blonde ten years younger than him entered the restaurant and were seated in the booth opposite the dark-haired man sat alone poring over the menu.

Brian didn't want to hang around too long: the meal was a token gesture, an opportunity to flash the corporate credit card, impress the girl with his music industry connections, go to bed and then home to the wife. The girl, the lead in an up and coming band, was under no illusions why she was here. She'd slept with managers, tour promotors and even roadies working for big name bands just to help raise her band's profile. If Esk let her have a few more column inches in exchange for a few of his own, then all well and good.

"I'll go and freshen up," she said once they had ordered, struggling to slip around the waitress who had taken their order as she was quizzing the man sipping water sat alone at the table opposite, felt certain she heard him apologise and say he'd give it another ten minutes. Brian was unaware of the waitress or the man, probably didn't hear the rest room door slam shut on the automatic closer, was engrossed tweeting his status to his myriad followers, head down in his mobile phone. The sharp pain made him look up into the eyes of the dark-haired man, who just raised a finger to his lips.

"That was a syringe filled with a lethal dose of heroin and barbiturates being slipped into your thigh," the man said quietly, "and if you don't cooperate with me then I'll push the plunger in. Death is certain within seconds," he added, in case the word lethal could be misinterpreted. Brian felt his bladder tremble, he could see the steel in the man's eyes and, critically, feel the syringe two inches from his scrotum. Cliff didn't wait to be asked any questions.

"Aiden McKie, where is he?" he asked, pushing the syringe with his free hand under the table for effect. Brian felt his mouth run dry and struggled to speak but was encouraged by the imminence of death being promised. Cliff added a sweetener. "If you tell me the information I want I'll pull the syringe out and leave you to your meal," he said.

"America, Los Angeles," he croaked, "to follow up some hare-brained lead," he added. Cliff's brain whirled as he wondered how much information the man had, how much he could obtain in the time available, hoping the wedge he had slipped under the rest room door held long enough for him to complete his business.

"When, how and do you have any flight details?" he asked, knowing it was a long shot. Brian nodded, flicked through his mobile phone, bringing his emails up and scrolling down one handed until he got to the email from his PA providing Aiden's flight details. Cliff fished his own mobile out one-handed and deftly photographed the screen details before pushing the plunger in hard, watching Brian's eyes glaze as the drugs rushed through his bloodstream, triggering a fatal heart attack in seconds.

Chapter 12

Sergei was bristling with anger, fuming with rage. Dimitri tried to calm his friend down, but so far it wasn't happening. "That old man, he is disrespectful, throwing those punches and kicks at me," he repeated for the fourth time in as many minutes. Dimitri nodded: he'd been brought up to respect his elders, especially coffin dodging hippies with long grey hair, but while this man had taken the piss, it was Sergei's temper that had brought them to this hell-hole of an island.

"It's not him that's the problem, it's here that's the problem," he said, also not for the first time. He nearly added that it was because Sergei didn't like to take no for an answer they were languishing in an otherwise idyllic setting. Crossing the upper echelons of the Russian mafia had put their lives in danger, making a deal with the previous manager of the island the only way they could see to survive and enjoy at least some of their money. Sergei believed that they would be forgotten now, that they could reintegrate into society. Dimitri knew Sergei had secreted some of their fortune away before they signed the deal that shipped them out of Russia and into the South Seas, with their cash shipped to the Cayman Islands.

"We need to find out when the supply vessels come and go, and we need weapons," he railed. Sergei stopped ranting and walked over to a bureau in their apartment. He often sat at the bureau, missing his computer with all his heart, scribbling down notes and performing arcane calculations. Dimitri left Sergei to his business, he had drink and pre-paid hookers to worry about. He looked up at the sheaf of papers Sergei was holding.

"Ten years I've been tracking the vodka stocks," he said. Dimitri furrowed his brow; there wasn't any access to any of the business markets, no access to anything outside of the island. Sergei noticed the look. "You and me, we drink vodka all the time," he pointed out. That old man was right in some ways, we do monopolise it. And sometimes it runs out," he said.

"Sometimes? At least three times a year we have to drink other drinks because the bar has run out," complained Dimitri. "And you won't let me accumulate a stockpile," he said, waving at the drinks cabinet. Sergei tapped his nose with a pencil.

"Before we were gangsters, I was a mathematician, one of the best in Russia. I noticed we ran out of vodka soon after we arrived here, assumed we had doubled, maybe trebled the consumption overnight. I started to notice how long it took for stocks to reappear, then worked on the assumption that when something runs out they need to wait until the next shipment before they can reinstate it. Thanks to their desire to serve they prioritise whatever has run out first when restocking supplies, so the vodka restoration probably happens within a few hours of the ship arriving.

"So, you know when the ships are coming?" asked Dimitri, suddenly interested. Sergei shrugged, scanned his notepad carefully.

"I'm fairly convinced there will be a delivery tomorrow, high tide is due after dark and I'm guessing that by the following night we'll have vodka on the menu again. The deliveries are fairly random in one way, very predictable in others. From what I can tell, they always choose dates when moonlight is at a minimum and high tide is at night. Tomorrow is a perfect fit and I think there is scope for another one nearly two weeks later as the moon is on the other side of its phase."

"So, the plan is?" asked Dimitri. Knowing the dates of the shipments was one thing, finding the boats was another, forcing their way on and taking control quite another.

"We get their guns, make them take us to the dock, wherever it is, and commandeer the boat. Preferably before they offload the vodka," said Sergei. Dimitri felt he was missing something, like "what guns?" OK, they all knew there were firearms somewhere on the compound but nobody on the residents' side had a clue. Sergei had a wicked look in his eyes.

"We engineer a way to make them crack their vault open. I've got a plan," he said.

*

Paul Riggs blinked in the Los Angeles sunshine, jet lag being washed away by the excitement of being that bit closer to having his script looked at by a major film producer. He didn't know it, but the offer had been made in the near full knowledge he wouldn't be able to make the journey within the timescales insisted upon, so the producer's admin team did the honourable thing and arranged for a limousine, five-star hotel room and a vague promise of being called forward if the producer decided to meet up with him.

Hauling his flight bag on his shoulder he walked to the edge of the arrivals waiting area, watching the stretched black car slowly make its way to him. Paul could just feel it in his water; this was it.

*

Aiden had woken up two hours later than he'd intended, with the mini-bar smashed, along with his head. He'd achieved two of the three objectives he'd set himself the previous evening but found himself arguing with check-in staff due to being late, attracting extra scrutiny from the security people who spent more time than Aiden thought was appropriate to view his junk on the full body scanner. By the time he was airside he was running late – bar or duty-free shop? No contest, his phone charger would have to wait until he was Stateside.

If his phone had been switched on, he would have received an urgent call from DI Morris who in turn had been alerted to a suspicious death in London of a colleague of Aiden's, notified by an algorithm in the National Police Computer Network. If he'd been flying later his check-in would have been blocked automatically. If DI Morris had realised that Aiden was flying to the United States, the US authorities would have been alerted to send him back on the next available flight.

*

DI Morris found himself linked into a teleconference with a Metropolitan Police task force dealing with organised crime. Brian Esk's body had been identified as a hit very quickly, the waitress alerted to the kicking at the rest room door noticing the male customer listed awkwardly in his seat as she passed. His lack of life was fairly self-evident; the reason determined within eight hours as a result of a tox screen and a pimple of blood on his thigh in the autopsy. The tox screen flagged a cocktail that had been identified in West Yorkshire a day or so earlier and DI Morris' name was all over the report.

CCTV showed the dark-haired man had staked out the restaurant prior to the attack and tracked him two streets away after until it hit a CCTV blackspot, from which point he disappeared from view. Facial recognition failed to throw anything up and a full forensic check of the restaurant, including the table he had sat at produced zip apart from some fibres that could have come from any supermarket clothing range. The detective quickly associated Esk with Aiden, noted that Aiden hadn't been particularly upbeat about the guy giving him paid work, realised that Aiden had been en-route to somewhere when he'd been contacted the first time, was attempting to check out of his hotel.

"I think it's likely Mr McKie is a person of interest, possibly at risk, probably involved in something shady," he offered as advice to the Metropolitan Police team.

*

Within half a mile of the Metropolitan Police task force, another teleconference was taking place, this time between Cliff and the Consortium. He confirmed that he'd ditched the wig, taking it off and wrapping his reversable jacket around it two streets away, dumping it a couple of hours later outside of the Capital along with the syringe and the latex gloves he'd worn since before entering the restaurant.

"Did you have any luck with the flight details?" he asked. The voice belonging to the technical expert on the other end confirmed that they had.

"Billed to the publishing house, with McKie travelling under an alias it seems," the voice said.

"Why would he need an alias?" queried another voice on the other end, accompanied with a rustling of papers.

"It seems he's on some sort of police watch list," replied the technical expert. "Became visible earlier today, but these things can take days to surface. I reckon they got wind and sent him undercover, like they did in the old days when he was their roving reporter travelling the world carrying out investigations into the darker side of rock and roll." Cliff smiled to himself; the heroin and barbiturate cocktail had been his idea, attempting to link McKie to the killings via their links to the music industry. It looked like the plods were acting more predictability than ever before.

"So, what's my next move?" he asked, knowing that most of the loose ends in the UK were tied up.

"Follow McKie, track him down and take him out," was the immediate reply. "He's probably going to try and hook up with Maggot's manager, but that guy has gone to ground. We've got someone else targeting him, but if you get the chance to take them both out, you'll be paid appropriately."

*

In an opposite time zone on the other side of the planet, Alec supervised the unloading of the supply boat, keeping the arc lights trained on the small army of ant-like people treading up and down the gangplank, boxes of consumable products, refrigerated cartons trundled on pallet trucks, some hardware to help maintain the old buildings and a bale of drugs.

"Have you seen the vodka consignment?" he yelled at one of the members of the unloading party. He turned to Tony. "We need to increase the order again just to keep up with the Russian demand, let alone the other guests," he said. He'd been trying to get Tony up to speed on the process all night with little luck; legend had it that Tony brought the island close to mutiny by the residents and staff dozens of times as under-manager, now he had the chance to do it all again. Apart from the little matter of attempting to kill a man, Alec had the prospect of having to pick up the pieces that Tony would undoubtedly tear his organisation into while Alec was Stateside.

Eventually the unload was complete, and the trucks loaded with the gear needed to replenish the needs of the residents, especially the Russians. "And that pain-in-the-butt Elvis," added Tony. Alec had recounted the stand-off earlier and hadn't stopped grumbling about it. "At least he's my problem for the next few days," added Tony, patting Alec on the shoulder. Neither man knew how long Alec would be away, both hoped it wouldn't be long, but for very different reasons. They both spent ten minutes checking the blindfolds on the hired help, before Alec boarded the boat. He found himself waving from the deck into the dark as the boat pulled out of the harbour, wondering when he would see the island again. It was strange – in many ways he'd hoped to leave for a break, but inwardly had harboured the ambition that he would take on Tony's job someday with the perk of travelling the planet to respond to the various potential residents. What he was embarking on wasn't in the plan, never had been.

*

Aiden tried to check into the hotel Esk's PA had booked just outside of LAX. There was some confusion due to his arrival being a day later than originally scheduled, so he had to trek a couple of blocks down to a sister hotel. He sat in the hotel bar attempting to formulate a plan.

He figured he was no fool: whoever had killed Ricky went to a lot of trouble but hadn't done their homework. He reckoned Derrick would have gone to ground – if anyone had realised Ricky had been killed it would be him, but all of his interviews since Ricky's death had been garbled, variable but consistently sticking to the story that Ricky had died during a routine operation. Derrick may or may not have known that Ricky didn't have an appendix to remove in LA, but the surgeon who attempted the operation sure should have noticed.

Aiden reckoned he knew how to flush Derrick out, but he wanted to grab a few more facts first. And the odd bourbon wouldn't go amiss, either.

Chapter 13

Derrick didn't know where to turn. He'd blown the police and press interviews, he knew that, but somehow thought he'd got away with it. He'd seen the calls from that fellow Brit who followed Ricky everywhere pop up on his phone a few times, had deleted the voicemails that had been left for him. To be fair he'd strung Aiden along in the past when it had suited him – the guy had produced the best and most fawning magazine copy for virtually everything Ricky had done, said or sung in the past ten years, but right now he didn't want to speak to any journalist, let alone the guy who knew more about Ricky than Ricky did.

He'd booked into a motel but found there wasn't a decent bar in the vicinity, so he'd moved further into the city, sticking to the outskirts, intending drinking anonymously alone in the bars that resting actors and musicians frequented. Partly he did this to see if he could discover the next Ricky, someone washing dishes who should be smashing up hotel rooms, partly he just loved their company, especially as they usually knew where the nearest drug dealers were located.

But the company he craved most was with other music managers in LA who congregated in one of two bars whenever they managed to get free from their stars. Fifteen percent might sound like a lot, but when you have to virtually wet nurse adults, be a drug

101

dealer, peace maker, politician, ambassador, legal eagle and be able to bury the bodies when necessary, sometimes literally, you earned it. Stick your act in rehab or get them married off and the manager is ready for maybe three nights of peace and quiet. That was when they let their hair down. Luckily rock stars entered rehab and got married so often some managers almost had normal lives. Derrick hadn't had that opportunity for years – the last two planning Ricky's demise had wrapped him up full time – and now he had, theoretically, the rest of his life to spend in either or both of those two bars he didn't feel it was safe to do so.

But the draw was so strong, the collective memory of the music world so fickle and anyway, he hadn't actually committed any crime as long as you ignored the falsification of the identification of a dead body, lying under both caution and oath, participation in the abduction and misappropriation of an unnamed dead person and the illegal, if consensual, trafficking of a person reported as dead. And that was without the usual minor transgressions involving supplying of drugs and whores. As far as Derrick was concerned, he was a pillar of society and consequently decided that he should shrug his reticence off and resume normal life.

*

The boat trip had been mercifully short and the sea thankfully kind. The flight in the Islander that only dropped off, never picked up, was bumpy and scary, being flown at around two hundred and fifty

102

foot above the sea on the blackest of moonless nights. The journey in the back of a beat-up Transit van over roads that had more holes than Blackburn, Lancashire apparently ever had had, culminated in a modern if third world airport hosting Boeing aircraft of a similar vintage to the Transit. Two changes of airport and airframe found Alec aboard a twenty-first century Airbus 320 drinking champagne from the first-class compartment headed towards LAX. In his gut he knew it wasn't an improvement.

*

"I told you," said Sergei, raising the tumbler of vodka, the best that Russia produced. Dimitri nodded and sank a couple of fingers himself, feeling the cold, sharp liquor attempt to shut his liver down.

"So, you think you know the date of the next delivery?" he asked, suddenly attentive. He respected Sergei, knew about his mathematical prowess long before being inducted into the Russian Mafia, hadn't seen any point of it on the island. But now Sergei had predicted the exact date the vodka would return to the bar with absolute precision all they had to do was complete the rest of the plan. "How do you expect to get your hands on their weapons?" he asked. Sergei smiled: his job had appeared to have become easier overnight.

"They run minimal management staff, as you know. That Brit Alec does the lion's share, Tony swans in and out without warning. Their next tier of staff are all pressed men and women – I expect a mixture of bribery and blackmail, coupled with overt threats to family members not on the island are used to keep them in check. When the residents revolt the top two, usually Alec, intervenes, divides and conquers. We need to ensure a coordinated revolt that includes some of the second-tier staff, not many but enough to persuade the management that words won't be enough. That's when Tony will crack open the arsenal," he replied. Dimitri wasn't convinced.

"But if we start something we're going to be on the wrong side of the argument, with the weapons pointing at us?" he asked. Sergei tapped his nose.

"We don't start the argument. We make sure we're not anywhere near it. We watch the management from a safe distance and once they make a move for the weapon cache we pounce," he said, smiling as he sank another draught of vodka.

"But there's two of them and two of us," pointed out Dimitri. He might not be a world class mathematician but he could count and his National Service had taught him the benefit of superiority of numbers.

"Have you seen Alec today?" asked Sergei, watching Dimitri rack his memories. They would be patchy this far down the bottle, but hopefully not totally ragged. Sergei continued, "He hasn't been about since last night. He's never sick, never off and that moron Tony is screwing up pretty much the whole hotel right now, just like he used to when he was the official deputy manager. Alec has disappeared and might be gone for a while," he surmised, admitting to himself he had no evidence for the synthesis. "My guess is he will return on the next delivery date," he said, "so we have to ensure we have the weapons, meet the boat as it comes in, overpower him before he realises what is going on and commandeer the vessel," he said. "There might be a few details I have to work out," he admitted. He could see Dimitri was crunching the data, had a furrow across his brow.

"Does Tony always leave on the delivery dates?" he asked. Sergei nodded – he'd noted this quite early on. His departures weren't predictable, but when he left, it coincided with a delivery. "And does he always return on a delivery date?" asked Dimitri. Sergei frowned, he didn't have an exact answer for this. He'd seen Tony arrive in the Land Rover when it wasn't being dried out after Moonie depositing it in the pool – which was becoming more predictable than the satellite he was named for – and he knew he appeared on dates that had no place in his calculations, but he did nothing around the resort so he was easily missed, he figured.

"Not sure, probably," he said. Tony's schedule was a worry and something he hadn't screwed down. "Yeah, I think so," he decided.

*

Elvis looked at the object in Ricky's hand. The technology was almost alien to him.

105

"So that's what the bat phone looks like now?" he asked. Ricky had given up trying to correct the old man, after all he'd kept up with a lot of other technology. They'd met in the recording studio where Elvis showed that he had a good grasp of what was needed to lay down a track. To be fair, Ricky was getting a little tired of Elvis' "trick" of recording analogue silence and playing it back at full blast – "see, not really silent at all" he kept saying as the one hundred-watt Marshall stack blasted out a deep white noise. Elvis said he was aiming at recording pure silence, but found the equipment wasn't up to it. Ricky didn't have an answer for that question, but he was able to confirm the appearance of the satellite phone he'd removed from Alec's safe when Elvis had kicked off with the Russians.

"Yeah, seems to be well charged and so far nobody has noticed it missing," he said, running his fingers over the controls and the keypad. Truth was, he was frightened of using it in case the frequency was being monitored by Tony or Alec. When he used it, he wanted to make sure it was used effectively. Until then it would stay hidden in the back of the Marshall stack that was currently deafening him with white noise.

"Ya'll notice what else is missing?" asked the old man. Ricky shook his head; he was settling in fine, but much was very new to him. He didn't have a sense of routine, wasn't sure that paradise should have such a sense. Elvis glowed, a smile splitting his face from side to side. "Alec," he said. Ricky scoured his memory but wasn't too sure who or what he'd seen so far that day having woken up with yet another beautiful but forgettable woman and yet another hangover.

"Maybe he's busy elsewhere," suggested Ricky, not really bothered. As long as he got the deal he'd signed up for he could tolerate the island until he worked out how to get away. Elvis was shaking his head.

"Tony's got the helm, y'all can tell. Nobody gets the breakfast they expect on time, first time. He doesn't know anyone's routine, can't tell his ass from his elbow, just like when he was deputy manager. Alec's gone, and that's the first time since he arrived. Either Tony's offed him or he's quit.

"Which means Tony's gonna be under pressure, cause as a manager he's darned useless." Elvis couldn't stop the grin widening even more. "Which means I can have a whole loada fun yankin' his chain," he said.

Chapter 14

DI Morris tried Aiden's mobile again. He'd stored the number in his phone and tried it on and off every couple of hours when he remembered. He was tied up with an outbreak of fairly serious juvenile crime and still had an unsolved murder on his plate. His boss was convinced he'd been too lenient on Aiden, despite the rock-solid alibi, citing research carried out in the senior officers' bar that anyone who needed an alibi was almost certainly guilty of something.

The teleconference with the Met troubled him. Both killings appeared heartless and cold – and his experience told him that Aiden didn't seem that way. He'd met psychopaths and sociopaths in his career and Aiden wasn't either, yet these killings suggested one or the other.

"What does it matter if it's a sociopath or a psychopath?" his sergeant had asked when he hung his phone up at one point. Morris considered the question carefully: for Aiden, probably not a jot. But it was a careful distinction that detectives ignored at their peril.

"Not all psychopaths or sociopaths are killers"' he noted, waving his sergeant to sit down, "in fact probably most aren't killers at all, but then again most could be with the correct psychological triggers," he said. Sitting back, he explained his professional view on the psychopath versus sociopath debate, a view built up through long and painful personal exposure to both profiles.

"Psychopathic killers can appear charming to many people who meet them, can appear to form bonds. But don't be fooled by their charm offensive, it's as shallow as the graves they dig afterwards. They can shrug off any and all social attachments like a bug off their shoulder.

"Sociopaths have similar levels of empathy by-pass hard-wired into them but can form social bonds. They rarely kill those they form bonds with, whereas psychopaths will readily kill anyone regardless of whether they have seemed to have formed a bond. Try speaking to the surviving parents of any convicted psychopathic killer and they'll tell you what a tough gig raising their kid was," he added.

"So, why's that useful for detectives?" asked the sergeant, intrigued. DI Morris pulled himself up in his chair.

"Well, it gives us a chance to narrow down suspects, especially if it's a sociopath. Who they don't attack is often the break we need – with these people that's as good as a break can get sometimes.

'But when it gets to the end game, who they use as a human shield depends on your approach – and they often use humans as shields. If we're dealing with a psychopath it doesn't matter who they have – it's a bloodbath from the beginning to the end. If it's a sociopath – well, let's just say the human shield might be disposable or may not be. That's why we need to understand the killer's diagnosis, and who he or she might have formed a bond with." The sergeant nodded, pretended to understand. He knew that the detective had been a high-profile big shot in murder cases back in the day, that his star had descended rapidly along with his family situation and his career. Best to humour him, he decided.

Morris continued: "What's more important is that we get a message to McKie, and quickly. This man – and it is usually a man – has taken down two people who are linked only by one thing – Aiden. That implies he's going to be a target. I can't do much to protect him, but I can warn him," he said. "I can't stop this, but I can give him a fighting chance," he said, flicking through the notes he'd made when interviewing Aiden. He came across a number scrawled across the bottom right hand margin at an angle, half crossed out – a throwaway point of contact Aiden had mentioned, but then discounted.

"I usually deal with Brian direct, but his PA does all the important stuff, like booking transport," he'd said, spinning DI Morris' pad around and scribbling a mobile phone number down, then starting to scribble it out again. "She probably wouldn't be any help to you guys," he'd said, only reluctantly allowing DI Morris to stop him obliterating the number completely.

When Morris looked up the Sergeant had taken the opportunity to back off, having left the mug of tea he'd brought initially. He picked up his phone, smiling inwardly. He knew his days of profiling were

over and he was quietly a bit of a joke in the
department, but he had to finish this one off.

*

When Aiden woke up it was early evening in
LA. He'd drunk himself pretty silly on the flight over
and virtually had to be manhandled off the plane.
The taxi had dropped him off at his hotel in the early
hours of the morning, his body clock had all but
deserted him. A quick rummage through the mini-bar
had revealed a tasty nightcap that he hoped Esk
wouldn't mind expensing, then he'd collapsed with
the "Do Not Disturb" sign hung on the doorknob of
his room after sending a couple of emails requesting
an interview.

Showered, sobered up and sat in a fast food
restaurant Aiden considered his first move. His emails
had borne some fruit; a hospital administrator had
agreed provisionally to try to see him the following
morning if he called in an hour beforehand, no
guarantee offered. More promisingly a contact in the
UK with an unhealthy interest in probing the deep
web, the company intranets beloved of all
organisations, had pulled out a name and shift rota
for a person of interest from the hospital itself.
Looking at his watch, now adjusted to minus eight
hours to compensate for Los Angeles' tardy progress
in time, he realised that he could tee up a rental car
and retire back to the hotel room to continue
recalibrating his body clock and preparing for an early
morning wake up. His brain complained that the new
plan pretty much insisted he dispense with a much-

111

needed top up to his alcohol-stream, but he knew he had work to do.

*

Derrick pushed the oak door open and felt the air-conditioned cool wave wash all over him. He'd visited the first watering hole that the music managers usually frequented and found it too quiet for his liking. He wanted a bit of company, lots of beer, some drugs and a shared background with guys who would understand the problems of earning their fifteen percent. This was looking more like it, with some of the most high-profile music managers in LA in attendance lining up the booze and the coke.

Better, there were a few who like Derrick had seemingly lost their acts tragically over the years, drawn like he was to the venue to shoot the breeze and occasionally something stronger. He'd paid them scant notice on previous visits, shunned them to a degree. But that was before Ricky had decided to bail out on the public life, had asked to become a resident of Hotel California. When the request had been made Derrick had made a bee-line for this bar and had pulled one of the displaced music managers to one side, suggesting he could provide some advice in exchange for alcohol, drugs and a foxy chick who was loitering nearby, a request that had been accepted.

The advice had been unequivocal: dissuade your client if you can, come and see me in my office next week if you can't. The meeting in the LA office had been held, the contact with Tony promised.

Derrick had promised to keep in touch, but the following two years was as his contact had suggested – a whirlwind of activity identifying fund flows, funnelling deals for box sets "just in case", meeting with shady go-betweens and blatant thugs whose only role in the process was to convince Derrick that loose talk was painful and generally fatal.

The go-between made his way to Derrick, hooked Derrick's elbow with his palm and guided him to a part of the bar that wasn't too crowded. They shared a dark secret, one that wasn't kept too strongly – Hotel California was discussed often enough by managers with clients and those whose clients no longer strutted their stuff, but the deal was that specifics were never sought or revealed, there was just a tacit agreement that there was somewhere for disenchanted celebrities to fade away to.

"I'm sorry for not keeping in touch," said Derrick. His confidant raised a finger to his lips.

"It gets busy, you missing Ricky?" he asked. Derrick nodded and signalled the barman to pour a couple of bourbons, taking the first one poured and sinking it. He'd ordered a replacement before his drinking pal had sipped his first taste. "It's understandable," added the man.

"It gets better, no more holding their hand, living any life you feel like, watching the payments slip in every month. Hell, I even tried signing a new act when mine left but then I thought 'why work all hours when you can live a good life for no effort?'

"And then there are the reminders," he added. Derrick looked up sharply. "Every now and then I find a note in my apartment, written on white card. I've changed the locks, put CCTV in, moved apartment without telling anyone – they still turn up. Each note is a cell phone number, dial it once and a pre-recorded voice reminds you to keep to your obligations, dial it a second time and it's unobtainable. Don't phone it within a couple of days and another note appears, a red card, another number. My guess is they don't issue a third note." He slipped the bourbon down his neck and ordered another round deftly, staring straight ahead.

"If they did, it would be on black card," suggested Derrick. "Straight out of Genghis Khan's playbook," he added, taking his drink once it was served. If the other guy understood the reference, he didn't show it. 'Genghis used to surround a city in a siege and set up in a white tent on day one. He'd send a message that if the city surrendered then everyone would be spared. On the second day the tent was red and the message was that if they gave up everyone except the men would be spared. Day three, black tent, no need to surrender," he said. His confidant nodded.

"They play rough, I'm told. Don't upset them, is my advice," he said. "But it's great to see you in circulation – put Ricky behind you, start living, keep shtum," he said, adding "I'm here for you, think of me as a mentor, but always remember the rules," he said, grabbing Derrick by the arm and dragging him over to

114

a group of managers having a party. One of the managers pulled Derrick over to him, told him he was his inspiration, pulled out his phone and within a minute a selfie was uploaded onto his Instagram account. Within half an hour Aiden knew where Derrick was.

As did Alec. And Cliff.

*

Dimitri crashed back into the apartment, tears rolling down his face.

"That guy Tony, he's so out of his depth. The old man, the one you keep picking a fight with, he's running rings around Tony. If you want your revenge on him for showing you up the other day, go and stir some shit with Tony, he'll believe anything about the old guy.' He looked at his comrade and was surprised to see he just had a smirk on his face.

'No, we leave Tony alone. It's Elvis we work on, him and that new kid who seems to hang around with him. We need Tony to reach breaking point, to decide to break out the weapons about the time of the next delivery so we can slip out of the shadows and take them. I calculate there should be a delivery in about a week's time.' He fished a slip of paper out of his pocket and perused it closely. 'Next Sunday, then we need to strike."

*

"So, how'd y'all cover your transition to the island?" asked Elvis, nursing a coffee. Ricky sipped his

115

cold beer before answering while looking into the middle distance.

"Same way as most, I guess, got a John Doe to substitute for me." The conversation had begun when Ricky asked about the guy who'd sang 'Annie's song' at the nightly karaoke. Elvis had explained how the singer had faked his death with the corpse of a down and out strapped to the pilot's seat of an experimental home-built plane that had been operated by remote control while he'd been shifted across country.

"Took ages to find a suitable double," Ricky moaned, reminded of the constant ups and downs – you're on, you're off. "Did you have that problem?" Elvis thought for a second before shaking his head.

"Two or three suitable contenders die in Las Vegas every week," he answered, "Usually on stage, sometimes permanently. I just needed the spunk to make the plunge. I soon realised I'd made a big mistake," he said, stirring his coffee slowly, watching the artificial sweeteners melt into the black liquid. "I was all messed up back then, doin' drugs, drinkin' way too much and eating junk food mornin', noon and night," he said, taking a sip. "Kept it up here awhile, too boy," he said. Ricky sat back, he'd heard this story several times already – how Elvis got fed up of waking up with puke in his hair and not being able to put his own shoes on.

"Pulled my life back together, stopped the drink and the drugs, started eatin' sensibly, takin' exercise,' he said, standing, running through a full Shotokan routine, punching the air and performing stretches that would shame a man half his age.

"I wanted to go back, melt into society, just retire normally," he said. "The only fun I get these days is giving the management the run around, but I reckon Tony won't take much more from me – he's out of his depth and would love to get rid of me,' he said. Ricky sipped his beer and nodded.

"How do you think we can get away?" he asked. He'd carried out rudimentary recces of the area and concluded there wasn't a viable landing site for a boat in walking distance. Elvis' eyes lit up.

"Two options. First, steal the Land Rover. They're terrible for leaving the keys in the ignition, either that or Moonie knows how to hot wire them," he said. Ricky made a note to ask Moonie sometime between midday and one p.m. – any earlier and Moonie would still be in bed, any later and he'd be too addled to make sense.

"What's the second option?" he asked. Elvis tapped his head with two fingers.

"There's an airplane that visits," he said. "I've got good hearing still, and I've heard it. Not sure where it comes from, but it usually coincides with the reappearance of Tony when he's been away. Your fellow Brit, Alec, drives off in the Land Rover and returns about two hours later. Sometime before he returns I hear the aircraft engines, saw it once as it crossed the horizon. If we can find a way to sneak on-board," he said, leaving the plan unfinished, exactly as it was formed in his head.

"I've an idea," said Ricky, taking his turn to tap his head.

*

Cliff pushed the club door open slowly. He'd allowed himself some time to let his eyes acclimatise to the low light levels, wasn't sure what to expect. It was the early hours of the morning and it was a stretch to hope that Derrick would still be in the bar. But it was the best lead he'd hoped for – Derrick was a bonus target and the Brit Aiden was almost certainly making a bee-line for the retired manager. He couldn't afford to off Derrick until he'd secured Aiden's whereabouts, so his plan was to befriend Derrick, use him to lead him to Aiden or Aiden to him, then off them both.

Looking around he could see a few heads lain on tables, glasses rolling alongside them, lines of coke etching messages in Morse code. In a corner there was a small group of guys sat around smoking dope and shooting the breeze quietly. Luckily for Cliff he recognised some of the guys; they were on the list of former managers he monitored and left calling cards for, listing a one-use only phone number reminding them of their obligations. Having clusters of former managers in certain locales around the world made part of his job easier. Setting himself up as a locksmith in LA targeting music and film managers made it ridiculously simple to keep on slipping the cards in periodically, keeping him updated on changes to their lifestyle and actually brought in some pin money as a bonus when they asked him to change their locks again. He recognised one of his regulars and hoped his locksmith disguise was sufficient to prevent the guy recognising him in his natural state.

He sidled over to the guy and asked about his day, offered him a drink and became his best buddy which, given nobody else was bothering with him at that point, wasn't much of a stretch. Some of the group quietly chatting took a bit more interest in Cliff than he preferred – his stock in trade was remaining as anonymous as was possible. The guy wasn't much help – had arrived late himself, knew hardly anyone and didn't know the guy who took a selfie with Derrick, although Cliff was very careful not to mention Derrick. As he got up to leave one of the group who were chatting wandered over to him.

"You looking for Frank?" he asked, mentioning the name Cliff had been asking about. Cliff sat back down, deliberately aiming at appearing non-threatening while keeping pressure on his left leg to enable him to move fast at virtually no notice. Frank was the guy who'd sent a selfie the previous evening.

"Yeah, haven't touched base in a couple of months, then saw a photo he posted on Instagram yesterday. Recognised the club, found myself a few hours away, thought I'd pop over and share a beer or two with him," he said. The guy wavered as he stood, finally steadying himself by leaning on the back of a chair.

"Why didn't you message him, let him know you were coming?" he asked, reasonably. Cliff shrugged.

'Tried calling, but he didn't pick up. Looked like he was having a good time with some Limey, guess checking his phone wasn't his highest priority,' he suggested. 'Thought he might have come back tonight,' he said, hopefully, looking around at the décor, realising it didn't quite match the décor in the snap.

"Haven't seen Frank in here for days, but the guy in the photo," the man said, pointing at Cliff's phone, "came in yesterday, had a drink, a quick catch up, then left. Didn't stay long, looked a bit lost, to tell the truth," the man said. "It's Derrick Moore, lost his client Ricky Maggott a few days back,' he offered. Cliff nodded reverentially.

"Yeah, great loss, guess it's hard," he commiserated. All that money for the rest of your life for no work, must be real hard, he thought. He also wanted to leave, having realised he'd chosen the wrong club, noticing the guy wasn't reading his body language, was moving closer, seemed to be inspecting him.

"One of those guys," said the man now towering over Cliff, "reckons he knows you," he said, nodding over to the group, most of whom were tacitly avoiding eye contact. One, however, was looking straight at Cliff with steely eyes, the owner of a large penthouse Cliff had visited twice in the last two months, once to place a card, then to change the locks. Cliff pretended to have not seen the man.

"Who? I don't recognise anyone?" he said, slipping his right leg forward, to provide access to the knife strapped to his calf. The guy turned and beckoned to the man staring at Cliff, who stood and waded over. He placed both hands on the table Cliff had sat at, scrutinised his face closely, so closely that Cliff could practically determine the brand of tequila the man had been drinking.

"It is you. I thought I recognised your voice, but your hair is quite different," he said, staring at Cliff's close-cropped head. "Why'd you change your hair? And what's a locksmith doing in a place like this?" he asked, waving his right hand behind him, nearly falling over in the process. Cliff was musing over flight or kill when the man interrupted Cliff's thought process.

"I think you're a scam artist," he said, stubbing his forefinger at Cliff's chest. "I've mentioned you to a few of my friends who have used you and they've all noticed that their homes have been effortlessly visited after you've changed the locks. I think you're passing lock details onto someone, and I've spoken to the police. Up until now they've ignored me, but when I point out you've been stalking this place and mention you're into disguises, I think they'll take a lot more notice," he said.

Cliff stood, wrapped an arm around the man's shoulder, steered him towards the main door. "You're wrong on many counts my friend, and I'm happy to call the police to prove I'm right," he said, noting nobody ventured to follow the pair out of the room.

"First, I have no idea what you're talking about," Cliff said, pulling the main door open and gently pushing the man through. "Second," he said, stooping long enough to draw the knife out of his calf holster, "you should understand you're in breach of your agreement." The man stepped back a pace, trying to work out what the guy he believed to be a crooked locksmith was saying, not registering the knife arcing towards his throat. "You receive a cheque every month for keeping your mouth shut, not blowing a very important arrangement out of the water," continued Cliff, twisting his shoulder to provide more accuracy to the slice, watching the man's eyes bulge as the arteries on both sides of his neck were severed, along with his windpipe. Cliff lowered the man carefully to the ground, cupping his left hand behind his neck, feeling the flow of blood run down his arm.

"I guess you've just saved my organisation a lot of future payments," said Cliff, watching the last vestiges of life ebb out of the man's eyes. Looking around he confirmed what he'd noted on the way in – the car park was empty, nobody was around at this time of night and the CCTV cameras were still covered in black spray paint, exactly as Cliff had left them fifteen minutes earlier. Dragging his thin jacket off,

Cliff wiped the blade, then his arms down, turned it inside out and walked away rapidly. Breaking into a slow, leisurely jog he made his way around the block to reach the panel van he'd parked up earlier. Within an hour the stolen vehicle, along with anything that could provide forensic evidence, was burned out on waste ground just on the edge of the city as dawn rose.

Chapter 15

Danni Wate rubbed water into her face, turning the faucet off. Looking into the mirror she saw that she'd sprayed cold water all down her scrubs and had created a pool on the rest room floor.

It was eighteen hours since she'd walked in to the hospital on her shift, another two at least before she could leave. As a newly qualified doctor she had to take all the shit and none of the bonuses of working in one of the highest profile hospitals on the West Coast; as a wannabe surgical resident she had to fight for each and every opportunity to take part in general surgery.

Being allowed to take the soiled instruments from the surgeon during a complex open-heart procedure and loading them into the autoclave was about as good as it got at the moment, but the game was to be there whenever they needed a hand, do anything they asked and hope that someone noticed you.

Her pager bleeped and a number scrolled across the screen.

"Uh, main reception," she muttered as she recognised the number. It wasn't her highest priority; she preferred to be contacted by the hospital administration staff looking for extra hands at no extra cost, but she wasn't one to turn her back on opportunity. She picked up an internal phone and dialled the number, announcing her name.

"Hi honey," said the woman on the other end, probably qualified to eleventh grade, stuck in the same job since leaving school, sounding like her mom and almost certainly on twice the money that Danni was on. "I got a Brit here, wants to talk to you," the receptionist said, dripping false charm. Danni didn't know any Brits apart from the characters on Downton Abbey and a nurse working the opposite shift who spoke in some kind of code with an accent that didn't sound like any British accent used in the films.

"What does he want?" she asked, looking at her watch. She really wanted to crash somewhere quiet, clutching her pager just in case something really sexy turned up, however she knew that was unlikely and didn't think the Brit was likely to be a visiting consultant wanting to pick her brain. She heard the question relayed.

"Coffee, hun," said the receptionist. "and a chat, apparently," she added, attempting to say "chat" in a British accent. Danni frowned. Sleep, chat? Chat, sleep? She looked at her watch again, decided that probably a coffee was more useful if the call came than a few minutes cat-napping, so decided to give the guy a chance – as long as he was buying. She told the receptionist she'd make her way down to her location in a few minutes and started walking.

*

125

"She's on her way, honey," said the receptionist, putting the phone down in the cradle and indicating where Aiden should sit. He followed her lead and sat in the plush waiting area, fighting the need to sleep himself. His body clock was all over the place and when he'd set out to follow up the lead his contact had provided, he felt he was like a spring lamb and now he was crashing again, such is transatlantic travel.

All he knew was that a name on the documents his researcher had dug up, Danni Wate, was almost certainly on duty until very early morning, then off for a vacation. That information had kicked Aiden into action – Danni's name was the only one that turned up in his contact's search and a week's vacation wasn't something he could risk.

The close-cropped afro approached at the reception desk and was then pointed towards Aiden. He rose and outstretched his hand, appreciating the twenty-something who probably regarded him as a parental peer. Within minutes they were facing each other in the staff café, nursing refillable coffees.

"A journalist?" asked Danni, looking at the middle-aged man in front of her. Part of her was on guard - journalists and hospitals made a poor mix and trainee doctors weren't supposed to talk to their landlords without clearing it with the hospital administrators, chatting at four in the morning in the staff café with a foreign journalist was as far outside of the rules as to be coming back from the opposite direction. But this guy introduced himself as a music journalist, and Danni's other love in life after medicine was music. She sat quietly as Aiden listed his credentials, covering the music papers he's staffed on, the bands he'd met and a brief sojourn into his Pulitzer.

"Never heard of you. Or most of those bands you mentioned, either," she said at last. But she didn't stand up and walk out, instead appraised the guy. Ageing, showing signs of alcohol abuse, nervous tic while he talked, scribbled what she presumed was shorthand but could easily have been random lines. "How can I help you?" she asked. Aiden fished a crumpled sheet of paper from his pocket and flattened it out in front of Danni.

"Is this you?" he asked. Danni leaned over and scanned the document, nodding as she ran her fingers down it.

"Yes, it's my name, but what's this to do with music?" she asked. Aiden took a deep breath.

"You ever hear of a guy called Jason Jones?" he asked. Danni shook her head, looked at the internal document with her name on, couldn't place the procedure. "You might know him as Ricky Maggott," said Aiden.

*

Tony was pulling his hair out, counting the days, no, the minutes until Alec returned. The Russians had, mercifully, become placid, helpful even. He put that down to the vodka. Elvis was creating shit

127

at every turn and the new Brit was like a lapdog, running around doing the octogenarian's bidding. Food orders were going wrong, complaints were escalating, the residents were baying for blood.

How Alec coped with this bunch of snivelling shits, Tony didn't know. He found himself jumping out of his skin every time one of them tapped him on the shoulder, wanted to run and lock his door every time somebody decided the cocaine wasn't the right fucking grade. He felt the situation spiralling out of control and he was certain that some of the residents were likely to be arming themselves with home-made weapons.

The last time he'd been worried about knives was when the Russians had arrived several years earlier. Back then he'd taken to carrying a Bowie knife in a sheath strapped to his back, concealed by his jacket because the Russians scared him, hell they scared everyone, still did. Now they seemed to be the only people who didn't seem to present a danger. Perhaps he should put everybody on a vodka ration?

He found himself gravitating to Sergei and Dimitri whenever there were more than a couple of residents around. He felt that should push come to shove they would back him, stand shoulder to shoulder. He found himself speaking candidly with the two men over a drink in the bar, confiding his concerns, begging for a little protection until Alec returned. Dimitri looked at Sergei carefully before responding to the request.

"You're not the only one worried," the Russian said, grasping his vodka glass tightly, taking a swig then circling the rim with his forefinger rapidly to encourage the barman standing discreetly a few feet away to top up the drink. Tony was taken aback by this, both Russians had a reputation for being tough guys who drank hard but fought harder. He thought everybody shat themselves whenever they walked into the room, but now they were suggesting they were the ones soiling themselves. Sergei was nodding vigorously.

"Yeah, neither of us feel safe these days"' he said, looking around suspiciously. "That Elvis guy, I'm convinced he has a gun," he said in his thick Russian accent. Tony was shocked at the suggestion, he'd factored knives, yes, but firearms?

"Nobody has a gun on this island," he lied, watching the Russians look at each other.

"We think the old man has a gun," said Dimitri, looking around. Tony tried to suppress a laugh but was shaken by the anger in the Russian's face. 'That new man he is with, Ricky, he's from Sheffield. Everybody in Sheffield knows how to make steel,' he said. Tony didn't know anything about Sheffield, wasn't aware that Ricky hailed from such a place anyway. It just sounded like a random fact that might or might not be true.

"So, what difference does that make?" he asked, noting both men becoming agitated.

"He could make a gun," explained Sergei, exasperated. Tony shook his head slowly.

"I don't know anything about making steel," he admitted, "but I'm guessing it needs a fair bit of space and heat. I think I'd have noticed the new guy melting cutlery in the compound," he said. Dimitri took the argument up again.

"We've heard rumours that the old guy dug a tunnel," he said. Elvis' tunnel was part of the island folklore – one of Tony's predecessors had practically rumbled it, had leant on the singer and the story went that the tunnel digging stopped. It was pointless anyway – where would it lead to, what use would it be?

"I've heard that, a long time ago. But he's still here, so if it's true I'm guessing it doesn't lead anywhere," he said, thinking that also described the conversation.

"But it would make a perfect place to 'melt cutlery' and make a gun," offered Sergei, jabbing a finger at Tony. Tony felt there were a few gaps in the argument, such as the skills and tooling needed to make a gun being noticeably absent, but he felt there was a bigger problem with the concept.

"OK, let's suppose Elvis has a tunnel and Ricky has the skills to melt and work steel into a gun," he said, finding that vocalising the idea created a feeling that it actually could be possible. "Where will they get the bullets from?" he asked.

"You can make a gun, you surely can make a bullet," suggested Dimitri in a flourish of logic, a leap that Tony felt didn't make full sense.

"Yes, but bullets are more than metal, they have gunpowder to propel them," he said, feeling quite relaxed. For most of the conversation he'd had an uneasy "this could be possible" feeling, but he knew there wasn't any stockpiles of gunpowder floating around.

"Can you account for every firework on the island?" asked Sergei. Tony felt his stomach tighten. They had regular firework displays to celebrate birthdays, new releases, national days for over twelve nations at the last count. Alec was in charge of the fireworks, kept them locked up for safety, not security, and was pretty thorough. But Tony couldn't absolutely confirm all fireworks were accounted for, because he never got anywhere close to details like that. That was Alec's department. He knew they always had less at the end of a display, but that was to be expected.

"And what about the old man's heart complaint?" added Dimitri. Tony shook his head at this change of tack – he'd been partly persuaded by the two Russians over the fireworks and now they were talking about heart complaints.

"What heart complaint?" he asked. The Russians had factored on Tony not knowing anything about these sorts of things.

"Angina," said Sergei, looking pleased with himself. He'd agreed with Dimitri that they'd settle on the common problem instead of inventing something more complex for effect. Tony just looked more perplexed than ever.

"Angina?" he repeated. "Has he got angina?" he asked, almost rhetorically.

"Nope," said Sergei, increasing Tony's puzzlement. Sergei didn't know anything about Elvis' medical conditions, but knew practically every old man back in Russia seemed to have heart problems, usually involving angina. "But he's been taking the medication for angina from the dispensary for years," added Dimitri. Tony shrugged, the dispensary was just a pick and mix sweet shop for drugs, recreational and medicinal. No prescriptions needed, if a resident said they wanted a drug they got it. If it made them happy with his service, a result. If it killed them, well also a result. The ultimate win – win.

"So, what?" he asked, wondering why the conversation had drifted so rapidly.

"The treatment for angina is a small amount of a drug under the tongue," said Sergei, relishing the point he was about to make. "The drug is nitro-glycerine," he added, pausing while the words sank in.

"Also known as dynamite," he said, as Tony felt his bowels start to loosen.

*

Danni held the sheet of paper up to the light, but conceded that as a photocopy it was unlikely to reveal any hidden information.

"I was on duty that night," she said, her smartphone open on the calendar function, "and I seem to recall it was a quiet shift. One of the senior consultants offered me and a couple of my colleagues the chance to play with a cadaver," she said, looking back at the sheet. It indicated she'd helped on a procedure that she didn't recall, and an insurance company she'd not encountered before had been billed for her services.

"The insurance company doesn't exist," said Aiden, sipping from his second coffee. Danni looked up, concerned.

"So, we won't get paid?" she asked, Aiden presuming she meant the hospital. The payment for care system was so ingrained in the US that even down and outs would express concern if a multi-million income hospital lost one payment.

"Actually, I'm pretty sure the hospital will get every penny it bills, and I'm certain your senior consultant will have received a good bonus, too," he said, offering a plate of cookies he'd picked up at the counter. "Given that I suspect you've been involved in a cover-up, you probably should have been bribed as well." Danni looked up suddenly.

"Are you accusing me...?" she asked. Aiden shook his head.

"From what I've seen, you've been used. But let me dig a bit deeper before you start accusing anyone – my picture is far from complete." He pulled an image of Ricky on his mobile phone, flicking through a gallery. "This is who you are billed as operating on, you might have seen him in his reality show," he said, finding a photo that showed Ricky almost looking normal. Danni scrutinised the photograph but showed no sense of recognition.

"I don't watch reality shows," she said, "and that face doesn't ring a bell"' she added. "To be fair, when operating we often don't look at the face – it's not usually the part we're interested in." Aiden shrugged, he'd had a similar experience with groupies.

"According to this you took part in an operation on a live, breathing person who, unfortunately suffered complications and died on the operating table," he said, repeating what he'd mentioned. Danni kept shaking her head.

"I told you, the only surgery I took part on was on a cadaver, a John Doe who had been donated to help with teaching practise." She ran her finger along her signature, saying, "that's my signature and I vaguely recall signing this, but understood it was some sort of release document, an audit trail for the cadaver. We did a minor surgical procedure, sewed him up and presumably left him for another group to play with. It was late at night, early morning really, I was very tired but excited at being allowed to wield a scalpel." She sat back, munching a cookie, noticing

134

that her shift was virtually over. "What happens now?" she asked.

Aiden clarified and double checked on the "minor surgical procedure", treble checked the date and the location, confirmed until Danni became angry that it was her signature.

"I'm going to track down the guy who signed off on the identification. If it was your John Doe he'd have known it wasn't Ricky," he said, stabbing the form with his index finger, "which suggests he knows what really happened to Ricky, why his death had to be covered up." Danni felt her pulse race; in part she was angry that she'd been used, partly she was intrigued by the subterfuge. She got the concept – a guy too famous to ignore, even if she'd never heard of him, dies or is killed in circumstances that are inconvenient so an "operation gone wrong" is fabricated to make his death more acceptable. She just couldn't see why it would be so important to Ricky's manager to hide the truth. Aiden fleshed out his theory.

"Ricky's had his fair share of illegal drugs supplied, and he's had more than his fair share of extra-marital relationships with some fairly high-profile individuals. Both groups provide a reason to remove him, I guess, and if it is drug dealer related then Derrick might have been leant on very heavily to keep the police out of the picture. If it's a high-profile affair, then who knows how much influence has been brought to bear. All I know is that there is both a

135

story to be unfolded and a right to be wronged," he said. Danni nodded, it made some sort of sense.

"OK, but I'm off shift in twenty, should be crashing for at least a day and then I'm supposed to be surfing for the next week. Except my surfing buddy cried off, too late for me to cancel my vacation days. If I can't surf, then turning detective sounds almost as exciting.

"I'm coming with you."

*

Cliff stared at the email again. He'd had bots working on the data he had about the Brit journalist, and they'd compiled an automated report. He'd been planning on letting Derrick lead the journo to him, two birds, one stone sort of gig, but the bots had turned up some useful information. They knew where McKie was staying, down to the room number. They knew the Brit hadn't used his room overnight, thanks to a code left by the housekeeping staff on the hotel database. He knew, down to the last miniature, how much bourbon McKie had drunk before leaving the hotel the previous day and how long he had left on his booking. He figured that if McKie had stopped out then there was a good chance he would touch base sometime during the day. Guessing that Derrick was sleeping off his hangover, Cliff decided he'd take a trip over to McKie's pad and see if he could eliminate him while he waited for the yardarm, or whatever other measure of useful time music managers used.

Then he'd finish off Derrick.

*

Aiden supped his third cup of coffee while he waited for Danni to rise. He'd felt jubilation when she'd hooked his phone up to the mobile charging block she had stored in her purse, especially when he'd accessed Instagram and found Derrick within a couple of minutes. But then the charger had switched off, dragging his phone down with it. She'd slipped into her bedroom, he'd crashed on her couch, too pooped to drive across town to his hotel. Her work lag was obviously stronger than his jet lag, and the occasional snoring sound reminded him that some people have real jobs. His heart rate increased as he heard her stumbling around her bedroom – he just hoped she remembered she had a Brit journalist crashing in her lounge, or whatever the Yanks called it.

"You want coffee?" she asked, her head popping around the door thrown open. Aiden nodded towards the percolator bubbling on the side.

"Already made," he said. He'd spent enough time this side of the pond to realise that nothing happened until the coffee flowed, at least until the bar opened. Danni wrapped her dressing gown around her and stumbled to the percolator, pouring herself a mug full and offering the glass bowl up to Aiden. He reciprocated by crossing the short distance and pushing his mug under the spout.

"You got internet here?" he asked, looking around the room. He knew there wasn't any relevant technology in the space he'd crashed in and had avoided wandering around the tiny apartment while she'd slept. Danni shook her head and explained that half the residents had had their flats broken into in the last year, insurance rates were sky-high as a result, so she kept her valuables to a minimum.

"Just me and a bottle of bourbon," she said, holding up the bottle they'd hit before crashing. "Well, half a bottle."

"I'll replace it," said Aiden. "You got anywhere I can charge this?" he asked, holding his phone up again for the second time in twelve hours. Danni took it, disappeared into the bedroom and returned thirty seconds later empty handed.

"It shouldn't take long, time for something to eat," she said, opening the door into the cramped kitchen she'd found the bourbon bottle and glasses in the previous evening. "Cereal OK?" she asked. Aiden guessed that was the totality of what was on offer, so accepted, even if the bourbon bottle looked more appetising.

"Sure. Look, are you still up for helping on this?" he asked. The hour or so he'd spent lying awake waiting for Danni to rise had been occupied trying to work out his strategy. He'd blundered across the pond in a hurry while the offer of the free flights was on the table, convinced he'd know what to do once he arrived. His instinct had been spot-on,

138

finding Danni and getting her to confirm what he already knew but couldn't prove, but now he realised he didn't actually have a plan. Danni confirmed she was on-board, nodding vigorously whilst shaking a cereal box at Aiden.

"You bet. Someone's made a monkey out of me and I want to know why," she said, pouring two large bowlfuls out. She brought the breakfasts through and thrust one into Aiden's hands, slipping a pair of spoons from her dressing gown pocket. "Don't worry, we'll eat some real food once we get on the road," she said. "That guy you found on Instagram last night, is he the one you want to talk to?" she asked, timing her question perfectly as Aiden shovelled his spoon into his mouth.

"Mmm mm," he answered, swallowing hard. "That's Ricky's manager, ex-manager, Derrick. We've met several times," he said, explaining the gate-keeper role of the artist manager. "He did the formal identification of Ricky – if he identified the same guy you worked on then he seriously needs to get his eyes checked," he said, recalling the description Danni had provided the previous night. "One way or the other he knows something, and I intend to find out what it is. I recognise the location, it's about thirty miles from here but will be shut until noon," he said, looking at his watch. Danni checked hers too.

"I'll just get showered," she said, standing. "Then we can get on our way. We'll pick your gear up from your hotel room on the way."

139

Chapter 16

Cliff looked around the hotel room, carefully felt the weight of the suitcase still propped against the wall, avoided disturbing anything. The latex gloves and the synthetic fibre clothing he wore reduced the amount of trace he left behind, his close-cropped hair leaving nothing of forensic value. The bed was made up, the wardrobe revealing a sparse traveller. Cliff liked that, he travelled lighter than most, only taking a carry-on for journeys most passengers would pay excess baggage for. Journalists had similar needs, he figured.

He surveyed every inch of the hotel room, quietly opening drawers and easing bedside cabinet doors, noting the empty spaces, closing everything behind him. He picked up and flicked through the Gideon Bible, watched the dust tumble through the air, guessing he was the first person to open the book since the hotel had been built. Probably the last, too. He found the safe, cracked the code within seconds and pulled out the laptop, surprised McKie hadn't taken it with him. Then he remembered reading how the Brit was old school, used shorthand in interviews, presumably word processed later. He took the laptop in case it contained any information that was of use to the police, hooking the bag over his shoulder.

Ending up in the shower room he lowered the toilet seat and slowly eased his bulk down, pulling a towel off the rail and laying it over the edge of the bath to create a platform for his tools. He lay his 9mm Glock on the towel and rested a pillow he'd liberated from the bed against the side of the bath. He then withdrew the blade he kept holstered to his calf and turned it carefully, checking the length of the blade, suppressing the desire to run a latex clad thumb along the edge, knowing if he did it would slice through the glove material and his skin effortlessly, laying it next to the Glock. Finally, he lay a syringe with what was becoming his favoured killing juice alongside the knife before concentrating on his breathing, slowing it down and regulating it so that he was almost using no energy as he waited, monitoring the app that tapped into the hotel information database on his phone while he waited. If housekeeping approached, or the elevator stopped at his floor, or if McKie made any request on arrival, he would know.

He had a few hours to spare, he might as well spend them here.

*

Aiden thought about checking for messages at the foyer as they entered the hotel, but decided to just grab a few things from his room and get back on the road. Danni, fresh from her shower, was half a step behind him, taking in the hotel décor as if weighing it up for a remodel of her sparse apartment. Perhaps she was considering the benefits of just living in a hotel. He pushed the elevator button twice, waited for the lights to indicate and turned on his heels as he realised the elevator was still going up.

141

"Do you mind stairs?" he asked. "Only the third floor," he explained, trying to remember if it was third floor American style or UK style. "Maybe fourth," he conceded, watching Danni's face.

"Sure, stairs are good for us," she said, the doctor in her surfacing, moving to the door leading to the stairwell.

*

Cliff heard the door handle rattle, the 'beep' of the electronic key, startled as he hadn't heard the elevator arrive. He tensed and strained every fibre of his body as the sounds of voices wafted in, detecting a degree of breathlessness. Two voices, one British, the other a woman; friendly, on good terms. The door snapped shut and a dull thud reverberated against the entrance wall. Very good terms, it appeared.

Cliff stood silently, although given the increased tempo of the sounds the other side of the wall, that was more habit than needed. Picking up the pillow in his left hand and the Glock in his right he paused at the door, waited until the rhythm started to reach a crescendo, the point where neither of the people would register his movement for at least a second given their self-made distractions. Swinging the door open he pivoted around, pushed the pillow against the back of the man's head and the Glock deep into the pillow, squeezing the trigger as the barrel sank into the down, watching the feathers fill the air as the red mist sprayed across the wall, with

142

both people sliding to the ground, both heads destroyed with the single bullet.

Calmly Cliff returned to the bathroom, leaving the remnants of the pillow for the LA police department to tidy up, slipping the knife into its sheath and the Glock into the shoulder holster, ignoring the towel as it slid into the bathtub as he turned. Checking he hadn't left any clues behind he slipped out of the room, crossed the corridor, entered the stairwell and made his way down to the lobby. Within minutes he was clear of the hotel, any remaining evidence bagged up and disposed in a trash can along with a time delay incendiary device that destroyed the evidence a few minutes later, and on a bus heading away from the scene.

One loose end less to tidy up.

Chapter 17

The LA detective hauled himself wearily up the staircase as the elevator was still being screened for trace. He knew the floor had been cleared by uniform and all the residents were being processed by junior detectives in the function room on the ground floor. The domestic maid who had discovered the bodies and reported the homicide was being ritualistically degraded down the precinct station to eliminate her from enquiries. Ducking under the 'do not enter' tape he made his way to the policeman managing the scene, holding out the badge that announced Detective Brown and signing the sheet that would record when he arrived and when he left. Hopping on one foot he managed to slip the overshoe covers on after donning the forensic white coverall he'd had hanging on his left arm since leaving his car. The disposable cap and beard guard finished the look as he entered the flat.

The view was grim: two people, a man and a woman, clearly killed by, he guessed correctly, a single bullet to the head. An execution by any other name, he decided. He looked at the drywall above the crumpled couple, following the red streak from the woman's head up to the indentation at his shoulder height, surrounded by a ring of smaller pink indentations created by bone fragments. The bullet would be under the couple, he guessed, again correctly. His experience of these crimes was that the bullet wouldn't lend much to the inquiry, but they'd invest a lot of time and resources into it anyway.

The pathologist was crouched alongside the couple; the detective wondered if suppleness was a requirement of the profession, what with dead people rarely ending up standing. The pathologist stood and waved his hand at the two dead people.

"Single shot, both killed straight off," he said. "Girl's local," he added, waving a Los Angeles Driver's License, "but the guy's a Brit," he said. Brown nodded, acknowledging the license and UK passport pushed into his hand. He flicked the passport open and took in the details, tried to compare both faces with the relevant ID, giving up thanks to the mess the bullet had made. Slipping the documents into an evidence bag he took a look around.

"Anything else?" he asked. The Pathologist shook his head and explained it was a bit early to provide any more information until he'd got the bodies back to the morgue, but the CSI detective, who had been processing the hotel room when he came in, stepped forward.

"Some prints, in fact lots of prints. Probably most belong to the Brit," he said, nodding to the body lying face down, not that there was much of the face left. "Can't say housekeeping looks too thorough, so there may be prints and trace going back weeks," he said, pulling a face. Hotel killings were often the hardest to glean meaningful forensic evidence, with lots of false starts and incomplete finishes. "Looks like trace of cocaine lying around and the minibar's taken a hammering too, according to the hotel records," he added.

"So, nothing to go on?" asked Brown, keen to follow up on the two IDs and running through any CCTV footage that the hotel had. The CSI smiled, his beard guard twitching at the ends and his eyes gleaming. He held out another evidence bag, the same size as the one the detective had used for the IDs. "Is that a syringe?" asked the detective, taking the bag and holding it up to the light. It was filled with an opaque liquid.

"Yep. Lying in the bath under a towel," he said. "Might be the dead guy's personal use," he suggested, adding, "looks unused but won't know until we examine the needle under a microscope."

"When will you find out what's in it?" the detective asked. The CSI shrugged.

"I've got a lot of ground to cover here," he said, looking around. "And there's only me to cover it. Of course, if you could get this back to my lab I'm sure one of my colleagues could help expedite it," he said, holding a sheet of paper that recorded the chain of evidence. The detective took the sheet, filled in his details, signed and passed the form back to the CSI for his signature.

"It'll be in the lab within half an hour," he said.

*

DI Morris should have been home hours earlier, but a pile of paperwork had landed on his desk with a note from the Chief Superintendent insisting it was cleared before the morning. He was just turning his desk lamp off when his mobile phone rang. Looking at the number he recognised the country code as being the United States, but the rest of the number was a mystery to him. Picking the phone up he was expecting some scam artist to be attempting to sell him dodgy pills, stocks or just inviting him to pass his bank details and provide access to his PC, so he was surprised when the voice on the other end introduced himself as a Los Angeles detective.

"How can I help?" he asked, looking at the clock on the wall, trying to work out what time it would be in LA. Recalling that there was an eight-hour difference he decided it was early afternoon.

"Your name has been flagged by the Interpol computer," said the detective, impressing DI Morris. He believed he was so undervalued and underappreciated that he doubted any police computer in Yorkshire would recognise him, let alone an international database these days.

"How so?" he asked, sitting, grabbing a pad and pen. The detective on the other end explained that he was investigating the brutal murder of a British citizen and a Californian resident in Los Angeles, and evidence led all the way back to Morris, via a number of unsolved cases. His stomach started to flip; he'd given up trying to contact Aiden McKie in the last twelve hours thanks to the workload he was trying to survive, now it looked like his instinct to warn him was both correct and ultimately too little, too late. He listened to the broad-brush details of the single bullet to the head through an improvised silencer. It was the description of the syringe found in the hotel room containing a unique mixture of heroin and barbiturates that matched a combination used in at least two homicides in the UK recently that had created a flag on the computer.

"I was hoping you could give us some information on the British victim, perhaps help us determine a link between his death and the two in the UK," the detective said. Morris felt his world collapse inwardly, he felt he should and could have done more for Aiden, wondered whether he'd helped flag him as a victim, or whether his intervention was irrelevant.

"I can give you a name for the victim, if you're struggling with that," he said, realising as soon as he said it that the American detective almost certainly would have Aiden's details seeing as he knew one of the victims was British. His offer piqued the Los Angeles detective's interest, though. "He's a writer," added Morris, supplying Aiden's name and offering to sort out the process for advising his family. The silence was palpable.

"Could you repeat that name?" asked the detective.

*

Tony held out the personal medical records associated with Elvis at arm's length. The island doctor had tried to stonewall him, citing patient confidentiality and his legal obligations, however Tony had simply reminded the doctor why he'd ended up working on the island, the outstanding arrest warrants and the fact that he had no legal obligations.

"So, he does have angina," said Tony, trying to decipher the medical paperwork. The doctor shrugged non-committedly.

"Maybe he does, maybe he doesn't. It's very hard to diagnose," said the doctor, not really remembering how easy or difficult it actually was. "Plus, it was a very long time ago, way before my time. According to the notes he presented with angina-like symptoms, but they are not dissimilar to indigestion. Or many other illnesses."

"But he was prescribed nitro-glycerine?" asked Tony. Another non-committal shrug.

"You know we don't actually prescribe anything here. Patient wants it, they get it," he said. "It's more like a recommendation, really. We only record what they take to ensure we keep supplies topped up," he added.

"But he takes it?" asked Tony, feeling exasperation well up in him.

"Sure. Every month, he picks up a fresh supply, twenty-eight days' worth. Has done for years."

"How many years?" asked Tony, running numbers through his head. A basic piece of research using the only internet connection on the island revealed that it would take ten years to accumulate enough nitro-glycerine to make enough explosives for a handful of bullets. The doctor flicked through the records swiftly.

"About forty," he said.

*

The events were zipping past Detective Inspector Morris faster than anything he'd ever experienced.

"You'll fly Leeds to Heathrow, change to the LA flight and liaise with the LAPD on arrival," said the Superintendent signing off on the travel costs. "A Met officer will be at Heathrow to update you on anything they've pulled together since you last spoke, so make sure you have that conversation. There's a three-hour gap between flights so you should have enough time," he said, handing the signed documents to Morris.

Looking at his watch, Morris realised he had exactly one hour and thirty minutes to pull his information together, get home to throw some stuff in a bag. If he'd had a normal career he would also have had to leave a note for the wife and kids before making his way to Leeds Bradford airport, but like many of his contemporaries his wife had left, taken the kids, only contacted him when she wanted to increase the maintenance payment amount. One job less to do, he guessed. He had his passport in his desk, a manila folder on top with hard copies of all the reports he'd been involved in, a laptop that had access to the National Crime Database from anywhere in the world and two bank cards with overdraught facilities, complete with overdrawn accounts.

He wanted more information, wanted to know why it was suddenly important to drop everything he'd been working on to fly halfway across the planet, to find out what specifically had changed. Importantly he couldn't understand why the Met were handing a high-profile case over to a provincial copper with less than two years left until retirement, especially as the destination was highly desirable.

Grabbing as many charging cables as he could find he stuffed them into his laptop case as full as he could. Scooping his mobile off the desk he tried to remember if it was set up for international calls, whether the battery would hold out without charging until he landed. He wondered what value he could lend to an investigation that spanned two continents, three police departments and four victims.

Chapter 18

The Met officer had arrived at Heathrow on time and had been allowed airside to speak to DI Morris. He described the British victim, glossed over the American, understood that they were dealing with the killing of a writer on US soil.

"What's the link?" he asked, not sure how well read-in this officer was. He could feel a fob off coming on, couldn't work out why.

"We know when and where his seat was booked; the paperwork in the folder shows an audit trail. It seems likely that information was known by other persons and he was targeted as much as the doctor in your patch and the music editor in ours. Looks like travelling incognito didn't fool anyone."

"You mean, someone followed him from Heathrow to LA and killed him in connection with the other two murders?" he asked. It sounded a stretch, a complete leap of logic. The officer shrugged non-committedly; he was only the messenger who had half an hour to spare and lived en-route to Heathrow.

"It's a working theory," he offered. He'd had a rushed briefing on the way out, told who he had to meet up with, understood he wouldn't get paid overtime, but time off in lieu was possible. "If it's wrong, there appears to be one hell of a coincidence going on," he noted. DI Morris had to agree and took the buff cardboard file the officer had brought.

"Everything we have is in there," the officer said. Within ten minutes Morris found himself stood alone in Departures, file in one hand, coffee in the other, boarding ticket sticking out of his top pocket. He got the impression that the Met didn't want to get involved in this part of a murder enquiry, that the brass didn't want to pick up the tab for a transatlantic flight to investigate a series of murders that hadn't caught the public attention and was almost certainly a red herring. Morris's boss, however, had felt a breeze of opportunity waft over the case and felt a little investment in air fares and budget hotels for a few nights might make him look good in front of the promotion board considering him in a month's time, given he'd been turned down for being too cautious in the past.

Responding to the call for passengers, Morris juggled the folder, coffee and his hand baggage as he made his way to the departure gate. At least he had some reading material while in the air.

*

The club was splendid from the outside, the stucco exterior painted white, with decorative mouldings edged tastefully in gold leaf, the Los Angeles sunshine reflecting fully onto Alec's sunglasses. Sat opposite the building at a coffee shop, occupying an outside seat that gave unparalleled views of all the main entrances, Alec could sit quietly sipping his milk-loaded froth while flicking lazily through the local newspaper left by the previous occupant. If Derrick returned to the club then Alec would see him, unless he took the unconventional approach around the back where deliveries and perhaps the odd celebrity might enter. He assumed that the ex-manager of a supposedly dead rock star didn't attract the paparazzi this long after the event and guessed that Derrick could walk in by the front door on stilts with a neon sign on his head and still not attract attention. Deep down he wouldn't be upset if Derrick did take the hidden view as Alec could justify his stakeout as a rational approach given his limited resources.

The journey by sea, air and hire car hadn't calmed his nerves, his stomach flipping each and every time he remembered why he was here. Managing prima donna guests in the most bizarre hotel complex in the world required him to be tough talking, aggressive even, on many occasions, but thankfully he never had to resort to actual physical violence, let alone kill anyone. He'd considered it a few times, but now he had to do it he knew he wasn't really cut out for this.

Maybe this was just a test, he wondered. The explanation that Tony was compromised was plausible, but the organisation had others better qualified to perform the blackest of hotel arts. Perhaps Tony had decided to retire – historically a difficult transition, as far as Alec was concerned no manager had achieved retirement in the conventional sense of walking away and settling down in a quiet community. He accepted that data on previous managers was limited to whatever the existing manager provided, in his case whatever Tony decided to pass on, and his knowledge appeared to be limited to what he had observed and been told. So maybe the whole thing was a crock of shit, a belief system designed to keep under managers focussed and in line.

Or maybe Tony didn't know he was about to retire.

Either way, Alec knew he had to follow through with this assignment. Perhaps all managers had to do a dirty deed to ensure their total loyalty, to become so compromised that they would become entirely committed to the corporate goals when free to roam the world outside of the island.

Alec drained his cup, the third he'd drunk since arriving and looked around to see if he could attract the attention of the barista, with no luck. Leaving his pile of papers showing the faces of the music industry managers and ex-managers expected to frequent the club he slipped inside to order a top up. While he was inside the staff running the club unlocked the front entrance, pushing the door momentarily and letting it close again on its hydraulic dampers. While Alec was relieving himself in the rest room a close-cropped man entered, the first customer of the day. Had Alec remained on his stakeout position he wouldn't have recognised the man as a fellow employee, even though he knew a lot about the man by reputation. By the time Alec returned to his seat Cliff was ensconced in a booth

155

overseeing the entrance in the main bar, with a soft drink in front of him.

*

Derrick had woken with the usual hangover, about the usual time just after noon. A quick review on his laptop, checking the news apps, his email and his online banking account revealed that since crashing for the night his lies about Ricky hadn't been rumbled, he wasn't being recalled by the police for further enquiries and he hadn't allowed himself to be fleeced, three of his recurring nightmares. His bank balance was still very healthy and, according to the information from the organisation, was about to get healthier in a day or so, the first of many monthly payments to keep shtum.

Showering, shaving and stopping off at a fast food outlet to take some nutrients on-board, Derrick sat with a coffee wondering what to do with the rest of the day. Inevitably the muse moved on to the rest of his life, with little more clarity. He knew he couldn't keep going to the club night after night, that he was wealthy enough to fly off to anywhere in the world and just have a fantastic, debauched life, but he knew he wasn't ready, like most of the kindred kin he was spending his nights with.

Checking his phone, he noticed his Twitter feed was going berserk, with comments about a music manager being killed a few miles from where he was sat. Checking out the local news sites he found out that the killing took place at the club he'd visited

156

briefly two nights ago. He didn't know the guy who had been killed, but noticed the inserted box mentioning the artist that the guy used to manage, a famous rock and roller who'd died too young, just like Ricky.

Just. Like. Ricky.

The thought circled his head as he pondered if the famous rock and roller was truly dead or, like Ricky, just conveniently dead-ish, that the man might, just maybe, have been pulling in monthly stipends from the same organisation that Derrick was waiting to see rolling in. He recalled the discussion with his mentor who'd warned him about the threats, the cards, the Genghis Khan school of persuasion. His brain went into overdrive, wondering if the man had broken the rules, had mentioned on social media that his artist wasn't as dead as generally believed, had spilled his guts out to a hooker while high on cocaine, had simply left a detail in the open. Three fears Derrick had, fears that meant he had tried to avoid social media, had rain checked most of the hookers since swearing blind the weird looking guy on the slab was Ricky and left him waking up paranoid every morning.

Christ, he missed Ricky too, the foul mouthed, erratic, ego tripping lunatic who'd caused him daily problems and periodic heartache. He wondered if other managers felt the same way, whether they wanted to talk to someone, anyone about what they had done, what they knew. He wondered if this guy had had those thoughts, had strayed from the script, had been horribly mutilated for his transgression. The news reports were necessarily vague, but clearly indicated the killing to be brutal. Derrick knew he needed to talk to someone and knew that realistically there was only one person he could talk to and, even then, the conversation was going to be circumspect. He just hoped his mentor was going to the club.

*

The club started to get busy just after three, a magic slice of time between breakfast and starting recording for many in the music industry. Alec watched as individuals, couples and groups of up to six arrived and left with increasing frequency. He realised that he almost certainly could have missed Derrick if he'd arrived, but in a strange way he'd enjoyed playing I-Spy with the industry managers. Some, he knew, were in receipt of payments from his organisation and he felt a few of his customers back on the island would be pleased to get an update on the guys who had been their ultimate confidants and middle men in their drug habit. He felt that waiting outside was likely to result in missing Derrick if he did turn up and certainly would prevent him finding out anything about his whereabouts by just watching. Plus, his head was banging thanks to the seventeen cups of coffee he'd consumed, perhaps beer would balance it out.

He was surprised at how dark it was inside the club, muted lighting barely showing the way to the bar. As he walked past the booths that sat either side of the route that skirted the dance floor and the tiny stage he was aware of various conversations between small groups of people, predominantly middle aged or older men, with the occasional young female voice repeating the scale of costs for her services. At least one booth seemed to house a single man, his eyes blazing out, cutting through the dark, appraising each and every person that passed. Suppressing a shiver, Alec approached the bar and sidled up alongside a man who he recognised from his list, a possible point of contact for Derrick. Trying to keep his options open he ordered a drink and, after a pause, offered the guy one too, an offer readily accepted.

"You in the industry?" asked the guy, only half interested. He'd got a free drink and someone to pass the time while he waited for the hooker he'd booked to arrive. Alec played it cool, saying he was on the periphery of the industry, dealing with the hospitality of the stars, suppressing mentioning a list of customers that between them accounted for over fifty percent of all-time record sales. The enormity of that thought brought a flush of pride to Alec's cheeks as he realised how blasé he'd become dealing with some of the most famous names in music and the occasional Russian thug. This guy had looked after just one of Alec's guests, had fleeced him twice that the musician knew of, had bedded his wife several times and had generally mismanaged his career while he was still officially alive. Now he was getting a monthly stipend that dwarfed Alec's wage just to keep his mouth shut.

They chatted about mutual acquaintances, with Alec drawing on the information supplied on his arrival by the organisation, peppering it with slightly modified tales from some of his more recent customers to give his story depth. Slowly Alec brought the narrative around to Ricky Maggott, mentioning how he'd sorted out the singer's rider on a number of occasions, rolling his eyes at some of the more extreme demands. The guy smiled throughout, then picked up his glass ready to leave.

"You another journalist?" he asked bluntly, taking Alec aback. With some conviction Alec denied the allegation, asking why he thought he might be one. 'When I get two people asking about the same dead guy in one short hour, I get suspicious,' said the man, nodding to the darkened booths. Alec turned instinctively to the gloom before turning back.

"Who else has been asking?" he asked, realising immediately that he was now sounding more like a journalist than ever before. Probably better than being outed as a potential killer, he thought. "And yes, you're right, I am a journalist, writing an article about Ricky," he lied, trying to show contrition. The man shrugged and turned back to the bar, picking his drink up, sinking the dregs.

"Booth on the right, second one in," he said, slapping a pile of notes to cover the drinks he'd had before Alec started pumping him for information. Alec noticed the barman counting the notes, looking at him. He slapped a few more notes to cover the drinks he'd bought and to cover the tip before moving back into the dark, towards the second booth on the right, the one where he'd felt a pair of eyes blazing out. He didn't know if it was the right or wrong thing to do, it felt as reckless as agreeing to kill a man he'd never met, but it was all he had.

*

Tony rummaged in the safe, pulling confidential files aside, moving blocks of gold he'd kept just in case he needed a quick, safe exit. He wondered if he'd be hauling some of those blocks anytime soon. Digging deep into the large steel container he found what he'd been looking for, the thirteen round Browning handgun a previous manager had brought with him, wrapped in oilskin. He looked behind him at the locked door, checked for at least the third time that he'd drawn the blinds and covered the CCTV camera, just in case someone had hacked the feed.

Digging deeper he found the two loaded magazines and proceeded to push the top rounds down to feel the resistance felt from a fully loaded magazine. A roll of gun cloth provided the material he needed to wipe the surplus oil off the outer faces of the handgun before he stripped it down for a thorough clean. Ten minutes later he had all the working parts lain across his desk, a manual open at the page showing all the components numbered and described, a pile of gun cloth scrunched up in a dirty, messy pile and twenty-six rounds stood like toy soldiers in a line.

The gun had never been fired in the years he'd been on the island, passed from manager to manager unused, unneeded and under a pile of confidential files. Now he was seriously considering carrying it in the worn and tatty British Army issue shoulder holster that was pushed into one of the far corners of the safe. Reassembling the weapon Tony decided against wearing it straight away but would ensure it was ready to use at a few minutes' notice. He pondered if he could slip away to set up a little target practise away from the compound without attracting too much attention. Since Alec had left Tony felt he'd had hardly a minute to himself and wondered if he could spare the two hours minimum he'd need. He wondered if he could spare any of the twenty-six rounds either?

Locking the weapon away, taking care to shield it from view even though at the moment he was the only person with access to the safe, he turned the two-part key and spun the combination lock. The outer part of the key went into the blister and the inner part, one of two copies, was slipped on a chain around his neck inside his shirt along with a master key to the accommodation blocks and the office itself. Alec had the other inner key and kept it as hidden as Tony ever did, and he wasn't here anyway. Tony hadn't mentioned the Browning in the years they had worked together, assumed that Alec easily could have found it while carrying out his duties, especially as Tony was often off-site, but if he had, he'd kept the fact to himself.

Perhaps they needed that conversation when he got back, for mutual survival purposes.

*

Cliff eyed the young man carefully. He knew about the under-manager brought over to hunt down Derrick Moore, understood that the organisation was concerned that he'd be tied up in the UK for an indeterminate time and wanted to try and expedite the whole process. But this kid? Fair enough the punk had come straight over to him, sat down and challenged him directly – that took guts.

"We're on the same team kid," Cliff said. Alec tried to process the single sentence for way longer than he wanted to. He'd realised he and the stranger were both looking for Derrick, wasn't sure why anyone else would want to, was trying to reconcile the use of the word "team". "We get paid by the same people," suggested Cliff to help Alec. "I normally work alone, leave virtually no trace, keep everything tidy." He paused for a moment before continuing. "You're starting to make me look untidy." Alec shuffled uncomfortably.

"You know me?" he asked. All he'd done was introduce himself by name, aiming to launch into a "What the hell do you think you're doing?" type tirade before being stopped in his tracks by the coldest, most evil stare he'd ever encountered. Cliff nodded, raised a hand to attract a waiter's attention.

"And I reckon you know me, by reputation," he said, adding, "your reputation is very highly

163

regarded, by the way. If I wanted a hotel manager, I'd like him to be as efficient as you're reputed to be," he said. Alec took a beer off the tray that floated under his nose, noted the man didn't.

"OK, we're both after Derrick," he said, taking a swig. The man sat opposite didn't show any emotion as he leant forward.

"It's a bit more personal than that," he said, watching Alec wince. "Look kid, I don't think you're up to this any more than I would be running a hotel. The bosses wanted this angle covered because it looked like I was otherwise indisposed, however it seems there's been a change in circumstances that means I'm over here now and I reckon you can stand down," he said. Alec felt a wash of relief flow over him, before a nagging thought returned. What if this was a deliberate challenge? He'd become convinced the whole thing was a test and this guy seemed to be confirming it. Cliff seemed to understand the look.

"Hey, you still want in?" he asked, leaning over and picking the beer bottle out of Alec's hand. "Personally, I don't think that's a good idea but if you're hell bent, then you need to keep a clear head," he suggested, unaware that Alec's head was too chock full of caffeine to be considered clear for at least twelve hours. The hyper-driven thoughts racing around in Alec's brain were verging on the paranoid mixed up with a life-long guilt trip.

"Yes, I'm still in," he declared, sitting straight and looking around. "I guess you're the expert and

I'm the student," he said. "I probably couldn't do this on my own, but as it's my duty I'd like to work with you to take this to its final conclusion," he declared, wondering how he was going to achieve this. Cliff looked at the kid closely, considering the options.

"What the hell," he declared as he came to a decision. Handing the bottle back he outlined his rules. "I reckon you may as well finish this, you'll probably need it. Stick close, don't get in my way, stay calm and don't leave any DNA anywhere," he said. "Now tell me everything you've learned," he added.

*

Derrick unclipped his seatbelt before the cab stopped, causing an irritating alarm in the car and an irritated tut from the driver. Handing the fare and a suitable tip over the seat Derrick opened the door, felt the LA heat hit him as the cooled air from the cabin escaped.

He hauled his bag off the seat alongside him, felt the heft. He'd checked out of his room, taken his hire car back and decided that after a few drinks he'd decide where to go next. He hoped this was the last time he walked into this club, not certain that it would be. He knew that if he bottled leaving town then he could get a room within walking distance; if he followed through with his plan he could get to LAX and onto the first flight that caught his fancy that had a seat. He had a valid Mastercard and passport in his back pocket, a wallet full of dollars in his front.

Just a few beers and a couple of shorts to motivate him, a chance to say his goodbyes and he was out of here. Turn his back on Los Angeles, the music industry, Ricky, the lot. That was his plan, his master plan. He just hoped he could see it through.

Feeling his shirt cling to his back he walked to the hydraulically damped door with the flashing "open" sign above it, pulled the door and felt the cold air wash over him, drying the mop across his forehead. He walked into the foyer, looking left and right, trying to decide which of the two bars to go to, the main bar or the more convivial smaller bar, wondering which one would be in favour today. Turning right he caught a glimpse of two shadows exiting from the door on his left, two people leaving, looking for another bar along the strip no doubt. One had a British accent, and he nearly turned to look at his fellow countryman but decided to continue to the right.

Derrick felt the buzz in his pocket, stopped and looked at the number flashed on his phone as he pulled it out, struggled to recognise the area code or the country of origin. Uncharacteristically he pushed the answer button and heard a very familiar voice reach out of the phone, a voice he assumed he'd never hear again. Staring at his phone, speechless, he failed to notice that the two shadows hadn't left via the front door but were right behind him. He froze as the bony hand clasped his shoulder.

Chapter 19

Elvis stared at the bat phone Ricky had snuck out of Alec's office when Elvis had created a diversion with undisguised contempt. "He didn't even answer ya," he said, clearly unimpressed by the guy who was supposed to be Ricky's right hand man. Ricky felt completely deflated. He'd chosen his time to call, had calculated as best he could a time that Derrick would be out and about, had racked his brain for days to recall a mobile number that was normally just a speed dial away. If he hadn't had to memorise it in the early days of their professional relationship to quote to police when arrested for smashing up hotel rooms he'd never have known it at all. He was convinced Derrick would talk to him, provide help, but it looked like he'd hung up as soon as he'd realised who the caller was. Sure, he'd spoken Ricky's name in surprise, but then nothing, silence. The line went dead suddenly after a few seconds of static.

"He did answer," he said defensively, irrationally wanting to fight Derrick's corner despite feeling abandoned by the man he paid to look after him. Or rather, the man he used to pay.

"He was frightened," he said, looking around the cove they'd snuck into to make the call, aware that other residents might turn up for a swim or a drunken beach-side barbeque at any moment. They'd hidden the sat phone under a rock more than halfway up the beach, well away from the high tide and sheltered from rain by a thick polythene wrapper to avoid carrying it to and from the recording studio.

Elvis considered the statement carefully; he'd come to appreciate the young Brit's instincts in the relatively short period they'd been friends. In fact, he realised that Ricky was probably the first real friend he'd had in years, with all the other residents at best humouring him as the elder statesman of the resort. This kid only knew of him by reputation, hadn't grown up buying his records, came from a different musical background. But he'd known poverty, like Elvis had. He'd fought his way into the business, again like Elvis. He'd trusted a manager who seemed like he'd let him down, again the parallels were compelling, although the manager part was accepted as an industry norm. More importantly, Ricky seemed to like Elvis for just being Elvis.

"I guess ya could be right, boy," he said, turning back to the path that led back to the compound. "Perhaps he was spooked by it," he suggested. "We can try again tomorrow, once he's had a chance to let it sink in," he added.

As they walked along the path, deep in conversation, neither registered the sound of the sat phone ringing from under its rock.

*

Alec replayed the last few minutes in his head, bewildered by the speed of events.

168

He'd taken a plunge, a leap of faith to side with the man with the blazing eyes who called himself Cliff. The man scared him, shitless to be blunt. The whole task he'd been given scared him shitless as well, had done so since he'd been taken to one side in the foyer and told he was going on a trip and wasn't coming back until a man he'd barely heard of, never met and didn't give a flying fuck about was dead. And by dead, they meant really dead, not the pretend dead like Alec's residents. Critically the man was to be dead at Alec's hands, and that was a huge deal. So, when Cliff agreed to work with Alec, act as his mentor, agreeing to let him deal the lethal blow that would seal his loyalty to the organisation while watching his six, providing tooling and, more importantly, providing training support, when all of this was offered Alec leapt at the man.

They'd thrown some notes on the table and decided to wait outside in the foyer. Checking each booth on the way out seemed almost automatic, sizing up the male occupants, listening for a British accent, hoping to fluke in on the target. They'd opened the double doors leading out of the bar discussing the general gist of the plan when they'd seen a few people milling around the entrance, with Derrick on his own deciding on whether to turn to Cliff and Alec's direction or away to the opposite set of double doors. Alec felt his stomach flip as Derrick paused to look at his mobile, a furrow cross his brow as he hit answer and listened to the voice on the other end of the phone, so distracted that Derrick hadn't noticed Alec or Cliff.

169

He stepped forward, intending intercepting Derrick stood at the opposite end of the entrance lobby when Cliff reached out and grasped Alec's arm with a firm, bony grip. "This is my part of the task," growled the assassin.

*

Derrick looked up, into the eyes of the man who had gripped his shoulder. He felt his heart sink as he realised who had intercepted him, knew that his plan for the day was screwed. Maybe his plan for the rest of his life was screwed. He looked down at his phone, realised whose voice it was he'd heard as he'd hung up the call, couldn't stop himself as he looked up again.

"That was Ricky," he said, his eyes welling up. He dropped his bag to the ground and found himself gripping the arm tightly. "He called me," he said, looking back into the man's eyes.

"Ricky? Really? Call him back." Derrick nodded, scrolled through the menu, dialled the last number in the list, the one that had piqued his curiosity, heard it ring out several times. He lowered the phone and his shoulders.

"We need to talk," said Aiden, picking up Derrick's bag. Derrick nodded, looked at the pretty young black girl stood next to the writer, wondered what the crack was. He barely noticed the two men who walked slowly past checking them out.

*

They sat in a quiet bar a few hundred yards from the club, watching the sun set through the engraved windows. Derrick was sweating despite the best efforts of the air con.

"How did you find me?" he asked. Aiden wrinkled his nose. The club was an obvious port of call for anyone in the industry, one of only a few such locations. The Instagram message helped as well, so Aiden showed it to Derrick. He looked at the photo with scant recall, didn't look like he actually recognised the technology.

"Did I do that?" he asked, pointing at the image.

"It was off his feed, but it bounced off your account, so you must have shared it with him sometime," he said, feeling a little uncomfortable. "I kind of hacked into your account months ago," he admitted. He shrugged at the look Derrick threw him. "I'm a journalist and specialise in Ricky," he said in way of justification. It seemed to work as Derrick's dark look softened.

"What do you want to know?" he asked, looking around. The memory of the conversation a few nights earlier poked back in, the talk of keeping the open secret more secret than open, the potential risks associated with talking about the arrangement. He looked at the girl again, realised that Aiden hadn't attempted to introduce her. Aiden saw the look, decided it was time he laid his cards on the table.

"I'll be honest, I really thought Ricky was dead, but I didn't believe the hogwash you served up," he said. He looked at Danni and waved a hand in her direction. "Danni is one of the doctors you used to fake whatever it is you were trying to fake," he said, noting the look of respect enter Derrick's eyes. Most in the industry liked to cultivate a strong relationship with anyone with a prescription pad and a qualification that allowed access to legal drugs, Derrick was no exception.

"How did you know?" he asked, genuinely interested. He knew he'd flunked some of the interviews, but the prep had been thorough, the backstory considered robust. What on earth did they miss? Danni decided it was time for the expert to take up the discussion.

"I was asked, no, encouraged to take part in practise surgery on a cadaver," she explained, "and Aiden traced my paperwork back to the paperwork associated with your friend's operation," she said. Derrick felt his heart sag; they had said the paperwork trail wouldn't be a problem as nobody would think to unravel it. Clearly, they hadn't planned on Aiden McKie entering the fray. Danni hadn't finished.

"I didn't register the cadaver's features, apart from being white and male," she said, establishing her medical training credentials, "and the procedure was fairly routine. Blood loss minimal – you get that with dead people – and I didn't even stich him up. One of my colleagues did that for the practise," she said. "But I did register the healthy appendix that I

172

removed and placed in an emesis basin," she added. Aiden noticed the querulous look from Derrick.

"We call them kidney dishes," he said, before continuing, "I have medical records from the Eighties that show Ricky had his appendix removed back then, you can't have it removed twice," he added, noting Danni's hand raise.

"Strictly speaking, some people do have two," she said, scouring her memory for the salient details, "but it is very rare and, more importantly, if one is removed because of inflammation then any competent surgeon would remove the other at the same time," she said, nodding to Aiden to allow him to resume.

"I've spoken to the doctor who diagnosed the appendicitis in the first place and he's confirmed Ricky had it removed. He saw him post operation and he promised to check his personal records to let me know who performed the operation." Derrick looked somewhere between impressed and deflated until Aiden dropped his bombshell.

"At least, he was going to but since I spoke to him, he's died. Approximately a few hours after I left him," he added. Derrick felt his blood freeze; this might sound routine to a journalist with half the story, to him it was big time.

"What I'm about to tell you might put your life and mine in danger," he said, looking around the near empty bar, noting the bartender was the opposite end watching the sports channel intently, "but it sounds like you might have passed that point already," he said, pulling Aiden and Danni into a huddle.

Outside the bar Cliff and Alec sat in Cliff's rental car, Cliff scowling as he stared at the door. Alec thought he understood that the other two persons were a complicating matter, but he'd never assumed Derrick would be alone, that he'd have to follow him and find an opportune moment to do the dirty on him. The company specialist, in his opinion, was a little unreasonable to expect to find the target alone and ready to be offed at the first opportunity.

"He'll probably split from them at some point," he offered. "Hopefully he'll be well smashed by the time they leave here, which makes it easier for us," he suggested, repeating something Cliff had suggested earlier. Cliff audibly ground his teeth.

"It's more complicated than that," he growled, not taking his eyes off the door. His head was spinning, he'd assumed the man with the British accent and the local hooker had been McKie. Certainly, the electronic audit trail suggested it was him, the hair colour, or what was left of it, matched, as did the length and his general build. He'd killed the wrong guy which would add a bit of extra heat to the local situation, but that wasn't the big problem here. He now had both primary targets together, which could be a bonus, but there was the young girl as well. She looked professional, possibly a cop, perhaps the dots had been joined up and they were onto him. Killing cops wasn't off the list, but it was definitely a last resort. Then there was his apprentice; with just Derrick to off he wasn't a problem, with up to three to coordinate he was more of a hinderance.

One solution he'd thought of was to get the kid behind the wheel and keeping the engine running. He could pull the automatic weapon from the trunk, walk in and spray everyone in the bar. Messy, indiscriminate and impossible to guarantee complete success. Plus, he had no idea how the kid would manage in that situation; the last thing he needed was a panicking escape driver doing a runner with the car keys or worse, with the car. Christ, he didn't even know how many were in the bar and where the targets were.

"I need you to carry out a recce," Cliff said, still looking at the bar door.

*

"How long will the battery be good for?" asked Elvis, sipping a long non-alcoholic drink. Ricky downed a short, very alcoholic version. They'd been talking about music, power chords and minor keys, so the switch to electrical engineering jarred a little.

"What batteries?" he asked. Elvis put his glass down carefully.

"The ones in the bat phone," he answered. Ricky shrugged, he'd assumed that satellite phones were designed to be efficient given they were associated with remote locations, but to be fair he'd never seen one in the flesh, let alone used one. It had taken him ten minutes to work out how to turn it on.

"Dunno, a few days on standby I guess," he replied. He thought Elvis had left that subject behind on the beach as he hadn't mentioned anything in the hour or so since. Ricky hadn't thought of anything else. He was sure Derrick had answered, was dismayed he might have hung up on him. Derrick was, he guessed, his only hope to get out and had said as much several times already. The octogenarian considered the point before declaring they should go back to the beach.

"Leaving it twenty-four hours is too long, we should go back an' try again," he said, seeing the light in Ricky's eyes return. Ricky shoved the empty glass along the bar to the waiting barman, who made to refill it. Ricky waved a negative, leave it, gesture.

"Come on, old man," he said.

*

Crushed between a man who should have had two seats and a woman who clearly hadn't had a conversation in years, John Morris sat at an angle trying to read the contents of the buff folder as the Atlantic Ocean drifted below the Dreamliner coasting towards the Eastern seaboard of the United States en route to the Western variant. Most of the reports were known to him; he'd generated at least three of them and just noted the comments made by Metropolitan Police senior officers. It was the faxed report from the LAPD that he spent the most time reading, smudged passport images, boarding tickets, itemised bills from the hotel that presumably was adding a room cleaning bill to.

He tried to ensure the woman didn't see the images of the double homicide by turning to the obese man's bulge, assuming the snoring noise confirmed he had some privacy. He was less concerned that he might shock her than start a new line of banal conversation. He read the notes concerning the man Paul Riggs, failed to make any new connection other than the coincidence regarding the seat booking. He read the statement made by Brian Esk's PA about how she'd released the seat, replacing it with a new booking of one twenty-four hours later, checked the airline statement that an administrative error had left McKie's name on the database even though the seat had been resold at very short notice and even shorter profit margin.

He looked at the list of homicides in the same district – short one-line descriptions of car jackings, liquor store raids gone wrong, gang warfare in the darker corners of LA, domestic squabbles involving firearms and a number of bar fights involving at least one fatality. Not bad for one week. Pulling a yellow highlighter from his jacket inside pocket, Morris drew a yellow streak over one particularly nasty killing downtown as the Boeing crossed the North American coastline, with a large part of the journey left to cover.

*

Aiden, Danni and Derrick had piled into Danni's car and headed up the freeway, having been spooked by the sight of a man standing in the doorway clearly casing the joint. "He looks a bit suspect," Aiden had noted as Alec had paused in the doorway and fixated on the only group of customers bar one. The stranger reminded him of something, maybe he was a Jehovah's Witness on a recruitment campaign, or perhaps the Salvation Army sent undercover operatives to bars in the US. Whatever it was, it sent a feeling of unease down his spine and encouraged him to move the party out of the bar through a doorway on the opposite side of the room, spilling out into a parking lot that bordered a string of small shops that served the hairdressing and nail beauty needs of the local population.

"My car's just over here," he said to Derrick as they walked rapidly down the parade of shops that ran parallel to the main street, crossing a piece of waste ground at ninety degrees and skirting a drain that seemed to run for miles in either direction by leaping over the concrete sides. Opening his car Aiden looked back to see if the lone man had followed them but couldn't see anyone in sight across the dead ground they'd just crossed.

"We'll just drive and check we're not being followed," he said, gunning the engine and shifting to drive.

*

Alec ran back to the car, his face flushed as much by being sussed as by the exertion. Cliff leant across and opened the passenger door, watching the Brit pile in.

"What happened?" he asked. All he'd asked the hotel manager to do was walk in, sit at the bar and take a look around, noting where they were sat, how many others were in there and some basic directions. How hard could it be.

"They spotted me," gasped Alec.

"How? At the bar?" asked Cliff in quick succession. Alec shook his head.

"I walked in and stopped at the door to get my bearings. The other guy, the one that intercepted Derrick just ahead of us, saw me and started talking about me straight away. I never got to the bar, they just got up and left by the rear exit," he said. Cliff allowed a microsecond to process the information, felt his anger rise as he realised he'd sent a rank amateur into the club to do a professional's job, realised that all the blame was on him. He looked around at the road, noted the steady stream of traffic running up and down, saw the odd car exit a side road a few hundred yards behind them, realised he had no idea what car they were in. The trio had left the club he'd staked out and walked the few hundred yards to another, quieter looking establishment and entered, talking all the way and totally oblivious to Cliff cruising slowly behind them.

"You didn't follow them at all?" he half asked, pretty much telling Alec as he was certain he knew the answer. Alec shook his head in final confirmation that they had been within inches of accomplishing their task and now were miles away from even finding Derrick. He decided he needed to read the young guy in, if only because the problem was now a lot more complicated.

"The other guy you mentioned," he said, noting that Alec was listening with maximum intent, "is a music journalist who's been asking all the wrong questions back in your home country and he's made a trip over here to try and track down Derrick Moore. He's the reason you were asked to off Derrick; I was supposed to dispose of the journalist over in the UK along with any loose ends. Unfortunately, he's made his way over here and, thanks to a mistaken identity, I've taken out the wrong guy," he said. Alec looked at the man, wondered just how deep this was going. He had accepted that Derrick had to be taken out, hadn't realised just how ruthless the process was, the clinical clearing up of anything that might rock the boat.

Cliff decided that as he had no quick way of locating the threesome he would explain as much as he felt he could to Alec, incriminating and implicating the young man as much as possible to keep him focussed while avoiding releasing any information that would swing a Grand Jury. Compromising a lamb awaiting slaughter was a delicate balance, he thought. After he'd run the story past his apprentice, he decided he ought to tidy up one more loose end.

"I'm going in to ask a couple of questions," he said, patting his left side, feeling the reassuring bulk of his Glock hanging just inside. He left the car with the engine running and entered the bar, walking over to the counter while taking in the information that he'd expected Alec to absorb, realising that he had years of training and experience behind him. Nestling on a bar stool he waited for the barman to approach, flicking idly with some pamphlets left lying on top, seemingly taking little notice of his surroundings. By the time the barman asked him what he wanted he'd established that there was one other person in the bar apart from himself and the barman, a man sitting along the counter nursing a drink and, presumably, a hangover given his look.

"A whiskey," he asked. "No ice," he added as he expertly followed the CCTV camera feed, locating the hard drive unit. The barman slapped a glass on the counter, poured a decent dash and was rewarded by a bullet to his chest fired from the silenced Glock. The man nursing his glass looked up, almost resignedly as another bullet smashed into his skull, slopping his body across the bar floor.

Cliff picked his glass up, slung the liquor down in one gulp and walked out, pulling the latex gloves off as he walked and stuffing them into his side pocket, carrying the hard drive he'd liberated from behind the bar just seconds earlier. He jumped in the car briskly, indicated and pulled out. Alec clearly hadn't registered the muffled shots from inside the building, as he just turned to his mentor. "What did he say?" referring to the barman. Cliff decided against repeating the cry of surprise and handed Alec the hard drive.

"He agreed to let us have the CCTV video footage," he said. "It takes our images from inside and outside of the club out of circulation and hopefully I can lipread something from Derrick and his cronies," he said. Alec briefly wondered about the persuasive powers of the man he was sat next to, but quickly realised that this was a very experienced operative.

"That should help," he answered as they sped off towards a motel Cliff had previously identified as suitable for his purposes.

*

The sun was dipping in the South Seas by the time Ricky and Elvis returned to the beach. The long shadows made finding the hiding place a little more difficult than before, plus a few of the residents were just wrapping up from having a dip in the sea. Ricky mentioned it was windier than of late, the sea choppier. Elvis stood and sniffed the air.

"Storm's comin'," he predicted, turning his head side to side. Ricky thought that the man was full of shit this time, it was just a little breezier, but conceded Elvis had lived there a tad longer.

They stood talking alongside the hiding place for a few minutes, waiting for the beach to clear before moving the rock and picking the sat phone up.

Unwrapping the lump of plastic, Ricky realised he hadn't powered the device down. Taking note of Elvis' earlier question about battery life he looked at the power indicator and realised that it was more than halfway depleted, much lower than he recalled from earlier in the day. He also noted that it had recorded a missed call.

"He called us back," he exclaimed, slapping Elvis on the back. The old man beamed, pleased that his initiative had been rewarded. Ricky's hand shook as he fumbled with the keypad, trying to ensure he returned the call, looking around furtively, stopping when he saw a silhouette appear on the horizon.

"Shit," he said as he recognised the man walking towards them.

Chapter 20

Ricky had his chin in his hands, his shoulders slumped. When Tony had turned up, demanding what the hell they were doing, Ricky had gone into auto-burble. He explained they'd been out for a walk, had kicked the stone and found the package under it. They had no idea what it was or how it had got there. Tony didn't look convinced, had a look that murder was close to the surface and the two residents the likely recipients. Elvis had played a blinder, backing up the story on the hoof, looking at the device as if he'd never seen one before. He'd drawn a sideward glance from Tony when he'd referred to the device as a bat phone, but Ricky assumed Tony decided he'd misheard.

Both had been relieved when they'd been told to "fuck off, pronto", and neither had put up any resistance. Ricky had resorted to good old-fashioned Anglo-Saxon verbiage, but that was just working-class bravado rising. Neither had any illusions that they were in deep shit. Elvis put up a brave face, insisting that the resort needed them more than they needed the resort, but Ricky knew that the resort had the piece of them that counted – their royalties. It wasn't like they could up sticks and leave; they were trapped and as far as Ricky could tell they'd just lost the only lifeline they possessed.

"We really need to get out of here," he said to Elvis as they collected a nightcap each. Even Elvis had ordered a stiff drink, the first alcohol Ricky had seen the old man drink since he'd arrived.

"Y'all need to get out of here," Elvis said, sipping his drink, his body shuddering as the liquor slipped down. "I'm too old, but I'll do whatever it takes to get ya away boy," he said. Ricky looked at the old man, knew he couldn't leave him alone and undefended.

"It's both of us, or it's neither of us," he said as he watched his friend enter his apartment. He bid him goodnight and made his way to his own pad, where he dug out a bottle of strong hooch from his sideboard and started to wire into a bender before realising that drinking himself senseless left him vulnerable. Putting the hooch back he finished his drink, pushed heavy furniture up against the front door and made sure every possible entry point was locked and blocked. It was going to be a long night.

*

It was dark when they pulled over, satisfied that nobody had followed them. There had been sporadic discussion in the car about what they collectively knew but most of the time Danni and Derrick had been watching the rear window to try and spot a tail.

"I think we're clear," Derrick declared as they pulled into a motel about forty miles outside of LA on Route 210. Neither he nor the doctor named Danni had any reliable way of detecting a tail, but had decided to assume limited resources. "It's not like we're dealing with the FBI," he'd suggested earlier, peering into the glare of headlights following their route. Keeping a track of which lights peeled off and which joined at each junction had become increasingly tiresome, so Aiden had pulled into a service area for twenty minutes to see how many arrived shortly after, where they parked and whether they pulled off. Five were contenders, one disappeared within five minutes, two more were gone by the ten-minute mark, one left just before they did and the final one didn't seem to move as they pulled out. Collectively they felt they were in the clear for the moment.

Aiden turned around in the seat to face both the other two occupants when he stopped outside the motel. "Look, people associated with me have been dying in suspicious circumstances since I started asking awkward questions about Ricky," he said. "It looks like I'm a marked man and have to assume my online activities are being tracked," he said. Danni furrowed her brow at this.

"What sort of activities?" she asked, wondering what she'd let herself in for. She'd developed a strong liking for the Brit but realised she didn't know diddly-squat about him. Brits and online activities were often in the news.

"This car was booked online, using my credit card, for starters," said Aiden. "I fuelled it up back there," he said, throwing a thumb back down the Interstate they'd just left, "using the same card. If anyone is tracking me, that'll put them ball park to where we are. They know I'm in LA, presumably," he added, "now they know which part of LA.

"We've got to assume you're being tracked, too," he said, looking at Derrick. "If I'm the marked man, then you're the obvious way to find me," he said, feeling bad for the manager. "If only you'd taken my calls after Ricky's supposed death, given me a mouthful of plausible bollocks, then I wouldn't have felt the need to track you down out here, you'd be in the clear. Now we have to assume you're as marked as I am," he said.

Derrick hung his head, his paranoia had been on high alert for days, since the police interviews if he was honest with himself, but he'd seen the blood drain from Aiden's face when he'd finally listened to the voicemail message left days earlier by some Yorkshire Copper describing the killing of someone named Brian Esk on speakerphone in the car. He knew that it was more serious than Aiden thought.

"They'll be after me as well, no doubt about that. If they know we're together I'm a target, if I'd called you back when you first tried, I'd have been a target," he said. Both men turned to Danni as they realised the situation she was in.

"There's no way they can know about you," said Aiden. "I didn't share the details of my plans with anyone, not even Brian," he said, adding, "especially Brian. If I'd told him what to do, he'd have cancelled my ticket and blagged the trip for himself," he said, noting that if that had happened, Brian might

187

well be still alive. "We need to ditch the rental, somewhere away from here. Rent a different one or use cabs," he said, thinking aloud, feeling the impracticalities mount up exponentially. "Above all, we need to get you back home, without us, without an audit trail that leads us to you," he said to the young doctor. He'd only known Danni a short time but had developed feelings for her; he liked her sense of humour, shared her taste in bourbon, fancied the living daylights out of her body.

Danni knew the logic was sound; she hadn't paid for anything by card since leaving work, knew nothing about Aiden, Ricky or Derrick and was just one random trainee doctor in LA taking up her annual leave rather than lose it. She hadn't called her girlfriends, against her better instincts, knowing she would berate any of them that undertook a road trip with a man they barely knew. But she'd taken a chance on Aiden that first morning and he'd been a real gentleman, hadn't taken any liberties, hadn't tried to. There was something sincere in his demeanour she trusted and she'd gone with her gut. Now she understood he was in danger and, by association, so was she.

"Why don't we go to the police?" she asked. Aiden and Derrick looked at each other; it sounded a sensible thing to do. Derrick looked hesitant.

"OK, I've told you Ricky is alive," he said, "and that we forged his death," he added, noting that he'd been complicit in a criminal action. Aiden and Danni sat impassively; this was nothing new. Derrick sighed deeply, he was a dead man walking by all accounts so what the hell, telling the whole story, albeit in an abridged form, couldn't condemn him any further. He cautioned Danni that she might want to leave the car as she couldn't unhear what he was about to say, but when she declined Derrick told the condensed version of Ricky's decision, the arrangements with a shady guy with an implausible if Rock n' Roll name, the shenanigans it took to disappear Ricky and the advice against disclosure he'd been given since. It took ten minutes and the car was cooling as the night deepened.

"Do you believe me?" he asked. Danni was scratching her head, but Aiden had a faraway look in his eyes.

"I've heard rumours of this, it's part of the Rock n' Roll legend," he said. "But I never believed it; nobody does, it's just one of those things we want to believe. We love to think that Buddy Holly or Michael Jackson are still alive and could return refreshed and restart their careers any day," he said. Derrick reminded him that Buddy Holly would be way over eighty now and unlikely to pick up a guitar even if the dream was true. "Just examples," said Aiden, defensively. Derrick acknowledged that but made another point.

"Fair enough. But you never believed it, and I don't know if you do even now, but do you really think the police are going to believe it?" he asked. Aiden conceded the point; he was still ambi on the idea but factoring in everything that had happened it

189

had a certain plausibility to it. But all told, the events in the UK, in the unlikely event the local police could find out about them, would appear at best circumstantial. All he had here was a gut feeling he'd had when a guy walked into a bar. It wasn't like anyone had made a direct threat to him.

"I'm staying," said Danni, taking both men by surprise. In their heads the decision had been made, if not articulated. "We can book in here under my name, use my card. We can take the car back into town tomorrow and drop it off at the rental company, take a bus across town and get my car," she suggested. Aiden complained that he didn't want to cost Danni anything, but noted he didn't have enough cash to cover the accommodation for the evening. Derrick said he had some cash, but he tended to live off his cards as well. Danni shrugged it off; Aiden could draw cash out tomorrow at an ATM anywhere that wasn't where they intended staying local to, she suggested. Realising that they had to stop somewhere, it was late, very late, and they all were pooped, they agreed. Aiden regretted not asking Danni to bring the half-finished bottle of bourbon with her, but to be fair they hadn't expected spending the night in a motel. A toothbrush would have been useful, too, he thought.

*

It was middle of the night when the Dreamliner touched down and Morris was surprised to find a reception from LAPD waiting for him. The detective introduced himself as Detective Mark

Brown, the same guy who had phoned the previous day, and explained he'd been investigating a number of serious homicides in the area that may or may not be linked to the crimes John Morris was working on. Wiping tiredness out from his eyes John followed the detective from baggage claim to the waiting patrol car, which drove him to the detective's office block.

"I guess you planned on grabbing some shut-eye," said Brown, "but things seem to be ramping up over here and I want to run some stuff past you," he said, opening the office door, revealing a desk overflowing with paper and a computer screen flickering a screensaver image. "You can decide if you want to crash once you've seen these reports," he said, picking up a handful of papers. Morris scanned the first report, put it down and fished the buff folder out, pulling the report listing homicides in the LA region over the past week, with the one crime lit by yellow highlighter. He held both reports up.

"This is the same guy," said Morris, pointing at his mark on the page. "You got any details?" Brown nodded.

"Loads. Witness statements, forensic from the scene, small amount of relevant trace," he said passing a thick folder over. Morris liked the way Brown worked with physical documents, most of his colleagues had swallowed the paperless office story whole. Flicking through the first few pages he didn't need to look too far, this wasn't unexpected.

191

"I'm guessing no prints, CCTV or usable fibres," he said, scanning the data. Brown looked suitably impressed.

"I was told you were good," he said, causing Morris to raise his head suddenly.

"Who by?" he asked, his stomach tightening. It had been fifteen years, at least one breakdown, an on-off battle with alcohol he frequently lost and a marriage that would never return.

"My mentor was Alby Watkins," Brown answered. "Alby was the best detective I ever worked for, always reckoned you were twice as good," he said. Morris hadn't heard Alby's name in over a decade, hadn't exchanged an email or Christmas card with the man he'd taught at Quantico and worked with on some of the worst serial killer cases on the West Coast. His jaw tightened at the mention of his old partner, back in the day when he'd been seconded to the FBI as a behavioural specialist training members of police forces inside and outside of the US.

"How is Alby?" he asked, not sure he wanted to know. "Did he ask for me?" he added before Brown could answer.

"Retired, lives south of 'Frisco, speaks maybe twice a year," said Brown. "I asked for you, recognised your name on the Interpol reports. Had to fight some brass in Scotland Yard who wanted their men on the trip, took a lot of arguing this side too.

Something to do with protocol," he said. Morris nodded, part of him wished protocol had won.

"Look, I don't do this stuff these days, just a provincial policeman with a background I'd rather forget," he said, absorbing as much information as his tired brain would allow. Brown pointed at the report Morris was scanning.

"That report, I've shown it to our best profilers along with the report for Riggs and the reports from the UK. None of them thought there was a connection," he said. Morris stared at the report, flicked a few pages over and drilled down into some detail.

"They're wrong, this is the same guy," he said, inwardly giving in. It was his case, he'd known in his gut the death of the doctor on his patch was a killing long before the pathology he'd asked for proved it. As soon as he read the details of the Esk killing he knew he was dealing with a serial killer and Riggs just confirmed some of the details. But this wasn't a drifting lone killer, this was a killer with an agenda, probably working for someone.

"Have you got any coffee?" he asked.

*

Cliff sat up in the chair at the tiny desk running the CCTV images from the hard drive through his laptop, slowing down parts and zooming in on mouths whenever they were in shot. The quality was terrible, the angle made lip reading more guesswork

193

than a science. Cliff had taught himself the skill over years of staking out targets and prided himself on his accuracy, although he'd never validated it. Generally speaking, the targets were dead and buried soon after having their lips read, so a scientific analysis was highly impractical.

He looked across at the bed, at the Brit lying askew on top of the duvet, surplus to requirement cushions thrown haphazardly around the cramped room prior to Alec crashing into a deep, dreamless sleep. He decided to go back to basics, seeing as he'd fouled up first time around. Using backdoor tools, he tracked Aiden's card usage. That led to Aiden's car rental, which gave him access to an encrypted data report from the rental company that stored the vehicle GPS data.

Sending the encrypted data to a dark web service he used on occasions he focussed on the recent transactions. A listing for a coffee chain in the commercial district in the early hours, followed by a surprisingly large transaction at a fast food chain several miles away over seven hours later indicated Aiden was buying food for more than one, which figured with the girl who accompanied him. Eventually he worked out where they had last fuelled the rental, which indicated the direction they were headed.

Cliff drummed his fingers while he tried to figure out the details. The girl was a curved ball; was she police or had he made a leap based on a hunch? Pulling up a map of the commercial district where

Aiden had bought coffee he saw that it enclosed a myriad of high and low tech manufacturing on the outskirts. Inside the zip code were high tech industries, start-ups, a peripheral residential area accommodating the industrial and tech space, a police HQ, fire department, hospital and all the usual support amenities. He looked back at the credit card statement; the chain was national, international actually, and had a presence in most of the larger public buildings on his screen. Finding which one could be problematical, but he looked back at the timestamp: how many people were up and about at that time of morning? Was she part of McKie's investigation or someone he picked up while having a coffee in the middle of the night?

The police worked nights, he thought.

He looked at the mobile phone usage. He'd initially tried tracking Aiden's phone when he crossed the Atlantic but it didn't seem to be active. Tracking phone locations had become more difficult since the Europeans had enabled legislation about digital privacy – the big players still ripped the data mercilessly, but the new laws made the data more valuable and it wasn't as easy to obtain without leaving a credit card receipt, or digital footprint as Cliff saw it, behind.

Cliff's overarching drive, his personal obsession, was to leave as little behind physically and digitally as possible wherever he went. He had taken his eyes of Derrick's phone, too. Like McKie, Derrick had taken to jumping on and offline since the news about Ricky had broken, and to keep his footprint down Cliff had stopped monitoring location data as he had felt he knew roughly where to find him anyway. That had now changed. He could look at tracking Derrick's phone in the hope he'd left it on, but his pattern over the last period Cliff had had it tracked showed that to be unlikely and risked exposing him. He would hope the GPS data on the car would be all he needed right now. It was a waiting game until his contact came back to him.

*

Morris had commandeered a separate desk, laying all the reports across in a way that made sense to him. Detective Mark Brown had cleared a large whiteboard that was mounted on one of his walls and had grabbed two flipcharts from neighbouring offices as well. Supplying the Brit with marker pens, copies of photographs and ample quantities of coffee he watched as the evidence was built up in a way he hadn't seen since Alby had retired. The new generation were all about spreadsheets, databases and electronic post-it notes on their screens. Morris hadn't even bothered to power up his laptop yet.

The killing of a barman and a lone customer in a bar in downtown LA interested Morris. The local detectives had flagged the theft of the CCTV hard drive early on and were busily trying to find out if it was one of the models that automatically sent backup images to the cloud. The management were being helpful, but the people who would know the answer to that question were out of town and wouldn't be contactable until the morning at the earliest.

"Same guy, almost certainly. The profile is that he works alone, but you guessed that, plus the reports from the club where he sliced a guy back it up. This is different, though. His MO is to render all CCTV in the area inoperative which suggests a high level of planning. We can infer his vehicle from the CCTV from near the club, so when you've collated all that footage we can find his car, find his location, find him. If this is him, and I think it is, we might have a short hunt here," said Morris circling a photograph of the club where the shooting took place and drawing a line to a box marked "unsub".

"We've got some of that footage, but the quality is poor so far," said Brown, clicking on his computer mouse. Morris walked over to the screen and squatted next to the LA policeman.

"Do you know when the shooting took place?" he asked, rubbing tiredness from his eyes.

"We know when the bodies were found," said Brown, pushing a transcript of the 9-1-1 report across, which Morris picked up and scanned. "Register was untouched, so in all probability the person who called it in was the first to enter the bar after the killing. No reports of gunfire on record, door to door has drawn a blank, but the whole area is generally quiet at that time. Place picks up as night falls.

"Preliminary forensics suggests a silencer by the fragment spread, which ties in with the hotel killing. Probably a Glock, definitely a nine mill," he added.

"Did you find that out from the hotel job?" asked Morris. Brown nodded, acknowledged that he hadn't had official confirmation on the bar killing yet. Morris made a mental note as he liked to compartment evidence into confirmed and suspected – one fact was established; the other was indicative. Morris continued with discussing the timeline.

"We've got one customer who's come forward and claims he left the bar earlier. He was with the guy who got wasted on the stool and we have back up statements to verify his timeline. We've swabbed him for GSR and checked out his apartment and currently he isn't a person of interest," he said.

"He says the bar was empty apart from his buddy and the barman when he left, so we've got a timeline," he said, searching the first video for the time he was looking for. He explained the CCTV was located on a traffic intersection two hundred yards from the bar and was aimed at recording traffic flow. "Doesn't have license plate recognition, unfortunately," he added. Both men sat watching the video, noting any plates that they could read for almost ten minutes. Morris stopped the activity by standing and stretching.

"We're going to have to get some extra personnel on this, I can't focus anymore and the car, if there is one, might not have passed this way during the time interval," he said, pointing at a map of the locality Brown had taped to one of the walls. "It may have been parked up before the time the witness left, for example, or our unsub might have been on foot" he added. Brown took his hand off the mouse and sat back, conceding the point.

"Like you said, we're close. If he's in a car and we can find it quickly before he changes it, then we've got a good chance of catching him. If we delay, he might get to your man McKie and we'll have another corpse to log on the file," he said, tapping the top of the folder on his desk. Morris rubbed his eyes again, then picked up the cooling coffee he'd been drinking on and off.

"You're right, but we're not firing on all cylinders. What we need to do is find Aiden, make him safe, then regroup on our unsub," he said. Both men were convinced that Aiden was the primary target, even though they couldn't fathom out the link to the bar. Brown had started the video running again in slo-mo. Watching with one eye while talking to Morris at the same time. Morris grabbed a marker and started making some notes on one of the flip-boards.

"We can ping his phone, see if he's brought it over. We know roughly what flight he was on, can obtain his credit card details and find out where he's used them," he said, trying to keep focus through the fog of tiredness. "Is there anyone who can do that, tonight?" he asked, wondering if Detective Brown was a one-man band. Brown looked up, a look that indicated he'd found something shining in his eyes.

199

"Sure, I'll get on it straight away. If you've got any additional information about him that wasn't in your original reports then that might make it quicker," he said, "but first, can you look at this?" he added, pointing at his computer screen. Morris wandered over to the frozen image showing three people walking towards the bar from the far side, about three hundred yards from the camera. "Two guys and a woman," added Brown, pointing to the group. Clearly the men were of an age, one had unfashionably long hair and the woman looked to be young, early twenties and black. "They walk into the bar in a few seconds," he said. Morris peered at the image intently, pointed at the guy with long hair.

"That could be Aiden," he said. "Image is too fuzzy to be certain, but I'm pretty certain that it's him," he said, excitement rising. Aiden hadn't ended up in a pool of blood in the bar so it was possible he was still alive. "Do we know when they left?" he asked. Morris dragged the bar at the bottom of the screen until the point the police car arrived following the 9-1-1 call, noting that only two persons entered and left during the period, both independently, both disappearing off-screen the way they had approached. "And one of them could be our unsub," he added, suddenly not tired at all.

*

Derrick found he couldn't sleep. They'd booked into two motel rooms with himself and Aiden in one, the girl Danni in the other. Aiden was sleeping like baby, probably because Danni had walked across the street to an all-night liquor store and bought a bottle of bourbon that all three had sat up and demolished. Unfortunately, the liquor hadn't had the same effect on Derrick that it had on Aiden and he found himself pacing up and down the room in the near dark.

He took his mobile out of the drawer by his single bed and turned it around in his hand a dozen times, looking at it like it was the answer to an important mystical question. In a way, it was. Ricky had found a way to call him, on a number that he didn't recognise. OK, so Ricky hadn't picked up when Derrick had called back, but there could be numerous reasons for that including the not inconsiderable requirement that all residents were forbidden from attempting to contact the outside world. Rule one, the man had called it when he'd briefed them both.

He played with the idea of powering it up, to see if Ricky had called again. He didn't leave it connected most of the time, partly because he'd become afraid the FBI or the LAPD would want to speak to him about Ricky's death, partly because journalists were tracking him down and asking questions that might end up with him contradicting previous statements. That was irrelevant now, he told himself. Despite his best endeavours their master plan had been rumbled, lain bare, destroyed. He didn't know if anyone was watching him, monitoring his calls or just hoping to sell him un-needed insurance plans, but he really didn't want to risk turning his phone back on. Plus, Aiden had said in the car that the phones could be tracked when powered up and had insisted everyone turned their phones off after he'd listened to the call from the UK policeman.

He stepped out of the room, wedging the door with a fist sized stone just outside to stop it locking. The night air, though cooler, was still warm. The cicadas were in full symphony and he was buzzed by a number of unidentifiable midgets in quick succession. Walking out into the car park he started turning the phone over again, as if it was a nervous tic. The turning on process was practically involuntary, the phone lighting up and running through its normal start up routine, the search for networks, the hunt for a Wi-Fi signal it recognised before settling down ready to roll. Derrick scrolled through the missed call list, remarkably short, probably because the main reason for it being long previously was snoring in the bed next to Derrick's.

His thumb hovered over the strange number that had called him earlier. Derrick looked behind him at the wedged open door and felt a wave of guilt as he pushed the number on the screen, listened to the silence as the network attempted to connect, heard a couple of clicks, then the buzz of the ring tone somewhere else a long, long way away. He was about to hang up when he heard the crackle as the phone call was answered, felt his pulse race as he waited for Ricky to answer, his heart turn to ice as the American voice he'd negotiated a deal with months before answered.

*

They'd been allowed to leave the beach, with Tony left behind holding the sat phone, staring at it, trying to work out how it had made its way out here, how come he'd not missed it. He suspected that Ricky and Elvis were way more involved than they'd insisted and a shallow grave was probably the best destination for both of them, but right now he was struggling to manage the day-to-day of running the resort without arranging the death of two high-profile residents.

He'd taken the odd resident out over the years, but it wasn't his core skill. That's why Cliff was on the payroll tidying up messes on the resort and back at home, wherever home was. Taking out the senior resident would send a really negative message out to the other residents at a time when he was struggling to keep them under control. He'd seen the resort rise up in revolt a couple of times before and it could get really ugly again, really quick. He needed as many residents on his side, because if they mobilised then the whole pack of cards would come tumbling down. He decided that he would need to give them the benefit of the doubt unless he came into any more compelling evidence.

Sitting in his office, having dealt with the last of the day's issues, Tony had placed the sat phone on the desk in front of him. It needed charging, he needed to check the call history. Or he would do if he knew how to do that – Alec was just so handy with technology that Tony generally left him to it. When it lit up he nearly stood with shock, but he'd looked at the display and gently picked up the phone, uttering the single word "hello." He knew he had to do something when he heard Derrick on the other end swear.

Chapter 21

Aiden sat bolt upright when he'd been shaken awake by Derrick. Part of him understood why he'd lived a solitary life, undisturbed in his bed at night once filled with whiskey, but deep down he knew there were other, more fundamental reasons as well. Derrick was babbling at him in a high-pitched voice that made understanding impossible.

"Slow down, I can't understand you," he shouted. Derrick sat on his bed and looked like he'd been condemned. In his mind, he had. There was a knock on the door and Aiden walked over, looking through the spyhole, seeing Danni wrapping her arms around her body and looking left and right furtively. He opened the door and answered the look that Danni was giving.

"Ask him, I think he's had a nightmare," he said, nodding at Derrick sat with a hung head. Danni entered and walked around to the music manager, wondering what she'd let herself in for. Derrick looked up as she lay an arm on his shoulder, then back towards Aiden.

"They know," he croaked.

"Who knows?" asked Aiden, adding, "What do they know?" Derrick held his phone up, now powered back down.

"I called Ricky back, Tony answered," he said. It took a couple of seconds for the seriousness of the situation to sink in, a few seconds more for Aiden to dismiss it.

"If we're right, then they knew already," he said. "All you've done is confirm their beliefs, I guess," he added. Derrick's eyes watered.

"It's not just us. It's Ricky, too. Now they know we've been in contact they'll take him out, he's broken his deal with them," he said.

"Then we have to get him out," said Danni, standing. Derrick and Aiden looked at her with surprise. Derrick expressed the biggest problem.

"We don't know where he is, the location is secret," he said. It did appear to present an insurmountable problem, one Aiden started to crunch.

"Someone knows, not just them, surely?" he asked, knowing that the answer was exactly that. He'd heard a rumour years ago that you turned left at Necker island, but that was just flippant and as nobody believed in it anyway, it was irrelevant. "Even if we knew, it would be too dangerous," he suggested. Danni felt anger well up in her.

"If what you tell is true, it's already dangerous, for you two anyway. Whether you do anything or nothing, by your reckoning they're out to get you, so you've got nothing to lose," she said, trying not to rant. "I'm the one who isn't known to them, the one who should be able to walk away without any risk, yet I'm the only one who seems to want to help," she said.

"So, what do you recommend?" asked Aiden, not sure he wanted to hear. Danni paced up and down the room while she enumerated the options that she could see.

"Both of you have extensive contacts in the music industry, one of your contacts will know something," she said. "You need to draw up a list of potential contacts and then work that list. We can pick up a disposable phone tomorrow, you can quickly suck all the relevant numbers off your existing phones and use the new phone to start calling. Somebody will know something," she repeated. The two men looked energised, Aiden pulled a pad out from the desk by his bed and started to list names. Derrick looked less motivated.

"They won't say, if they've done this, if they've sent one of their clients to Hotel California, they'll be too afraid to spill the beans. Most won't know anything anyway, the organisers are very careful to keep specifics to a minimum," he said, watching Aiden tear the first page of his list off the pad. Danni tried a more supportive tone.

"You're right, but we only need one to break ranks, one person who has found out by hook or by crook the location. If you promise you'll never reveal your source, and you must mean it when you promise it, then someone will tell us," she said gently. Derrick didn't answer, but pulled a motel pad from his drawer and also started writing names in a list.

*

Alec sat motionless in the passenger seat of the car as Cliff drove swiftly but safely to the target, avoiding breaking any road rules and attracting any attention to them. He'd slept like a log when they first booked into the motel, but after about an hour Alec found himself wide awake watching Cliff poring over a laptop or walking outside to make a muffled call on his mobile.

The caffeine driven euphoria that Alec had felt in the club earlier had worn off, leaving a feeling of dread turning his stomach over and over. He'd reluctantly accepted the need to despatch a client who allegedly had reneged on the agreement to keep shtum, but now the requirement had been extended to include a journalist that Cliff insisted was "one of yours" to Alec, which he took to mean another Brit. Plus, the girl who neither he nor Cliff knew anything about was supposedly in scope too.

While Cliff was still notionally handing the honours for killing Derrick Moore to Alec it was unclear who was slated to kill the journalist but Cliff had bagged the rights to take out the woman, which Alec felt was creepy. Deep down he wasn't sure he was up for killing Derrick, but felt the other two killings were driving him down a route he'd never signed up for.

Cliff had roused Alec about twenty minutes earlier, not realising that he'd been awake for some time, and announced he knew where the targets were staying and insisting that they made their way there straight away before dawn arrived. As they pulled off the Interstate Cliff pointed at a lit motel sign five hundred yards ahead and announced they'd arrived before pulling up well short of the facility.

"We have some CCTV to sort out first," said Cliff, pulling a kit bag off the rear seat.

*

Morris wondered aloud how seriously the LAPD were taking this task. Despite Brown's insistence he had people who could take up some of the grunt tasks, there was little evidence of that happening. Brown sighed.

"You see the unsub as a serial killer, I see him too; my colleagues see the double homicide in the hotel as an act of vengeance by the hooker's husband, pimp or some disgruntled customer, the barman as an act driven by anger, both acts as isolated, one-off incidents. Those are day jobs – wait long enough for the remorse to kick in and the unsub will turn his gun on himself. A new carpet, walls painted, case closed.

"We know this is a serial killer and time is of the essence. If I could persuade our people of it then there would be a full ops room buzzing down the corridor," he added as the door opened and a wiry geek walked in with a handful of papers.

"Got a hit Mark," he said, holding up a sheet. "Rental company got straight back to me. Normally they only operate a one-way street with data – one of their cars gets stolen, they expect us to respond immediately, we want GPS data they want a court order," he said. "luckily one of their top-level programmers is in, something about a security breach on the GPS data so he had what we wanted to hand," he added, blinking as the two detectives rushed out of the door after scanning the sheet.

*

The lists were growing fast, with Aiden producing a two-page list with numbers alongside. "Every one of these has some association with an artist who died prematurely," he said, tapping the top page. "Given what we know it's likely some of these artists are residents at Hotel California, and some of these people must know something," he said. Danni looked at his list, admitted she had no idea who these people were, or the artists they had represented or known.

"Where are they based?" she asked, noting that it was five in the morning, one o'clock in the UK. I've got my cell phone charging next door. I'll just give my provider a call to check I'm allowed to call these UK numbers within my call plan," she said, "the furthest I've ever called is Mom and Pop in Kern County." Aiden looked up.

"It should fine," he said, not feeling particularly confident, not arguing further when Danni ignored him.

"I'll be back in a couple of minutes," she said, leaving the room.

*

Alec watched as Cliff worked his way around the site, systematically taking the CCTV out, working out the dead spots so he didn't appear any time during the circuit. Cliff appeared to have a tool for every situation placed about his person. Eventually he finished and walked back to the car, slipping tools into various pockets and compartments as he went.

"One more thing and we're ready," he said.

*

Danni wasn't getting much joy out of her provider, partly because she hadn't thought to bring any of the lists being compiled next door with her, so when the operative on the other end asked for an example of the numbers she wanted to call she couldn't be specific. She'd spent perhaps three minutes sat with her back to the door talking the operative through her needs when she became aware of sounds outside. She turned to see two male silhouettes stood in her doorway, illuminated from behind by arc lights dotted around the car park. Suddenly the power died around the site, plunging her room and outside into deep blackness. She stifled a scream as one of the men flicked a Zippo lighter and illuminated his face.

*

"Danni's a long time," said Derrick just before the power died. Aiden looked up and checked his watch, noting that she'd been almost ten minutes.

"I'll check on her," he said. Inwardly he'd become very fond of the young woman over the last couple of days. In between tracking down clues and crashing in adjacent rooms, he'd built a real, natural rapport with her, finding that despite her lack of music industry knowledge matching his lack of knowledge about medical issues they shared a common sense of humour that kept bouncing off each other as they went about their task.

When the lights died Aiden was halfway to the door and he faltered for a second, before rushing headlong out of the room and turning towards Danni's. Pushing her door open he found two men stood around her, Danni looking shaken and one of the men holding a gun. He turned towards Aiden and levelled the weapon straight at his face, stopping him in his tracks. There was an extended pause as everyone in the room took stock, with Morris putting his hand on Brown's, lowering the gun to point at the ground.

"It's OK, this is Aiden," he said.

"What are you doing here?" asked Aiden, shaken by the Yorkshire accent. Morris brought the

Zippo closer so that everyone could see each other in the flickering light, the shadows bouncing in waves all around them.

"Come to try and keep you safe," he answered. The full response needed more time than he was prepared to spare at the moment, given the situation. A clatter and a cry from next door stopped everyone in their tracks. Danni was past the three men and out into the car park in seconds, and was greeted by the shadows of Derrick being dragged backwards by another man who'd wrapped a waist belt around Derrick's throat. Derrick was grasping at the leather, tearing his skin as he was dragged backwards out of the room towards the parked car twenty yards away. Danni stooped and picked up the rock that Derrick had used to wedge the door open earlier and was about to throw it when the man dragging Derrick dropped the body to the ground and pulled a gun on her. He stroked the barrel with his free hand, curling his trigger finger under the guard, lifting the gun to take careful aim, ignoring the writhing man at his feet.

Suddenly Alec jumped in-between Danni and Cliff, blocking his view.

"Move," shouted Cliff as he tried to take aim, cutting and running as he realised there were others converging on him. Brown sped past the supine figure lying in the ground while Morris skidded to a halt, kneeling and pulling the belt free. Aiden rushed to Danni, wrapping his arms around her momentarily until she realised that Derrick needed urgent medical intervention.

Detective Brown stopped as he hit total blackness, with the noises of the medical emergency behind him rendering following the sound of footsteps impossible. A car engine started and he ran towards where the sound was, but found himself side-swiped by the car as it swept past, knocking him to the floor, causing his Colt to spin a few feet away. By the time he'd recovered the gun and put himself into a suitable firing position the car was long gone, being passed by the patrol car he'd been calling in when Aiden had tumbled into the room.

Limping back to the group he found Danni checking Derrick's vitals, aided by the British detective. He limped over to the man who had jumped in front of the gun and stopped the unsub from shooting the girl, cupping him by the elbow.

"And just who might you be?" he asked.

Chapter 22

By the time the smartly dressed lawyer had turned up unannounced Alec had been fingerprinted, DNA swabbed and sat in an interview room for at least half an hour. The interview had just begun and all they'd established was his name, when he'd arrived in the US, which apparently was on vacation, and where he'd been staying. Brown was attempting to get Alec to open up to reveal his reason to be in the car park of a motel almost thirteen miles from his stated accommodation at just gone five in the morning when the process was promptly stopped.

The first thing the lawyer did was have John Morris ejected on the grounds he had no jurisdiction in LA. He didn't say it, but he didn't want any unknown UK policeman attempting to apply British jurisprudence logic to a case that he could easily tie up in knots using the Californian Statutes. He then advised Alec to say nothing, confirmed whether he had been read his rights and when, then asked to be briefed on the reasons for his arrest.

"So, my client actively put his life at risk to protect an innocent bystander?" he asked. Detective Brown squirmed as he knew he had to answer this question accurately.

"Yes, he did. He came out of the shadows and put himself in-between the assailant and Miss Wate, but so far he hasn't given a reason for being in that location," he said. The lawyer looked up suddenly.

"Was he breaking the law being there?"

"No, but..." answered Brown.

"And does he have to give a reason for being in a public place? I think the fact that he was there and he intervened in such a way was very fortunate for Miss Wate, and I'm sure she's very grateful for his intervention," he said.

"And you have stated you believe he was involved in the shooting at the club downtown yesterday evening. Did you swab him for GSR?" he asked, knowing that they had and had found no trace of residue. Without waiting for the response, he continued, "in fact you have a very blurry image of a person who looks similar to my client, but do you have any physical evidence to suggest that he was actually in the location or indeed involved in the shooting?" Brown shrugged.

"We believe he was with the man who tried to shoot Miss Wate and practically strangled Mr Moore this morning," he said.

"Believe? Has my client suggested that to be the case? Is there any physical evidence to link him apart from a couple of blurry CCTV images around the time the bar killing may have happened? I understand you've been working on the killing at the bar being linked to another homicide in a hotel a few miles away?" he said. Brown nodded. "Are you aware that my client was disembarking from a flight at LAX at the time of the homicide? Does that sound like an accomplice?" he asked.

Within ten minutes Alec was bailed, had surrendered his passport on the advice of his lawyer and advised not to leave the city limits in the next few days. Outside the building, as the morning commuter traffic built up, the lawyer shook Alec's hand. Reaching inside his jacket he pulled a new passport out and handed it over.

"Make your way back, take care regarding the route you take in case you're monitored, try to prevent it becoming compromised," he said, turning. Alec stood and watched the lawyer blend into the sea of commuters making their way to their normal, violence-free employment, wondering how the hell he ended up in this mess. He turned to walk in the other direction to catch a cab to find that Aiden was blocking his path.

"We need to talk," said the journalist. Alec looked around and found that Danni was stood alongside a few feet away, lounging against the wall, and the British policeman had circled to block his exit. "Ricky is in trouble," added Aiden. Alec felt the weight of the whole world press down on him.

"Let's grab a coffee," he said.

*

Ricky sat up listening to the wind building, the old man was right. He pulled back the curtains and

217

looked out into the pitch-black night, trying to see the palms he knew were thirty yards from his apartment, to see if they were bending in the wind. Apart from the odd flash of light in the night sky, which Ricky assumed was sheet lightning some miles away, he couldn't see anything.

Checking that the furniture he'd pushed up against the door was still in place he returned to bed and pulled the sheets up to his chin, something he hadn't done since he'd been a boy. Pulling the pillow over his head he tried to cut out the sound of the wind from outside, and the fear in his heart. It was turning out to be a long night and the storm outside was nothing compared to the one brewing in his head.

*

They sat in a booth in a city diner watching business people grab a quick coffee on their way to work. There were about four booths occupied, mostly by solitary diners shovelling food down before leaving in a rush, whereas their booth was a sea of calm in comparison. Alec naturally was defensive, especially as he didn't know anyone in the party apart from his brief introduction to a policeman from Yorkshire earlier during his interview. Aiden decided to move the whole thing forward as the food arrived.

"I know about Hotel California," he said, adding, "and so does she," nodding at Danni. "This is Detective Inspector John Morris, and currently he doesn't know anything about it," he said to an impassive Alec. Over the next twenty minutes Aiden outlined what had happened and what he'd learned, watching Morris, trying to gauge his reaction. Sentence by sentence he noticed the man called Alec crumble and by the time he'd finished they'd needed top ups on the coffees and Morris needed a time out with Aiden. They stood aside from the booth while they talked.

"Is all that for real?" he asked, trying to keep an open mind. Aiden confirmed that, as far as he could tell, it was.

"It's been rumoured for years in the industry, but always treated like an in-joke. Turns out that it really exists."

"You have proof, evidence?" asked Morris, wondering how he was going to use this.

"We need to go one more step to obtain the level of proof I need as a journalist," he said. "But I can prove Ricky didn't die as a result of an appendectomy by any legal measure and I can prove that there was a concerted process used to fabricate that belief," he said. You know that a number of people have been killed as a result of my investigation," he added. Morris had briefly appraised him about the hotel homicide and the bar murder and his belief that they'd been carried out by the same person.

"I still believe you're connected to the killer, despite what your lawyer says," he said to Alec when they sat back down, waving his hand, "and I get it that you won't confirm or deny anything. I now know we're dealing with a sociopath and that's what saved you this morning," he said to Alec, but including Danni with his hand gestures. "My personal evaluation is that he's going to go to ground, regroup and come back hard," he said, trying to impress the group with the importance of the situation, "and to that end my LAPD friends are mounting a round the clock guard on your friend Derrick in hospital.

"But I still don't believe this story about an island that nobody knows about." Alec stirred his coffee, looking at the swirling pattern on top intently before speaking.

"It's real, I work there. Or I used to; once word gets out about today, I'll be as marked as Moore or Aiden here," he said looking up and staring at Aiden. "You said Ricky was in trouble, how do you know that?" Aiden had brushed over the phone call Derrick had made that morning, how he'd recognised the American voice of the man he'd negotiated Ricky's departure with, how he'd spoken and therefore given his identity away. Alec looked subdued at this.

"If Tony knows Ricky's been calling home then he's a marked man," he conceded. "But if Ricky's in trouble then my guess is that Elvis is in trouble too – they were as thick as thieves when I left the other day." Alec looked up at the three faces staring at him, realised that he'd struck a nerve. "Same guy you're wondering about," he confirmed, "elder statesman and biggest pain in the ass on the island." The reality was that although Elvis caused Alec daily grief, he was also his favourite guest. Ricky had the potential to become his second favourite.

"When you say marked and in trouble?" asked Morris. Alec looked up, his eyes welling.

"I mean they're both scheduled for a shallow grave. Tony will take them out, first opportunity, no doubt," he said.

"Surely, we can stop that?" asked Morris, wondering aloud whose country the island belonged to, realising he was being sucked into the belief system. Alec allowed himself a smug smile.

"You won't find the island on any map, not on Google Earth, not on any publicly available satellite image. Your country," he said, nodding at Danni, "and mine won't raise a finger to interfere with the island, they both have secrets buried there they'd rather never got dug up," he said. After a pause he added, "remember it was set up during World War Two. Just after the war it was considered expedient to allow some individuals to join the island and disappear from public view forever."

"You mean?" Aiden started to ask, interrupted by Alec.

"Let's just say that the autopsy on one of the early residents, according to records stored in my safe, confirms he really did only have one ball."

"So, if governments won't help and the island isn't under any country's jurisdiction, then we have to go there and pull Ricky and Elvis out," said Danni, joining the debate for the first time since they'd arrived. Looking at Alec she threw the gauntlet down. "How do we get there?" she asked.

*

Morris met with Brown, who'd spent most of the morning after the interview in the Emergency Room having his thigh looked at.

"Muscle damage, bruising, gonna be painful for a couple of weeks," he said. "How did the pow-wow go?" He'd seen Morris in conversation with Aiden and Danni outside the interview room and noticed they'd followed Alec outside.

"What are you like on the weird scale?" Morris asked. Brown shrugged, weird was fairly normal in LA.

"How weird?" he asked. Morris outlined the concept of an unmarked island that celebrities went to, to retire from public exposure with deaths faked to make the transition to privacy total.

"Like Wacko?" he asked, not taking a position, just exploring the weird level.

"Don't know if that's specifically one of the alleged celebrities," said Morris, deciding to avoid mentioning Elvis, "but they reckon Ricky Maggott is there and they believe he's in danger," he added. Brown probed to find out about who had responsibility about the island, was perturbed to find it didn't even have an official name, but agreed it was way outside of LAPD's sphere of responsibility.

"What about Aiden and Danni?" he asked.

"They're looking at travelling there, Alec has given information that he thinks will be sufficient to get them to it. I'm thinking of joining them," he said, admitting that although he was still on the fence regarding Hotel California, he'd travelled over primarily to help identify an unsub but also to protect Aiden from being a victim. "If they leave LA they're not your responsibility anymore, and I can't protect them from the unsub while they're travelling," he said, adding, "who may well follow them." Brown considered this for a moment; Morris had straightened out the behavioural analysis on the unsub, he had little to no confidence that he'd ever see Alec ever again but had no grounds to physically restrict him, and he agreed that it looked like the unsub would travel to follow Aiden, so letting Morris follow would be best in everyone's interests.

"Alec has said the guy you're looking for is known as Cliff, by the way," added Morris. "I actually think that's as much as he knows about him. His description is less detailed than yours, and you spent most of the thirty seconds chasing him looking at the back of his head." Brown wondered if the information Morris had gleaned was sufficient to pull Alec back in, but reckoned the fancy lawyer would cite entrapment or some other legal escape route. Better leave this to play out, he decided. He did wonder if he could help protect Alec, though.

"Is it worth pulling Alec back in, to keep him safe while this plays out?" he asked. Morris shook his head.

"Long gone, shot off as soon as we let him. I don't think you'll see him again, nor will we," he answered.

"Pretty much what I thought. I don't blame him, to be fair. I've set up protection details for the other three for the next twenty-four hours. If they can let me know where they'll be over that period, I'll have a patrol car outside. If they need longer then just keep communicating and I'll see they're safe while in LA," he said, writing notes down as he spoke. "Take care, and if you're travelling to the legendary island let me know when you get back," he added, patting Morris affectionately on the shoulder. "Take care John," he said, turning back to his desk.

*

Ricky banged on Elvis' door again, thought he heard movement in the apartment. "Elvis, it's Ricky," he repeated. He heard the sound of furniture being dragged and the locks being undone. The door opened a crack, revealing an old man with bags under his eyes.

"Let's grab breakfast," he said, positioning his foot to wedge the door if needed. Elvis looked to be in a terrible state.

"I'll order in," Elvis grumbled.

"No way. If they're going to take you out, poison is the easiest method," Ricky said. In the restaurant we can get them to cook to order, can watch them make it," he said. Elvis opened the door a little more and beckoned Ricky in.

"We can't live like this, watching our shadows," he said. "It's my fault, making you go back for the bat phone."

"It was just bad timing. It could have happened any time," said Ricky, entering the room and closing the door behind him. "Get a shower and freshen up, you look like shit," he said. Elvis started to shuffle towards the en-suite, pausing to mention it was the storm brewing that was causing him to lose sleep.

"Which one? The one raging outside or the one that's just for us two?" he asked. Elvis looked up and stared straight at Ricky.

"This'll be y'all first tropical storm boy," he said, which brought Ricky up short as he realised he'd only been on the island just under a week. All he knew was that he hated it, had made a major mistake.

"And my last," he said before correcting himself, "our last. We only need to survive long enough to escape from here," he said, knowing deep down he didn't have any semblance of a plan.

"It's taken me forty years so far," grumbled Elvis, "just saying," he added as he continued his shuffle to the shower.

Aiden tried to persuade Danni that this wasn't her fight, but she'd countered that the moment the maniac pointed a gun at her head, it was. They'd reconvened after a sleep at a hotel booked by Detective Brown and were running over the details Alec had provided at the diner before shooting off.

Alec had drawn a rough map of the Pacific, adding features such as Hawaii. Drawing a line down and slightly west he circled a ring of tiny islands.

"Is that it?" Aiden had asked.

"Those are the nearest inhabited islands with reasonable communications and landing strips," said Alec. "Some of the locals know the island exists, many have provided personnel in the past, less often now they have contacts with the outside world." He'd noticed the looks all three gave. "We import labour from mainly depressed parts of the world, compensating their families for their services," he'd said, expanding, "of course they rarely return home."

"Because they love the island?" Aiden had asked sardonically. Alec bristled, but continued.

"I treat the staff well, look after their welfare. Working on the island is a one-way trip for them too, but we provide security for their families that they would be unlikely to provide by staying at home," he argued. "Anyway, there are a limited number of people on these islands who will ship you across for a price," he said, tapping the sketch. "Good luck," he added.

"You planning on staying here?" Morris had asked. Alec shrugged; he had no idea what he should do, but waiting to be hauled back in by LAPD or targeted by the consortium were low on his priority list.

"If Cliff follows you guys, he's leaving me alone. I might be able to disappear," he'd said, fully expecting Morris to feed this back to the LAPD. He hardly cared any more. Morris leaned in.

"What if he chooses to stick with you and follow us later?" Alec's face drained as the concept sank in.

*

Sergei looked at Dimitri before answering Tony. "You want us to kill Elvis?" he asked.

"And the new kid," answered Tony, pleased that the Russians appeared on-board with the idea. Letting them do the deed took the pressure off him and gave him someone to blame if the resort erupted.

"What do we get out of this?" asked Dimitri. Tony was wrong-footed by this question; he always assumed they liked killing by the way they acted day to day.

"Privileges," he said. "Like extra vodka."

"We have unlimited amounts of vodka," Sergei pointed out, "until it runs out, then we have none."

"If we do this deed we would be very unpopular with the other residents," said Dimitri. "I don't think they like us much anyway, this would make it worse."

"Why don't you do it?" countered Sergei. Tony liked to act tough on the resort, but he didn't really have the stomach to carry this out on the elder statesman, the backlash would be too much to manage on his own.

"We have people who do that sort of stuff for us," he said. "Just thought you might like to do it," he added, turning. "It was just an idea," he said, reaching for the door handle. Sergei raised his hand.

"Whoa, hold on. How about a trade?" he asked.

"A trade?" repeated Tony, wondering what he could possibly offer now the Russians had identified they could have practically anything they wanted without lifting a finger. It was, after all, one of the resort's finest selling points. "What's your price?" asked Tony.

"Two tickets. Off this island," answered Sergei.

Chapter 23

Morris strapped himself into the economy seat, looking at the back of Aiden's head two seats in front. Danni was located somewhere behind him. Finding three seats to the staging point that made a connection to the group of islands took some doing, the small narrow body jet running the route well past it's use-by date. Most of the passengers sat around him were black, looked poor and at least one smelled. At least it was cheap.

The sun was setting over LA and the flight was scheduled to take about six hours, then there was a two-hour layover before undertaking another half hour flight in what sounded like a crop duster. Deep down Morris had no idea what he was doing – he was way out of his authority, wouldn't have a leg to stand on when he returned to Yorkshire, had no idea what he expected to achieve. At least Aiden had a reason and, critically, a belief in the concept of Hotel California; Morris still didn't buy it but he had no alternative explanation to counter with so decided to follow his nose. He'd sent a brief message to his superintendent back home, timed it to ensure he wouldn't be around when the refusal email bounced back, the ultimate assumptive sell meaning he had half a chance of recovering his expenses.

Several airlines had cancelled due to worsening weather conditions in the area the plane was headed, which was why this flight was so well booked. The pilot and co-pilot looked reasonably well turned out, which suggested they hadn't been flying long enough to create appreciable wear on their flying uniform; the trolley dollies looked worn, haggard and desperate. In fact, Morris now knew who the smelly person was.

After take-off Aiden unstrapped and walked back to speak to Danni, tapping Morris on the shoulder as he passed. "Team meeting," he said. All three stood near the galley, watching the stewardesses shuffle overpriced drinks and packs of pretzels up and down the centre aisle, while they discussed their plan, such as it was.

"If the weather forecast is correct, we might not make the second stage," said Aiden.

"How far is the second island from Hotel California?" asked Danni.

"Hard to say, Alec's sketch was hardly Ordnance Survey standard and I couldn't find any of the islands he suggested as suitable leaping off points on any of the maps at the airport," said Aiden, holding his laptop case up, indicating he had filled it with useless maps. "But it's a half hour hop on a tiny plane so not too far. After that we have to convince someone to set sail to take us the final leg which might be a challenge given the weather," he said.

"We can't do much about the weather," noted Morris, "so we might as well make as much progress as we can and then wait for it to pass.

"Anyone up for pretzels?"

*

The day had been fraught for both Elvis and Ricky. Breakfast had been spent sat with both backs to the wall, watching out for each other as they arranged their food to be cooked. Mid-morning they'd reconvened in Ricky's apartment, watching DVDs, occasionally getting up and placing an ear to the door if either thought they'd heard something. Outside the wind was rising and lowering, but always present. Waves could be heard crashing on the shoreline two hundred yards away and the sky was purple.

"Next time we go to the restaurant we stock up on food. I can cook here," said Ricky, waving a hand behind him at the ever-mounting pile of dishes.

"Or you can let the help in to do the washing up," suggested Elvis. "They'll cook too, if y'all ask them nicely."

"Aren't you worried in the slightest about being poisoned?" asked Ricky, looking at his friend with concern.

"Sure. That's why I'm suggesting y'all let the help cook," said Elvis.

*

The old fisherman and his young assistant pulled hard on the ropes mooring the ketch to the harbour, trying to reduce the amount of freedom the vessel had in the building waves. The man might be old, thought the young man, but he works hard. They'd managed to lower the mainsail but had struggled with the foresail with the wind whipping up so strongly. Hauling as hard as they could they locked the boat off and resumed working on the foresail, which was whipping around them.

The young man knew they'd be back out several times over the night to adjust for the rise and fall of the tide and to check for damage. The old man wouldn't let the storm that was brewing to interfere with his drinking, so would become an increasing liability to the younger man, but would still pull harder than men a third of his age.

Fishing had been poor; the storm would make it worse before it got better. The younger man knew the old man had drunk his way through most of the cash they'd been paid the previous week to ferry the funny guy off the TV. He'd spent some of it, but most had been placed in the tin on the shelf, the one he was using to save up to get married to his childhood sweetheart, but like the old man he could do with more, fast.

They retired to the bar opposite the marina, the old man buying himself a stiff drink to compensate for the battering his body had taken wrestling with the ropes and the wind, eking out his remaining cash for himself. The young man bought a soft drink, knew he'd nurse it through the long evening and longer night. He commandeered the TV remote and turned on the channels that showed all

232

the reality show re-runs, found the one that seemed to broadcast the one he loved the most, the eccentric British singer who trashed his mansion in a heartbeat, the guy who'd been a passenger just over a week earlier. He loved the show, hoped the madman would return to make more soon. Checking his watch, he made a mental note to stir the old man after two episodes to adjust the ropes and settled back in the wicker chair that he thought of as his in the bar.

*

It had been a long journey, with turbulence increasing every half hour until they'd reached the point that everyone was strapped in and the cabin stank of vomit. Even the smelly stewardess didn't seem to smell too bad any more when compared to the overarching whiff of spew. Aiden was convinced that he'd emptied his stomach of every drink, meal and pretzel he'd taken onboard in the previous twenty-four hours, and hoped that he couldn't dig any deeper. The crew had appeared to have an infinite amount of barf bags on hand initially, but it was clear that they were running out and were probably holding a few back for themselves, but regardless of how many they had left they were going to need a major clean-up operation when they landed to clear the sea of vomit running up and down the aisle.

If they landed, Aiden corrected himself.

Morris was having similar thoughts. He'd had some rough flights in his time, especially when criss-crossing the States pursuing serial killers, but this was the worst. He'd long closed the blind on his window to stop the sight of the horizon pitching up and down in an erratic rhythm, convincing himself that the pilots would emerge as veteran fliers when they landed, then echoing Aiden's alternative thought.

A voice crackled over the sound-system, a voice that sounded dry and wretched. Clearly the boys at the front weren't having a fun time either. "Please remain seated," the voice implored, even though Morris doubted anyone could actually stand at the moment, "We've been given clearance to land and are circling to line up for approach," the voice continued to crackle, with a spontaneous if half hearted "hooray" rising throughout the cabin.

"We hope to be on the ground within four minutes, if God spares us," the pilot said, turning the tannoy off with a loud, if final, click. Across the cabin those who had a God prayed, those that had lost one started to revaluate their relationship, those that had never had one invented a belief for the duration.

The aircraft aligned with the runway, the wings rolling up and down to compensate for the buffeting wind. Morris leant across the back of the passenger bent double sat next to the window and returned the blind to the up position. He caught sight of the wind-sock in the distance stretched tight at right angles to the approach, felt his stomach ratchet in even tighter than the sock. The pilot was clearly fighting hard to keep the aircraft level, winning about half of the battle. He could just see the trailing edge of the wing from his seat and watched the flaps lower, noticing the pitch slip distinctly nose up; then he heard the deep rumble as the undercarriage was lowered and saw the nose pitch lower. The ground was approaching rapidly, yet appeared to be too far below for a landing in his experience. Suddenly the horizon flashing past his window rose rapidly as the aircraft lost height in the blink of an eye and landing, if not crashing, now seemed inevitable.

A crunch, a bounce, another crunch and the cabin listed dramatically to the right. The view out of the window showed Morris' side of the aircraft slewing, leaving a trail of earth spraying up from the side of the runway. He saw the right wingtip dig a furrow in the soft earth as the aircraft skidded to a stop, oxygen masks pointlessly dropping to dangle in front of every passenger and warning lights and alarms sounding all around the cabin. He was aware of the smelly stewardess making her way to the centre access door, pulling herself along the by the right-hand seats, slipping on the sea of spew washing from left to right across the centre aisle. Pulling at the lever on the door she pushed it clear of the cabin and released the emergency chute, beckoning to the passengers nearest to her to disembark and was practically mown down in the rush by all to leave. He felt a hand on his shoulder, looked up and saw Danni stood next to him.

"Any landing you can walk away from is a good one, eh?" she said, miraculously managing to smile.

*

Communications had struggled since the storm had started, with Tony suspecting one of the aerial masts by the vehicle compound being damaged. Alec usually looked after technical things like that, having done all the courses before arriving. Tony's predecessor had also done all the courses and Tony had been slated himself, but a little problem involving Tony offing his erstwhile boss after a disagreement a few years earlier had put paid to that, putting him off killing as it was very messy and nearly backfired, plus he knew he was gammy-handed with a wrench.

However, the VHF receiver did seem to work, if intermittently, and it was by chance he learned that the Islander aircraft was inbound. Light was failing and he knew he'd have to make his way to the landing strip adjacent to the vehicle compound immediately if he was going to be able to sort out the landing lights. Looking out of his office window he saw Ricky and Elvis walking back to the accommodation with armfuls of food in tins and packets. Looking beyond them he saw the Russians loitering, noting the progress of the two men keenly. He still wasn't sure if he had a deal with the Russians, wasn't convinced they took his offer to repatriate them seriously, wasn't quite sure how he'd handle the situation when they realised he'd reneged. He'd probably leave Alec to sort that one out, noting that as Alec was inbound, he could sort out Elvis and Ricky too.

Opening the safe Tony retrieved the Browning and holster. Drawing the blinds, he strapped the weapon, now loaded, on. The holster sat just under his left armpit and the Browning weighed heavily, if solidly, in place. He slipped his dark jacket back on, buttoned up the centre button and slipped the spare loaded magazine into his left-hand pocket, causing the jacket to sag to the left-hand side. Grabbing the Land Rover keys and kicking the safe shut, Tony opened the office door and looked outside, checking it was clear of residents. Locking the office door, he exited the complex by the opposite end to the Russians and made his way around the building to the Land Rover, staggering under the building winds buffeting his body. He started the vehicle and drove off, only putting the lights on when well clear of the resort.

The journey was hard enough under the blistering heat and light of day; at night with a storm brewing it was a bone-jarring white-knuckle ride of a trip, with potholes appearing at very short notice challenging the Land Rover suspension. Checking the time, Tony realised he had about ten minutes to spare, enough time to unlock the panel that controlled the lights and turn them on, nowhere near enough time to replace any blown lamps if needed.

Digging the key from the hidden storage box Tony walked headlong into the wind, putting his right arm in front of his face to minimise the effect of the whipping sand particles, turning to walk backwards every few steps until he stumbled over an object causing him to resume the Zorro stance. Reaching the panel, he fumbled as he heard the twin Lycoming turboprops struggling against the weather as it approached, passing overhead ready to bank and turn. Pulling the lever down caused two lines of bright, white lights demarking the edges of the strip to illuminate. Noting that several weren't operational he made a mental note to task Alec with sorting them out once he'd showered and fed himself, perhaps after the storm had passed.

The aircraft levelled itself up and waggled its progress towards the landing strip, counteracting a small amount of shear as it approached. Tony was surprised but not worried that the pilot hadn't put any lights on for the approach – it was a few years since he'd been on the reception party side of the airstrip, so assumed protocols had changed since his day as deputy. The Islander was bouncing around in the air as it approached, understandably given the weather conditions which now included driving rain, soaking Tony to the skin in seconds. It dumped down and the nose dug in hard, the wings wavering side to side as the turboprops were put into reverse pitch, the gas turbine engines popping and spluttering under the load of the deceleration. Tony admitted it was far from the most elegant landing he'd seen, but again weighed in the weather conditions as mitigation.

Stopping, the aircraft sat panting, the propellers chattering as they rotated while they were eased off back to idle. Tony's brow furrowed as the engines were shut down one at a time, the clattering and whining dying down rapidly, being overtaken by the whistling of the wind and the rain. In all his time on the resort he'd never known the pilot to stop; most knew something about Hotel California, none were fully read in. Generally ex-military pilots for hire, they carried out a DOFO operation – Drop Off and Fuck Off. Clearly the weather was an issue, what Tony did with the pilot would be a challenge. There was silence as the props stopped apart from some banging and clattering inside the cabin, eventually the cabin door swung open and a man jumped out, leant in and started to drag at something from inside. Tony approached cautiously, certain of two things – he knew the man and it wasn't Alec.

Cliff turned around, pulling the man in a pilot's uniform by the collar. "Help me drag him out, then we can tie this beast down," he said. "Difference of opinion," he said by way of explanation for the dead pilot.

*

"Y'hear that?" asked Elvis. Ricky stood and walked to the door and placed his ear against it.

"I can't hear anything," he answered. Elvis just shook his head.

"Not the door, the 'plane," he said, pointing out of the window. Ricky shook his head, he'd been

239

reading a book while listening to some of his old music at an unreasonably quiet volume when Elvis had spoken. "Y'need to get your ears washed out boy," said the old man.

"How do you know it's me, my ears are a lot younger than yours," he answered, defensively.

"They might be younger, but they're not as keen as mine, that's for sure," said Elvis. "That's why I'm aiming to record perfect silence, because I'm so blessed with this good hearing. You'll never understand," he said, walking over to the window. All Ricky could hear was the wind howling.

"So, you should hear it leaving in a minute, then," said Ricky, picking his book up. He didn't know if Elvis could hear the aircraft or not; nobody else seemed to be able to hear it, so maybe it was just wishful thinking. He looked up to see a look of concern on Elvis' face.

"I think it's just shut down," he said.

"How can you tell?" asked Ricky.

"I know silence, boy, I know silence."

*

Disembarkation had been relatively swift. None of the three had brought any meaningful baggage, all belongings had been carried on. Aiden had his laptop and a clutch of maps he reckoned were useless, Morris had picked up three toothbrushes and some toothpaste at LAX and Danni had procured a couple of bottles of Bourbon. Aiden thought he loved Danni, for all the right reasons.

"What now?" he asked as Morris returned from the flight office.

"No more flights until the storm has passed," he answered, agreeing to take a swig of the bourbon. "I reckon we find somewhere to stop, get a shower, buy a change of clothes," he said, lifting his foot up and scraping puke from the sole as best that he could, "and then get a meal and a drink. There's a taverna down by the quayside that's supposed to have some rooms," he added.

Chapter 24

Within an hour all three had found rooms in
the taverna, had picked up replacement clothes from
what appeared to be an all-night mini-mart and had
showered and changed. Despite the events of the last
few days and the dramatic flight none of them felt like
sleeping. It was Aiden who suggested the bar.

"Just a nightcap," he said, checking his wallet.
He'd drawn some cash out at an ATM in LAX and
found himself effectively a millionaire in the
community they were staying in. Danni and Morris
were up for a drink too, both knocking on Aiden's
door a few minutes before the agreed time. They
made their way down to the bar and Aiden pulled
three stools up to the wooden structure.

Predictably the bar was quiet, with a sleepy
barman rubbing his eyes and an old man slumped
over on a table in the middle of the room, a glass of
some unidentifiable spirit half drunk and a pool of
water around his chair where rainwater had dripped.
In a wicker chair in the corner a young man sat
sipping a coke and staring up at the TV, which had the
sound turned down to a minimal level, also dripping
wet. Aiden looked out of the window into the dark
night and noticed the rain streaking down the pane,
became aware of the sound of it lashing against the
glass.

"Even I would have stayed in on a night like
tonight," he said, turning back to the barman and

ordering a round of drinks, amazed at how far his dollars had gone. "Could be a long night here," he suggested. Morris and Danni took their drinks and raised a glass each in toast of surviving the landing. Both Aiden and Morris started reliving the event with each other, but Danni wanted to forget so she wandered over to a spare chair and started to stare at the screen. The fly on the wall reality show was familiar in the way that all such shows are: people you hope know better demonstrating that actually, they don't. A British guy was up to antics in a LA mansion, wiping value off everything he looked at as far as Danni could tell. The programming looked dated, tired, as did the young man sitting watching with a fixed smile on his face. He asked Danni a question but realised quickly she didn't speak his language. He changed to the English he'd learned watching the reality show and comparing the words to the subtitles.

"You like this show?" he asked. Danni looked at the screen and decided the familiarity was fleeting, the feeling she knew the programme an illusion no doubt reinforced by the high-octane end to her day.

"Never seen it," she admitted, noting the young man turned back, pointed at a particularly wasteful act on screen and laughed with a real belly laugh. He started to try and explain what was going on, why he found it amusing, how he learned his English from watching the show. Danni conceded his English was significantly better than any foreign language she'd ever tried to learn and started to wonder if watching a similar show from a Spanish station would improve her skills.

"That man, Ricky, he is so funny," said the young man, before confiding a personal story that he felt gave him status. Danni listened with a dropped jaw as he related a journey undertaken just over a week earlier. She got up and walked over to Aiden, who turned and asked her if she was ready for a top up.

"Never mind that," she said, "you've got to listen to that man over there," she said, pointing at the man in the wicker chair.

*

Tony drove back a lot slower and more carefully than he'd driven to the airstrip, avoiding trees blown down in the storm. He'd known Cliff, on and off, for several years. He'd pointed out targets who had become mouthy, had acted as intelligence briefer on new customers. He'd pointed Derrick out to Cliff a couple of months earlier when the deal was being finalised.

"I thought you were Alec returning," he said as they drove through the appalling weather, both having got soaked to the skin tying the Islander down and loading the dead pilot into the back of the Land Rover.

"He hasn't arrived yet?" asked Cliff, staring at Tony as he drove. "He's become a bit of a problem," he said. He explained that Alec had disappeared from view, his cell phone had been found in the trash not far from the police precinct and his credit card activity had ceased. Either someone had done Cliff a favour or Alec had gone dark. Either way, Alec was doomed.

"And this is sanctioned?" asked Tony, swerving to avoid a pothole. The silence was telling, but seeing as Tony was considering a similar unsanctioned killing he couldn't, in his heart, blame Cliff.

"I've got a problem or two that needs your skills," he said to break the silence, explaining about Elvis and Ricky. Cliff listened carefully and maintained his silence for a good thirty seconds after Tony had finished. Eventually he whistled.

"Wow, you challenged me over offing Alec without sanction," he said, noting that at worst that created an administrative Human Resource issue for the organisation. "It just means they've got to find and train a replacement," he said as if that was a trivial task. "It's not like you haven't got previous," he said, reminding Tony about how he got his current position.

"But offing guests? That's extreme," he said. It wasn't unknown, but generally lawyers back where the residents escaped from wanted proof of existence on an annual basis – verifiable fresh DNA, video showing the resident reading a dated newspaper or, preferably, new material recorded in the studio every few years. All the royalties destined for the organisation were funnelled through the lawyers who

245

held onto them as long as they could justify to accrue themselves interest in addition to their fees, with the ultimate sanction being withholding all funds unless they believed the client was still alive.

"Off Alec, that's not a real problem, off the biggest cash cow along with the new kid who could provide another lucrative income stream – that'll piss the organisation off," continued Cliff. "Plus, I'm not convinced by your logic; I've never heard of someone making gunpowder from heart medication," he said, making a mental note to investigate the process to see if it could provide a new tool for him.

"And just because Ricky's from a steel making town doesn't make him any more likely to know how to make steel, let along fashion a gun and ammunition, than a person from Memphis is likely to be a Rock and Roll legend," he said. Hearing it laid out like this made Tony feel a little sheepish and he realised he'd become quite paranoid. Perhaps it was the cocaine, he knew he'd been hitting it hard lately.

"I think you should shelve the idea of killing Elvis and Ricky," said Cliff. Tony tended to agree, but realised there was one little detail he needed to share with the company hitman.

*

Sergei wrangled his hands as he decided whether they should take Tony up on his offer. "What if we do this and he doesn't let us go?" he asked.

"Then we have a third person to kill," said Dimitri, who didn't have any qualms about the hit. An old man and a middle-aged man with no track record of violence shouldn't present too much of a challenge. At least Elvis had studied Martial Arts. "Those two have taken to clinging to each other; that means we have to take both out together at the next opportunity," he said.

"But if the residents see us do the deed, or work out it's us, then our life here will be intolerable if we stay. Taking out Tony might be a popular move, but we'll be ostracised totally by the rest. And who knows who will take over from Tony? They might send someone to take us out – remember all we have is kitchen cutlery and anything we can use as a club," countered his friend.

"Then we do what we did in the old days, revive the Russian Mafia, make this our place totally," said Dimitri. Sergei had believed that Dimitri had wanted to run the resort like a Russian fiefdom for some time, old habits being hard to break and all that.

"So, what's your plan?" he asked, resigning himself to Dimitri's dominance, as he usually did unless anything other than brute force was required.

"Sneak into their apartment," he said, brandishing a set of homemade skeleton keys. "We know they are sticking together, so whichever apartment they choose. We need to go in the middle of the night when most of the other residents are too drunk or drugged to hear a thing. Go in hard, take one each, show no mercy," he said, as if mercy had a place in a contract killing.

"Do they work?" asked Sergei, looking at the keys Dimitri had brandished. Dimitri flushed at the question.

"They will, soon. I just need to work on them a little bit. Plus, I'm a little rusty," he added.

Chapter 25

Elvis was set up to stay awake all night; Ricky had tried to sleep but felt a need to keep the old man company, at least until he could persuade him to sleep or at least take turns.

"It didn't start up again," said Elvis. It was two hours since he said an aircraft had landed. Ricky couldn't tell, the wind was howling around the window. A plane could have landed on the roof and he probably wouldn't have noticed. "And the Land Rover is back," added Elvis.

Ricky walked to the window and peered into the dark at the front of the building in time to see a man hauling something heavy out of the back of the Land Rover, a sack or some sort of bag, he thought. Tony got out and helped, dragging the sack into the foyer and towards the office.

"Looks like Alec's back," he said in confirmation. "Fair enough, your hearing is something else." He had a plan hatching in his head, but wasn't sure how to make it happen, but felt there was a window of opportunity.

"I've got an idea," he said, noting Elvis didn't look enthused.

"Last time you had one of those we stole the bat phone," Elvis pointed out. "Look where that's landed us."

It was more a matter of negotiation, partly with the two fishermen, mainly with the detective and Danni.

"I think we should go now," Aiden insisted, bracing his back to the wind and rain, his long hair whipping around his head and slapping over his face, some of it sticking thanks to being wet. The fishermen were reluctant to set sail in these conditions; they'd sailed in worse, mainly because they'd been caught out in the ocean and had no choice, but right now they were on dry ground, well soaking wet ground, but ground all the same. Aiden knew that there would be a tipping point, he just didn't know how much it would cost.

"What have we to lose if we wait until the storm passes?" asked Morris, with Danni nodding in agreement.

"Elvis. And probably Ricky," said a voice from behind them. "If it's cash we're arguing about, I'll pay," said Alec.

*

"We'll bury him in the morning," said Tony, "or as soon as the storm passes. If it takes more than a day, I've got access to a freezer we can dump him in to stop him smelling," he added. Cliff wasn't bothered, it wasn't his office. "The residents are used to me carting the odd dead body over to the graveyard," he explained. "Once they've done a head count and realised it isn't one of them they'll be fine about it. They'll probably assume it's Alec, to be honest," he said, scratching his head.

"If I had my way, it would be," said Cliff. "Where can I crash?" he asked. Tony reached into a cabinet and brought out a set of keys.

"Why not Alec's room?" he suggested. It didn't look like Alec would be needing it anytime soon. It didn't look like he'd be needing it anytime at all.

*

With almost every piece of furniture jammed up against the door and the balcony window blocked by the bed turned up on its headboard and blocking entrance through the sliding doors, Elvis looked ready to sleep. Ricky had made them both a hot drink to wash away the taste of his cooking and to settle them down. He'd rigged up the master and spare mattresses on the living room floor in a way that permitted easy access to all amenities and drawn up a roster, digging out a wind-up alarm clock from a cupboard. Checking it was still working as it looked like nobody had bothered with an alarm since the resort was started in the mid nineteen forties, he wound it up and set it for two hours.

"I'll take the first stint," he said. I can't guarantee I won't fall asleep over the two-hour period, but the alarm should wake me and you, letting us swap. We can do this all night and at least we'll get some sleep." Elvis pondered the clock for a moment; Ricky had looked at it like it was an antique, Elvis had used one very similar to it each and every day when on tour before he disappeared.

"Y'all don't use alarms anymore?" he asked, checking that Ricky had set it correctly. Satisfied, he put it down, plumped up a pillow and lay his head down. "There's one last thing I need to do before we put your plan into operation," he said, starting to drift. "Do it first thing," he said, snoring as soon as he finished the sentence.

Ricky picked his paperback book up and continued reading where he'd left off an hour or so earlier, felt his eyes grow heavy, but resolved to fight it. For at least three minutes.

*

The ketch pitched violently, then rolled as a massive wave crashed over the top, soaking the two fishermen who were struggling to manage the mainsail. The four passengers were partially protected from the worst of the weather in a makeshift cabin, but all were effectively dripping wet. Morris wondered why he'd bothered refilling his stomach as he lurched to the side rail once more. Aiden, holding onto the table, was interrogating Alec.

"I thought you'd done a runner," he said.

"I did, then changed my mind. I know this organisation, and Cliff's reputation is renowned. He'll find me, and he'll kill me, so running doesn't necessarily help," he said. Morris returned to the table wiping his mouth, having heard the tail end of the conversation.

"He might not, he could have back in LA and didn't," he said. Aiden pitched in to help.

"Morris is a profiler, he's profiled Cliff and it seems he has a soft spot for you," he said. Morris bristled at the trivialisation of his profile but decided to keep it in lay terms.

"It isn't sexual, but he may see himself as being in a mentor role with you, so he'll cut you more slack than others." Alec just shrugged at this.

"Anyway, whatever, I decided I couldn't run forever so decided to make my way back to the island. At least if Cliff comes for me there, I'm on home ground and stand a fighting chance. Plus, I know where there's a gun and some ammunition in the office, so I might get the edge over him," he said. He obviously read something into the three pairs of eyes burning into him as he continued, "the organisation isn't like most. Taking a colleague out isn't too bad a misdemeanour in their view, so it would probably blow over if I got in first," he added.

"But that wasn't the main reason for coming back. Elvis is like a father to me, more than a father," he said. "I haven't had time to bond with Ricky, but he was my favourite musician growing up, so I don't want to see him come to harm either," he said.

"That was a dramatic landing your aircraft did, by the way," he added. "I'd been hanging around the airfield for about an hour when I heard the emergency announced. My trip was bouncy, but yours looked positively crazy," he added as Morris headed back to the rail.

*

Dimitri beamed as the apartment lock turned effortlessly with the modified skeleton key. Sergei really didn't care anymore; it was the middle of the night and they'd agreed they wouldn't try until the following night once they'd sorted some weaponry out and had done a proper recce of the apartments.

"See, it works," Dimitri said, raising his hand for a high five, lowering it when it was left hanging.

"It works on our lock," said Sergei.

"But all the locks are the same on the complex," pointed out Dimitri. Like Sergei he was dog tired but now he was fired up by his success. He felt like he presumed Sergei felt when he found another prime number, as if he didn't have enough already.

"They're the same type, but you've modified that pick to suit our lock all night. It might work generally, but then again it might not. I don't fancy hanging around if you start making the noise you made with that when you started," said Sergei. Dimitri agreed and felt a little deflated that the work he'd carried out might not work on Elvis' lock. Or Ricky's, depending on which apartment they chose to stay in.

"What if we use this on an empty apartment? If it works first time it proves it will work on their locks," he said. Sergei shook his head; he might be tired, but he was too much of a mathematician to let that logic slip by.

"It's not proof, not by a long chalk," he said using a phrase he'd heard the under manager, Alec, use. "It's indicative, sure; proof, nah. Maybe we can try an empty apartment tomorrow to see how universal it is," he suggested. Both men knew that was a fraught strategy, the residents and various staff were random elements that became more random in daylight hours. The storm would keep more residents indoors and therefore more likely to rumble them breaking into an apartment than ever. Dimitri voiced the opinion that had formed concurrently in both heads.

"We need to try this tonight. We need an empty apartment to play with, though," he said, pondering where they could find out that information. Sergei's eyes lit as he realised he knew an empty apartment just across the hall, about four doors down.

*

While the storm made sailing difficult, the prevailing winds were in their favour.

"We've made the crossing in record time," said Alec, leaning over the bow, an oilskin jacket protecting his back. He'd explained to the others that the organisation used this route occasionally instead

255

of transiting to one of the smaller, barely populated islands that were literally a hop and a skip from the resort that he'd recommended back in LA. Dawn was struggling to push through thanks to the weather, but he'd recognised enough of the headland in silhouette for a few brief minutes to get the old man to steer to a point he preferred to land.

"We don't want to land too close to the resort, automatic sensors will detect us coming, and we don't want to land too far; it's a big enough lump of rock to make that a real ball-ache," he said. "When we land, we will need to help these guys to moor the boat," he said, waving at the dog-tired fishermen. We'll probably need to drag the boat onto the shore as there isn't a proper jetty, so to speak, at the compound. There's one further down the coast, but we normally drive to that one," he explained.

"Then we'll need to agree an exit time for them; if we don't get back by that time we should let them leave."

"How long should we allow?" asked Danni.

"Twelve hours," suggested Alec, reaching. In reality he didn't have a plan, had no idea how easy it would be to sneak in, extract Elvis and Ricky and then leave. If he got the boat close enough to the compound, then grabbing one of the spare Land Rovers should be simple enough; one of his many duties was to keep all the equipment at the compound in a serviceable state and it was one he took seriously. Tony had let the stock of equipment deteriorate in the time he'd been the under manager and Alec had worked hard to bring it back up to standard. The journey time, if stealth wasn't a priority, was twenty minutes tops.

"We should be back at sea long before that time. If we aren't, we're never going to make it," he said, adding, "you're never going to make it. I'm not returning."

*

There were six apartments per floor, three floors per block with a penthouse suite on the top floor of each block. Apartments were furnished to the residents' specifications but were essentially the same layout. Based on a nineteen-forties design, updated in the seventies, they probably would have benefited from input from the Property Brothers had they been prepared to spend the rest of their professional careers on the island, reliant on royalties from their property programmes funding their lifestyle. Sergei and Dimitri knew the apartment they needed, all of the residents knew it.

Dimitri slid the skeleton key into the lock and probed as he twisted, backed off when he felt resistance, struggled as it seemed to fight back. Suddenly the door swung open and a mountain of a man reached out into the corridor grabbing Dimitri around the back of the neck, dragging him into the apartment, slamming the door behind him. Sergei pounded on the door as Dimitri screamed for mercy inside, tried the handle but realised it had deadlocked behind the two men.

Turning, running, ignoring the residents who had ventured out to see what the commotion was about, Sergei reached the elevator and pushed the up button, waited a fraction of a second before darting to the stairwell, pounding up the stairs to the penthouse suite. Banging on the door, shouting for help he practically fell into Tony's arms as he opened the door clad in a blue dressing gown.

"What the fuck's going on?" growled Tony, trying to wake up. He'd fallen into a deep sleep as soon as he'd hit the sack and had been startled awake by the pounding on the door and had been pushed onto his backfoot by the Russian falling into him shouting unintelligible nonsense. Pushing Sergei back into the corridor he focussed on the Russian babbling manically.

"Dimitri, he's being killed," shouted Sergei, trying to pull Tony's sleeve. Tony shrugged it away, he'd had plenty of incidences where residents had gone postal after a drugged-crazed night; experience had shown him keeping out of it was the safest solution, bollock the survivor, bury the other. Sergei was still babbling, and something registered that struck fear into Tony's heart. He pushed the Russian back against the corridor wall and pinned him by his shoulders.

"What has he done?" he screamed as he started to piece the babble together.

"He wanted to test a skeleton key, to break into Elvis's apartment," Sergei said, "so he tested it on an apartment he knew was supposed to be empty."

"Christ!" shouted Tony, dropping the Russian and darting for the stairs, running down them two stairs at a time, skidding around the corner and pelting to Alec's front door, beating on the wood ferociously.

"Cliff, Cliff, stop, for fuck's sake," he shouted as he heard the door unlock, braced as the door swung open. Cliff stood there, a smear of blood on his cheek, a trail weaving an undulating pattern along the hall wall behind him leading to a prone figure surrounded by a pool of blood in the living room.

"Shit," said Tony, turning to Sergei who had just caught up, restraining him, pulling him away. "Go back to your apartment Sergei," he shouted, struggling to hold the Russian, practically wrestling him. If only Alec was here, he thought, he'd take over managing Sergei. Then he realised that if Alec had been here, nobody would have needed to. A couple of the permanent night porters arrived, awoken from their night shift duties by the noise and they dragged Sergei away at Tony's insistence. He scanned the corridor and watched as doors were hurriedly slammed shut.

"Fuck, this is a mess," he said, looking at the dead Russian on the floor.

"He was breaking in, he was going to kill me," countered Cliff. Tony sighed inwardly; this was going to take some sorting. The storm was still raging outside and he was running out of freezer space, housekeeping were going to be very unhappy and the residents were already on the edge of rebelling.

"He thought the apartment was empty, he was testing a skeleton key," said Tony, stepping inside so he could close the door. "He was hoping to break into Elvis' apartment and take him and Ricky out," he said. Cliff stared at the hotel manager with disbelief.

"Why didn't he just ask you for a master key?" he asked. Why did people make killing folk so fucking difficult was the question he really wanted to ask. Tony didn't have an answer, he'd been persuaded by Cliff to stand the Russians down, just hadn't had the opportunity to do so, hadn't considered they'd still be up plotting when he'd arrived back at the complex. He had to sort this out and he needed to keep Cliff out of the way while he did so. It looked like it was going to be a long day.

*

"They won't stop," shouted Alec over the wind, holding his soaked hood with one hand, cupping his mouth with the other. "They haven't brought enough food to keep them going for twelve hours and they don't want to hang around a barren piece of land in a storm in the off-chance that we'll return," he added. For Alec it wasn't a problem; he'd decided to stay. For Aiden, Morris and Danni it was a little more problematical. "You can go back with them if you like, I'll do what I can to keep Elvis and

260

Ricky safe," he said, not knowing how he would achieve that aim, "or you can stay and I'll try to get these guys to return after the storm. We have a radio and I can arrange a call sign. If we can get Elvis and Ricky to the compound without Tony knowing I can cover for them for at least a day, residents often disappear into their apartments for days on end, only surfacing when the drugs or food runs out," he explained.

"I'm staying," said Aiden. He hadn't come this far to risk not having a story to tell.

"Count me in," added Danni.

"And me," said Morris, who had realised that for the first time in a decade his life had a real purpose.

"Great," said Alec flatly, "the four fucking musketeers ride again."

Aiden nodded to the young man, shouted some words into his ear and handed a wad of sodden dollars as a bonus for getting them there safely. Alec added instructions about the radio, then all four slipped over the side of the ketch, climbing a rope ladder down into the rubber dinghy the fishermen had inflated and dropped overboard. Morris grabbed an oar and started to paddle towards the shore, now fighting against the wind as it had chosen to turn at the point they needed it to least. Aiden grabbed the other oar and used it to push away from the ketch before dipping into the frothing sea, hauling as hard as his muscles would allow. Danni and Alec started scooping water out of the dinghy to keep it afloat for the short journey.

By the time they dragged the rubber vessel ashore the ketch wasn't in view. It probably wasn't that far away, but visibility was extremely limited. Alec insisted on dragging the rubber dinghy further up the beach than the other three seemed prepared to, based on his knowledge of the local tides, and all four weighed it down with rocks.

"No point disguising it, Tony's never going to come out this far in the next few days. By the time he does, hopefully you three, Elvis and Ricky will have used it to return to the ketch," he suggested. He stood up and scanned the beach. "The compound is on a promontory," he said, pointing to the elevated land alongside the beach. "There's only a couple of places you can climb up safely from this part of the shoreline," he said, recognising a weather-beaten track used by wild animals and occasionally himself when taking a little personal time. With Alec leading the way, they made their way up to the top of the track, to the compound.

Alec stopped more suddenly than he'd intended, the sight of the Islander aircraft tied down greeting him where an empty airstrip should have, taking him by surprise. Aiden looked impressed; he hadn't appreciated how well resourced the organisation was, this was way beyond his wildest guesses. "Can you fly?" he asked Alec, who shook his head.

"As far as I know, nobody on the island staff can. This presents a new problem," he said as the other three gathered around. "Clearly the pilot's decided the return journey is too dangerous right now, but he's going to want to leave as soon as possible. Tony's probably keeping him away from the residents, keeping the purpose of the island as secret as possible and will want him to leave as soon as the weather permits," he said.

"Is that an opportunity?" asked Morris, trying to work out the logistics they had to overcome. Transport was looking increasingly to be the largest problem; a twin turboprop could be a convenient solution.

"Probably not," answered Alec. "We'd have to lure him away without Tony knowing and persuade him to take on a host of passengers. The pilots know we're up to something here, probably have their pet theories, but we try to keep them as much in the dark as possible. They're all ex-military or CIA trained pilots and understand the need for secrets. That's probably part of why they like the work, the covert nature. He'll not want to alienate the people who pay the pipers," he said.

They approached the Islander, walked around it carefully to confirm it was empty and then found themselves congregated by the side access door. Morris pointed at the blood drips running from the bottom of the door and pushed the locking catch, released the handle and opened the door. "Look at this blood," he said, pointing at the slug-like trail

263

along the floor, starting between the pilot and co-pilot seats and terminating at the door. "Looks like he had a rough landing, too," he said. "Perhaps we don't have to worry about him returning to the compound in a hurry after all," he added.

They closed the door and walked over to the Land Rovers parked up, three in total, all looking identical. "We don't like the residents knowing we have spares, so we make it look like we use the same vehicle all the time," said Alec, adding, "Keys are hidden over here." He walked a few feet from the vehicles to a large rock and rocked it enough to reveal a cluster of keys, scooping one with the toe of his shoe to bring it clear of the rock. "Keys are different, though," he said, opening the Land Rover driver's doors one by one and trying the key until he found the vehicle it fitted. Aiden climbed in the passenger seat, with Morris and Danni jumping in the back.

"I'm not using the lights, so it might be a little bumpy," he warned. Although technically dawn, the light levels were still very low. Spinning the wheels, he drove out of the compound and onto the rough track back to the resort.

*

"We'll need to move the body," growled Tony to Cliff. He had to clear Dimitri from the block before the room and the body became a resident shrine. "I don't think I've got freezer space so we'll have to take him to the graveyard and leave him there. I'll bury him when the storm passes," he said.

264

Both men rolled Dimitri into a large rug and picked the lifeless body up, both men grunting under the weight of the muscle-bound Russian. Standing the body upright in the elevator they travelled to the ground floor, with Tony breaking off to fetch the Land Rover key from the office, and carried him out to the Land Rover waiting outside, dumping him in the rear compartment. Rain tracked down Tony's face and soaked his dressing gown.

"I probably should have got dressed," he said, "but I really want to get this body out of the way," he said, climbing into the Land Rover and starting the engine. Cliff got in beside Tony, feeling the benefit of being out of the elements immediately.

*

"Do we really need all this food?" asked Ricky. Elvis had found bags and backpacks he'd been stockpiling for years, squirreling them away for future use. Ricky hadn't considered that his island mentor was the male equivalent of a bag lady.

"We might have to go to ground for some time before we can escape," replied Elvis, who didn't have a Plan B and admitted Plan A was tenuous at best, "so just in case," he said. Ricky wasn't at all sure about this plan, no matter what letter Elvis assigned it, but he knew they couldn't spend many more nights like the one they'd just had, cowering in the apartment. If they managed to keep out of the way of Tony for a few days, maybe a couple of weeks, then perhaps the threat would pass, maybe he'd be promoted or something.

He lifted the two largest bags and shook one onto his back, heaved the other onto one shoulder. Elvis picked up the smaller two bags, took a quick look around the apartment, then moved to the door. It might have felt like a prison cell for the last forty years, but it had been his cell and he knew that in a perverse way he was going to miss it.

Leaving the accommodation block was uneventful; most of the residents had decided on a duvet day given the weather raging outside with some, unbeknownst to Elvis and Ricky, simply because they literally feared for their lives. The wind caused them to tilt into it and to peer through squinted eyes, while the rain drove into them, soaking them to the skin as they walked. The bags weighed heavily on their shoulders as they absorbed the rain, slowing them down. They were about twenty yards from the recording studio when Elvis heard the unmistakable sound of a Land Rover approaching, accelerating, bearing down on them. He turned and uttered a single word as the vehicle slewed to a stop alongside them.

"Shit."

*

The night porters had long left, both nursing injuries caused by the angry Russian. Sergei had stewed in his apartment for a while, trying to obey the message Tony had conveyed, recognising that this was something that had spun out of control. He'd been friends with Dimitri for as long as he could remember, certainly since university. Dimitri had been a drop-out, Sergei the grade-A student. Dimitri had shown that crime paid way more than academia and Sergei had done the math.

Eventually he'd edged out of his apartment, saw that the porters had left and nobody was guarding his door. He made his way back to Alec's apartment but found the door locked and no sounds coming from inside. He assumed Dimitri was still in the apartment and he desperately wanted to see him, to hold his hand. He knew the key to paying his respects to Dimitri before he disappeared into a shallow grave was to cow-tow to Tony; he realised that Tony had had some part in the death of his friend, didn't know exactly what and was certain that he'd make the man pay in time, but for the short term he had to put that to one side.

Looking at the time he decided to see if Tony was back in his penthouse suite or in his office. The suite was closer, so he retraced his journey to the top floor and knocked on the door, was surprised to see the door swing open. Forgetting that Tony had rushed out and downstairs half an hour earlier clothed in a dressing gown without locking his door, Sergei decided to see if Tony was inside.

He left a happier man two minutes later.

*

Ricky spoke first.

"Alec!" Elvis was surprised and pleased to see the under manager, was concerned by the entourage piling out of the Land Rover.

"C'mon old timer, we've come to get you out of here," said Alec, stepping out of the Land Rover and taking Elvis by the elbow. Ricky moved around to the rear of the vehicle and readied to put the heavy bags in, noting that he vaguely recognised one of the group, dismissing the others. He assumed Derrick had put two and two together and assembled a crack rescue squad.

"Not yet boy," said Elvis. "I've got one last thing to do 'fore I leave," he said, shrugging Alec's hand off and heading to the recording studio. Ricky saw the potential to lose an opportunity and called after Elvis to stop, to forget the task he'd planned, but Elvis was having nothing to do with the plan until he'd done his last act, turning to the studio clutching his two bags. "I'm taking care of business," he shouted over his shoulder as he entered the building.

Aiden and Morris looked at each other, part of them considered manhandling the aging rocker without actually verbalising it, but eventually just followed him into the studio entrance, with Danni joining them. Alec sighed and got back into the Land Rover, parking it outside the main complex in its usual location, partly out of habit, mainly as a result of his OCD tendency.

When he got into the studio foyer, Elvis had disappeared.

"Wants to make one last recording, apparently," said Aiden. "Seemingly it's virtually finished, he just needs to tee up a tape or something," he added.

Alec felt the situation getting out of control; he'd expected to have to run around the complex to round Elvis and Ricky up, had been overjoyed to see them both together in the street, ready to be picked up and shipped out. Now it had the potential to fall apart, especially as he spotted an identical Land Rover flash between the buildings and presumably park up at the rear. There was only one person who was likely to be driving that vehicle.

"Tony's back," he shouted, although nobody in the group, including himself, had known Tony was away.

"One more minute boy," Elvis shouted back.

*

Tony and Cliff walked in through the back entrance and checked carefully before they proceeded to Tony's office.

"I'll let you in," he said, pulling his office key from the chain around his neck, "and then I'll go to my apartment to get changed," he said. Once Cliff had ensconced himself, Tony walked to the front of the building, aiming to cut across the frontage to get to his accommodation block. As he exited the front he looked across at the recording studio, drawn by movement that he hadn't expected, saw Alec walk out of the door and then dive straight back in as soon as he'd seen Tony. He ran back to the office and called for Cliff.

"I've no idea how he's done it, but Alec's back," he said, grabbing the Land Rover keys off the desk and running back to the front.

*

"He's seen me," Alec shouted as Elvis left the recording studio.

"Who has?" Elvis asked, a patina of sweat on his face. He'd been rushing, that was for sure, and to be fair the pressure had ramped up for all of them. He could see the panic in Alec's eyes and knew straight away the answer to his question. He ran to the door and saw Tony and Cliff leave, with Cliff brandishing a handgun.

"We gotta go," he said to the crowd that had gathered behind him. Alec in particular looked desperate and confused by the old man.

"Our transport is over there," he said, pointing at the Land Rover that Tony and Cliff were walking past. Elvis didn't even look perturbed.

"No problem," he said, turning back towards the studio.

*

Tony and Cliff walked briskly across the frontage, Cliff checking his weapon was loaded, cocked and with the safety removed.

"Is there a rear exit?" Cliff asked. Tony racked his brain, it was a while since he'd been involved in that level of detail.

"No, you have to exit from the recording studio via the mixing desk room, then via the foyer," he said as they approached. He added, "I think there was someone else, at least one other person, in there." Cliff didn't break step, pause or otherwise waste time on the statement.

"Then I guess they may end up being collateral," he suggested, breaking into a jog as they got close to the front door, Cliff with his Glock levelled and ready. Taking the lead, he kicked the door open, then swung left and right to cover all arcs of fire.

"Foyer empty," he said, looking up to confirm there wasn't an upstairs to house an attacker.

"They must be in the studio," said Tony, wondering where the hissing noise was coming from. Cliff continued in the lead, edging up to the studio door, swinging around the corner when he got there.

"Wait here," said Cliff, disappearing into the studio itself, letting the door swing shut behind him. Tony listened to the banging of doors as Cliff swept the rooms dedicated to making music, then concentrated on the hissing noise that had distracted him. By the time Cliff reappeared Tony had identified the source of the noise.

"They're not here," said Cliff, perturbed by Tony raising a hand warning him to be quiet, edging towards the massive Marshall stack. Tony beckoned Cliff, put his ear close to the speakers, heard Elvis' last attempt to record silence amplified by some of the most powerful electronics known to the music industry and pushed through some of the biggest speakers. They were about a foot from the speakers when the final part of the recording boomed out.

"Elvis…has left the building," it boomed, rattling windows and shaking the fabric of the room, reverberating around the complex, rattling windows and knocking Cliff and Tony to the ground. Cliff dropped the Glock, loosing a round that embedded itself in the door leading to the recording studio while he placed his hands over his ears. He thought they must be bleeding given the pain he felt. Tony looked up at Cliff and realised what was about to happen.

"Run!" he shouted, standing and grabbing Cliff by the arm as the forty years' worth of nitro glycerine ignited, blowing the speaker cabinets apart, shattering the one-inch thick plywood and sending molten metal mesh around the room, throwing both men back to the ground as dust and debris billowed all around them. Cliff scrambled for his Glock while Tony watched the tunnel entrance behind the Marshall stack collapse, throwing more dust into the air and blocking the escape route Elvis had spent the best part of his residency constructing.

*

Aiden and Morris supported Elvis by an armpit each as they ran and dragged him along the low tunnel, barely lit by the flashlamps Elvis had stored by the entrance. Danni jogged alongside with Alec and Ricky, each turning in a concerned way at the old man. The explosion had occurred about a minute into the tunnel, sending a cloud of dust and soil billowing past them as they run.

"Where does it come out?" shouted Alec, nominally to Elvis. Ricky shouted back, in-between drawing deep breaths.

"Some compound. Elvis tells me he's timed how long it takes to walk there, says he's seen you meet Tony off some aircraft a couple of times. He never planned on making this journey at this pace," he added. Danni shone a torch at Elvis' face and started to crunch the data – age, weight, pallor.

"We're going to have to stop," she shouted above the clatter of five pairs of shoes and a sixth pair being dragged.

"We haven't time," shouted Alec. "If Tony works out where this leads to he'll cut us off."

"We have to make time," she shouted back, running ahead, turning and blocking the party. She shone the torch in Elvis' face again. "Lay him down, loosen his clothing," she said, pressing two fingers into his carotid, measuring his blood flow the old-fashioned way. Aiden and Morris did as Danni instructed, with Alec pulling his jacket off and tucking it under Elvis' head gently. His lips were turning blue and his breathing had become rapid but shallow.

Everyone could see he was in trouble, Danni knew the diagnosis.

"He's having a heart attack," she said, laying her hand on Elvis' forehead, wishing she had some medical resources on hand. "We'll have to take him back, I take there's a medical facility on the resort?" she asked.

"If we do, you'll all end up staying here," said Alec. "Let me take him back, you lot get away, whatever way you can," he said. Danni shook her head.

"You're never going to get him back on your own. I'll stay, everyone else leave," she shouted, noting nobody moved. Elvis grasped her arm and pulled her to him.

"I'm dying, girl, leave me here. Alec knows what to do," he said so quietly she had to strain to hear.

"What did he say?" asked Aiden. Danni looked up at Alec.

"He says that if he dies here, he wants to stay here, and you know what to do?" Alec nodded, but before he could speak, Ricky jumped in.

"He's not going to die, and he's not staying here," he said. Morris grabbed Ricky by the shoulders and pulled him gently away from the old man; he'd seen this played out a dozen times in his career and knew it rarely panned out well. Danni looked around, returning her gaze to Ricky and Alec.

274

"Is he on any medication?" she asked, continually running her fingers over his pulse, feeling the clamminess of his skin, gently stroking him to keep him calm.

"He takes nitro-glycerine tablets," said Alec.

"For angina," surmised Danni. "That would help. Does he have any with him?" she asked. Ricky looked wistfully down the length of the tunnel the way they'd just come.

"I think he just used the last of them," he said, startled as Danni began CPR without warning, pounding Elvis' chest and then giving mouth to mouth. Morris knelt down and teamed up, taking turns to apply compressions while Danni inflated his lungs and checked his carotid time and again. After a few minutes she stopped, tears running down her face. She looked up, scanned the assembled group.

"He's gone. Sorry," she said, feeling Aiden wrap an arm over her shoulder and helping her up. "He said you knew what to do, what did he mean?" she asked Alec.

"He always said he'd get home, it was a running joke because that's exactly the opposite of the deal. But he used to say that, in the unlikely event he didn't get home, that if he died on the island, he wanted to be buried here. To be fair, that is exactly the deal. He meant it. I'll make sure it happens." Ricky's eyes were streaming tears and he started to shake.

"No, we take him. We have a plan, we can get him home, bury him with dignity in a decent plot," he ranted. Aiden stepped in, pulled his idol to one side, reminded him that Elvis had the perfect grave at home, admired by thousands every year, that nothing they could do would better that.

"OK, let's honour his wishes. We can carry him to the end of the tunnel and load him onto one of the Land Rovers he told me about. Now let's get the fuck out of here," he said.

*

Tony and Cliff had escaped from the recording studio just in time. The explosion had blown their eardrums in, rendering them both deaf as posts, so they had both been oblivious to the creaking of the ceiling joists as the weakened structure buckled. As they staggered outside the roof collapsed, producing another mushroom cloud of building dust and flying debris. Falling to the floor, Tony tried to keep his bearings. He knew where the Marshall stack had been located and he knew the general direction of the tunnel they'd used. As the building finally imploded he realised he knew where the tunnel led.

"Come on," he shouted at Cliff, his words muffled in his own head, totally unaware whether Cliff had heard him or not. He slipped his hand in his dressing gown pocket and felt the Land Rover keys, stood and staggered over to the waiting vehicle, returning to tap Cliff on the shoulder as he struggled to stand. He pointed at the Land Rover, shook the keys, pointed randomly in the direction of the compound and staggered back to the four-wheel drive truck once Cliff had nodded acknowledgement.

Tony sat in the driving seat, checked the stick, dipped the clutch and tried to push the key into the ignition, fumbling partly because he was shaking, mainly because it was the wrong ignition. Frustration built up and, against the background white noise that was washing across his brain at maximum volume, he kept stabbing at the lock, trying to make the key fit. He registered the passenger door opening and turned to shout something to vent his frustration at Cliff, only to find himself looking directly at Sergei, who raised the Browning pistol he'd liberated from Tony's penthouse suite, pulled the trigger and blew Tony's face off.

Sergei stood and looked at the slumped figure, watched the blood ooze out of the gap in the back of the head, the dyed black hair matted with brain matter. Turning he found himself face to face with a loaded Glock. One second later, he lay dead across the body of the hotel manager.

Chapter 26

They found the tunnel terminated with a
sheet of corrugated iron that Elvis had managed to
cover with a smattering of earth some fifty feet from
the compound. Alec was impressed at the location;
he could imagine Elvis waiting for him to leave, with
Alec taking the scenic route to avoid letting residents
know where he was going but actually giving Elvis
time to get there before him. From his vantage point
Elvis would be able to watch the Islander stop,
disgorge Tony and leave.

Ricky whistled when he climbed up out of the
tunnel. "The old man was right," he said, pointing at
the Islander rocking in the wind.

"He knew it was here?" asked Aiden. Ricky
looked at the long-haired man, tried to work out how
he knew him.

"Reckoned he could hear it arrive and leave,
said it hadn't left this time. Are you a journalist?" he
asked. Aiden nodded, relieved that Ricky had
recognised him.

"What the fuck was Derrick thinking, sending
a journalist out here to rescue me?" he asked, helping
Danni out of the tunnel. Before Aiden could think of
anything to say in reply, Ricky had started walking
towards the Islander. Meanwhile Morris helped Alec
lift Elvis to the surface then quickly caught up with the
group while Alec fetched a Land Rover.

"Does anyone happen to know how to fly one of these things?" he asked. Ricky turned and started walking backwards in the direction of the plane, shielding his face from the rain and allowing him to be heard.

"I do. Learned to fly in LA years ago," he said. Aiden searched his memory about this.

"You had a single engine Cessna, didn't you?" he asked.

"Until my ex took it, yeah," answered Ricky, running through the pre-flight checks in his head for the first time in years."

"This is multi-engine," chimed in Morris. Ricky cast him a look, wondered what his part in all this was.

"Yeah," he agreed. He had a sarcastic numeracy put down ready if needed.

"I just wondered if you'd ever flown multi-engine before?" asked Morris, wondering if this was relevant. It certainly caused Ricky to bristle.

"How about I leave one engine turned off?" he asked. Danni just laughed, partly to defuse the situation. Morris managed to blush, despite his face being lashed by the rain.

"Fair enough," he answered. Aiden decided it wasn't the time to mention Ricky had had his licence suspended for life by the FAA for flying under Brooklyn Bridge, given the prickliness of the situation.

He recalled Ricky had been a talented, if show-offey pilot and had performed some really stupid tricks in the early editions of the reality show before having his licence lifted. Ricky picked up the pace, running ahead of the group and reaching the aircraft first, starting to untether the mooring ropes.

"Can we fly in these conditions?" Morris asked. Ricky shrugged; he guessed there wasn't an air traffic control he could consult. He wasn't sure hanging around was much of an option either.

"If it's got fuel, a map and a mini bar, I'm sorted," he said, adding, "only joking about the map."

"I've got maps," said Aiden, thankful there might be some use for the bagful he'd carried from LA. Ricky looked at Aiden, Dannie and Morris again, turned to the cabin door and opened it.

"I think it's time we had some introductions," he said.

*

Cliff dragged the bodies out of the Land Rover and tried the ignition, experienced the same problem Tony had before realising the problem. Swearing, he ran through the building to the Land Rover parked at the rear and jumped in, gunning the engine and driving off. The track wasn't particularly well marked, so he had to try and recall the route, having travelled to and from the resort only a handful of times before. It took him longer than he'd expected, but eventually he started to notice some familiar landmarks.

Reversing back to a track he'd driven past, Cliff pulled on to the track that led to the compound.

*

Ricky stared at the controls in front of him. He'd done a rudimentary walk round, pulling at the propellers and kicking the tyres, but he felt a little inadequate sat in the pilot's seat. It wasn't just that there were double the number of engines he was used to, they were gas turbines, not piston engines. The fuel system seemed so much more complex too, what with collector tanks and cross feed valves the permutations and complexity seemed far higher than he'd expected.

Behind him he could hear the others exploring the seating options and opening and closing panels to see what was behind them. Morris came forward and sat in the co-pilot's seat.

"Problems?" he asked. Ricky pointed at the panel and ran through the issues with the higher level of complexity.

"Look, I really appreciate what you guys have been through to rescue me and," he said, staring out of the rain-dashed window at the parked Land Rover, "Elvis, but I'm not sure I know how to fly one of these things, especially in these conditions."

"I wish I could help," said Morris in all earnestness. After a quick round-up of who was who and why they all were there, Ricky had mellowed. To be fair he'd just lost a good friend and probably had been over-compensating, so Morris had decided to cut him as much slack as he could. "You've never flown anything this complex, then?"

"Not outside of an Xbox," said Ricky, adding "there's nothing you can do. I need to carry out a test flight with everybody off the plane. If I crash and burn then only I perish; sure, it leaves you all stranded on the island, but still alive. If it all works out OK I'll land, let you all get on-board and take off again," Morris looked in the singer's eyes and recognised the look; there wasn't going to be a debate, so he moved aft and started moving people off.

Outside the Islander Alec, Aiden, Morris and Danni stood to one side, shivering in the driving rain, waiting for what appeared to be an age as Ricky worked out the start sequence. Suddenly one of the engines started winding up, with the propeller commencing rotation, followed by the other engine, a heat haze wavering in the exhausts behind the engines. The sound of the engines increased some more, and the aircraft crept forward before dipping at the nose as Ricky tested the brakes. Then it started to turn to face the opposite direction, the tail waggling as Ricky lined up for take-off.

Alec and Morris pulled the other two away and made them turn their backs as the engines ramped up, leaving the aircraft straining on its brakes. Suddenly the Islander shot forward, accelerating away from the small group. As the aircraft grew smaller in the distance it seemed to pivot on the mainwheels, with the tail slipping near the ground and the nosewheel lifting in the air. Then it was airborne, climbing into the low clouds, wings rocking up and down as it faded from view, with the sound of the engines growing less with every second.

Aiden threw a fist in the air and shouted encouragement that Ricky could never hope to hear, Danni felt her eyes well up again. Alec was about to enter into a group hug when his arm was tugged by Morris and his gaze was redirected to the Land Rover bearing down on them.

*

Cliff saw the group stood out in the open, away from the cover and potential escape the Land Rover parked nearby could have provided. They were clustered together, soaked through and about to die. He mooted just driving into them and mowing as many down as possible, but felt that they would separate as he approached, making him make split second decisions as to who to take out, leaving the others free to circle him or escape.

He particularly wanted to exact retribution on Alec, who'd betrayed him at a critical point of a killing and he decided he wouldn't mind making the girl suffer a bit. In fact, he favoured keeping her alive the longest so that he could torture her to death.

Slamming on the brakes, Cliff was out of the vehicle in seconds and had the Glock pointing at the group. He was relieved that nobody had the common sense to bomb-burst, running in all directions. All he saw was the look of resignation he often encountered when victims realised they'd been outclassed and outmanoeuvred. He noted the long-haired man pushed himself in front of the pretty young girl, started to wonder whether he should make the guy watch the girl die before he died, or maybe vice versa.

He spotted that Alec was looking braver than of late, had adopted a defiant pose and an indignant look that he decided was about to turn to one of terror. Cliff wasn't sure Alec deserved to live longer than any of the others, especially with that look, and decided he probably should be first. He'd thought a lot since Alec had fouled up the killing at the motel and he'd reconciled that the under manager had to die.

He then looked at the dark-haired stranger who had turned up at the motel with the black policeman who'd chased him to his car, and he felt a pang of disappointment that he wouldn't be taking the black policeman out as well. Not this time, perhaps he needed to torture him to glean vital information about the policeman.

He circled the group, stood about ten yards from the nearest one, taking aim from person to person, not worrying about time as none of them appeared to be armed and there literally wasn't anyone out here to hear them scream when he started. He spoke softly but had no idea if they could hear him as the buzzing in his ears from the explosion was still there, and although it had started to fade he knew casual conversation was unlikely to work. He slowly approached them as he circled, watched them form a rotating pack as he walked around, each one waiting to hear the sound of the gun go off, each one wondering who would be first.

He saw they were agitated, which was the effect he wanted, but increasingly they weren't looking at him, which wasn't. A shadow appeared on the ground alongside him and a noise started to filter through the white noise the explosion had left Cliff with.

He turned to see the Islander aircraft bearing down on him, the port engine headed straight at him, the aircraft flying at below head height, approaching rapidly. Side-stepping to his right, Cliff found himself clear of the propeller as it almost drew level, avoiding being hit literally by a fraction of a second.

Then Morris hit him, rugby tackling around the waist, pushing Cliff straight back into the path of the propeller, slicing his head clean off.

*

Ricky pulled back on the yoke as the arterial spray hit the front and side screens. He banked right and pulled the aircraft in a tight circle, noting the group two hundred feet below him scattering from the inert body. The journalist named Aiden waved and gave a huge thumbs up sign, before pointing to the runway. Ricky swing the aircraft away so that he could circle and line up. He wasn't sure he was flying the Islander as well as it could be, but he felt he had a fair feel for the controls. He waggled the wings in agreement and prepared to land.

Morris picked himself up off the sodden ground, surveyed the bloody mess of the man who'd been pointing a gun at them all seconds earlier. Part of him realised that he'd done the only viable act possible in self-defence; that his actions were justifiable.

But deep down he knew he'd crossed a line, a line he'd stopped short of crossing many times before in his career. This was why he'd walked away from profiling, had secured a dead-end job in a backwater police force, had watched his life disintegrate around him, his family disappearing from view forever.

He'd come close to killing before, had found a way out of it every time, but now he'd done the deed and knew he didn't feel the revulsion any normal human being should feel. In his mind he was as bad as the serial killers he had tracked over the years.

Aiden clasped a hand on Morris' shoulder. "Brilliant move, fucking great," he said, turning to Danni and giving her a massive hug. "We'll be on that 'plane in a few minutes," he said, jumping with excitement. Morris looked back at the prone, headless body.

"I won't be coming back," he said.

Chapter 27

Aiden answered the call immediately, recognising the number as the one he'd arranged for Ricky after sneaking him back into the UK some months earlier.

"Hi mate, how are you doing?" he asked.

"Great, just wanted to wish you luck for today," answered Ricky, sounding brighter than ever.

"Thanks," said Aiden. "How's the job working out?"

"I never thought I'd like shelf stacking in a supermarket, but it's great," answered Ricky. "No responsibility, nothing mentally taxing, keeps you fit. No wonder Elvis said it was his dream job. I might try for a job working in a chip shop, too," he added. Aiden laughed.

"I don't think that was Elvis' idea," he said, also smiling. "What else are you doing to keep busy?" he asked.

"I've joined a Death Star tribute band," enthused Ricky. "In fact, that magazine you sometimes work for ran a competition for the best Death Star tribute band last month, we sent in a recording and came third," he said. Aiden continued smiling; he was deputy editor on the magazine now, had initiated the competition and recognised the former front man straight away from the recording.

He'd bumped the entry down to third to avoid drawing too much attention to Ricky.

"I must come to one of your gigs some time," he said, "let me know when and where."

"Will do. Look, I'm on my break and need to grab a cuppa, so I'll hang up," said Ricky. "Just have a great day, right?"

"Sure, great to talk," said Aiden, closing the call.

*

The drive from Kern County had taken nearly six hours. Danni's mother had wanted to fly but her Pop had insisted on driving through some of the most inhospitable country in the West. He'd been unhappy and unhelpful since learning that his girl was marrying a man she barely knew, was almost as old as he was and was white.

"He's British," Danni's mother had said, in way of compensation, "and a journalist."

"A music journalist," corrected Pop. Of the many branches of journalism, he insisted, that was the one that mattered least. "He writes about music we don't listen to. Danni doesn't listen to that music either," he said, pulling on the bow tie his wife insisted he wear to the wedding.

"And why do I need to wear a bow tie? It's over eighty degrees and forecast to be higher," he grumbled.

"Because it's a wedding. Because it's our daughter's wedding. Because she's got herself a residency in a British hospital and we won't see her for months on end. Do you need any more reasons?" she asked.

"OK, but why here?" he asked, looking around at the gaudy décor.

"Because," said Danni, joining him in the entrance hall wearing an elegant summer dress. Mom gave her a peck on the cheek and held her hands.

"You look lovely, Danni," she said. "I'll wait inside, you walk down the aisle with your father," she said, giving Pop a stern look. Danni grabbed Mom's arm.

"Is Aiden in there?" she asked. "Can you check?" Mom stuck her head around the door and quickly returned it.

"He's there, looking very dapper," she said. "Even seems to have had his hair cut," she added, looking at Pop before disappearing into the main room. Pop turned to Danni.

"You know we love you, I love you. If this is what you want, then you have my blessing," he said. Danni wrinkled her nose a fraction.

"But?"

"But why here? Why like this?" he asked for the hundredth time since Danni had announced she was getting married and had brought her fiancé home.

"Pop, honestly you'd never understand," she said. "Listen, they're playing the entrance music," she said as the opening bars started.

"And why this music?" Pop said, hooking her arm in his, straightening his bow tie and walking to the door that seemed to open on its own. In front all he saw was a sea of family and friends turning to look at his beautiful daughter, the journalist Aiden, and the reverend dressed up as Elvis Presley. He knew "Love Me Tender" was going to be their entrance tune; Danni thought he was going to be apoplectic when he realised "Jailhouse Rock" was going to be the tune they walked out of the Las Vegas chapel to.

*

Derrick turned the buff envelope over a few times in his hands. A friend had spun by his crib and picked up his mail and this looked very official. Aiden had visited him when he'd returned to the UK and briefed him on Ricky's situation, told him that Ricky had been forbidden from making contact and asked that Derrick didn't try to find him. Now this letter was in his hands and they trembled as he tore the sealed flap open.

Inside was a very legal looking document from the law firm he'd used for his part of the transaction, an otherwise nondescript outfit from Gloucester. He scanned the document and ascertained that as they had not received any confirmation that the package he'd sent had arrived safely then the agreement was deemed unfulfilled. To that end, apart from some sunk costs and of course, their fees, the financial arrangements were to revert to the way they used to be.

In other words, Ricky's royalties would continue to flow into Derrick's bank account and onward to whatever Ricky had arranged before the disappearance. Derrick realised that even if Ricky's ex made a claim on the estate, a highly probable affair, Derrick would absorb large quantities in interest for the rest of his life. More importantly, it looked like he was off the hook for Ricky not staying on the island.

*

Alec patted the soft earth down with the entrenching tool, tidied up the shallow grave so that it looked respectable. The burial had been for a workman who'd fallen from the roof as part of the recording studio repair squad and would have survived without the excellent medical team on the island. He turned as John Morris approached, two mugs of steaming hot tea in his hands.

"Good send off?" he asked. Alec took the tea and waved his free hand across the graveyard.

"As good as you can expect. A few turned up to help dig the grave and said a few words, then went back to work," he said, taking a sip. The one thing he'd always missed under the old regime was someone who understood how to make a decent cup of tea.

"Not as grand as Elvis', though?" asked Morris, nodding to the only grave that had been allowed to be marked. The residents had insisted upon it.

"I never realised how popular he was," said Alec, "although to be fair he was always my favourite, so there you go.

"In fact, I was just thinking about Elvis a few minutes ago," he added. Morris raised an eyebrow. "He spent the best part of forty years digging a tunnel, rigging up an explosion and monitoring my activities at the compound and never got rumbled," he said.

"But when I think about it, he spent most of his time either at the recording studio or here, tending to the graves. I think I've worked it out," he added. "Obviously he needed the time at the recording studio for most of the period to dig the tunnel, but he had to justify spending a lot of time there. That's where his quest for recording perfect silence came in. If he'd been pretending to lay down new tracks there would have been an expectancy of some material coming out every now and then," Alec said, packing the digging materials away in the back of the Land Rover. "But nobody was interested in listening to his latest attempt at silence. Christ, I even had a state-of-the-art mixing deck put in to help him achieve it," he said, laughing. Morris smiled, the detective in him jumping the gun.

"And he got into the habit of visiting the graveyard to distribute the soil he'd dug out during the sessions," he surmised. Alec nodded.

"In one. Probably a good job we didn't have a detective on the staff back then, things would have turned out quite differently.

"By the way, are you still happy to be under-manager?" he asked. Alec had suggested that the old order be replaced by a more democratic system, with both managers sharing the trips home over time as soon as Morris was trained up on hotel management. Morris' eyes gleamed as he nodded.

"Hell yes, this is the dream job of my life. I'd never thought of working in the hospitality industry, but this mixes the challenges facing a young copper on a Friday night with the organisational skills needed to staff a manhunt for a serial killer," he said, lifting his face to the sun. "And I get a tan in the process, try getting that walking the beat on a Friday night or sitting in an Ops tent in the cold."

"I knew I had to get out of police work, that my time working on serious crimes had damaged me, my family life and my sanity," he said. The answer obviously worked for Alec.

"Great, because I'm off next week to start negotiations in Europe with a new client, then stopping over in Memphis on the way back for a couple of days to hook up with Aiden and Danni on their honeymoon. We're off to Gracelands," he said, adding, "so I need you to run the shop on your own if you think you're up to it?" he asked. Morris nodded agreement.

"Anyone I know?" he asked, closing the rear door on the Land Rover.

"German opera singer who's had enough of fame and fortune," said Alec, climbing into the driving seat.

"That should make karaoke night a bit more interesting," said Morris, throwing the remainder of his tea over the grave that had just been filled in. "At least Freddie will be pleased. Now let's get the spare Land Rover pulled out of the swimming pool," he added. "Bloody Moonie."

The End

If you enjoyed this book, then please consider leaving a review on Amazon. Also, tell your friends on social media.

If you want to contact me then email:

raysullivan.novels@yahoo.com

Also by Ray Sullivan:

Parallel Lives

The Journeymen

The Journeymen II: Day of Reckoning

Skin

The Last Simple

Project: Evil

Digital Life Form

Assassin

32762202R00168

Printed in Poland
by Amazon Fulfillment
Poland Sp. z o.o., Wrocław